Darkest Desire

Books by Tawny Taylor

Darkest Desire

Dangerous Master

Darkest Fire

Decadent Master

Wicked Beast

Dark Master

Real Vamps Don't Drink O-Neg

Sex and the Single Ghost

Darkest Desire

TAWNY TAYLOR

APHRODISIA

KENSINGTON PUBLISHING CORP.
www.kensingtonbooks.com

APHRODISIA BOOKS are published by

Kensington Publishing Corp.
119 West 40th Street
New York, NY 10018

All Kensington titles, imprints, and distributed lines are available at special quantity discounts for bulk purchases for sales promotion, premiums, fund-raising, educational or institutional use.

Special book excerpts or customized printings can also be created to fit specific needs. For details, write or phone the office of the Kensington Special Sales Manager: Kensington Publishing Corp., 119 West 40th Street, New York, NY 10018. Attn. Special Sales Department. Phone: 1-800-221-2647.

Aphrodisia and the A logo Reg. U.S. Pat. & TM Off.

ISBN-13: 978-0-7582-6566-1
ISBN-10: 0-7582-6566-2

First Kensington Trade Paperback Printing: September 2012
10 9 8 7 6 5 4 3 2 1

Printed in the United States of America

To David.
Forever yours.

ACKNOWLEDGMENTS

A huge thank you and big squishy hugs to Sierra Summers.

1

Beautiful.

Exquisite.

Thoroughly, utterly, intoxicatingly sexy.

And as deadly as a cottonmouth.

That was Malek Alexandre, summed up in twelve concise words.

A spectator at the private bondage club, standing in the shadows at the back of an open dungeon, Lei Mitchell moved aside to let a slave wearing a black thong and dog collar pass. Her gaze never left Malek. Not for a second.

This was an opportunity she couldn't deny herself.

For once she was free to just . . . enjoy. Without fearing she'd be caught by Malek, one of his brothers, or her sister, Rin.

Lei's hungry gaze wandered up and down his body at leisure now, taking in the full glory of his heavily muscled form. He was wearing a simple outfit—black, snug-fitting knitted shirt and tailored trousers, no leather for this man—but still Lei could make out the rippling bulges and clean lines defining each muscle as he lifted his arm and flicked his wrist. The leather tails of his flogger sailed through the air toward their target, and Lei's breath caught in her throat.

Malek was not just any dom. He was *the dom.* The one who made her blood pound hard and hot through her veins. If only submitting to him wouldn't mean her destruction.

Warm and tingly all over, even though her insides ached a little at knowing she would never—could never—know the pleasure of submitting to her master, Lei stood in that dark corner, just out of his sight, and watched as Malek trained a submissive. The sub, a male, clearly enjoyed every stroke of the lash, as evidenced by the look of utter rapture on his face . . . and the large bulge pressing against the only garment he was wearing, the snug black G-string. Like Malek, the sub was lean, firmly muscled, bronzed, attractive. He was also delightfully responsive. She wouldn't mind taking him back to her private suite sometime.

Since being rescued from a nightmarish life as a sex slave, Lei had come to this private bondage club to exorcise her demons. One of her previous owners had trained her to dominate him. As it turned out, his kink had become her salvation. Now she was the one in control. She was the one holding the whip, tying the knots, instead of receiving the blows or being bound and forced to fuck.

Free now from that horrendous life, she couldn't seem to stop herself from seeking out opportunities to dominate men. She wasn't sure why. She received no sexual fulfillment from it. She received no emotional fulfillment either. She was still the empty shell of a girl she'd been the day her sister had bought her out of hell.

But now she was an empty shell with a compulsion.

And a fascination with a certain dom.

As Malek released his submissive from his restraints, in preparation for a change in position, Lei tried to walk away.

But she couldn't. Her feet simply wouldn't move.

Her body was tight. Hot. Her heart was pounding. It was as if she were lowering to her knees before Malek, waiting breathlessly for his next command.

Malek ran his fingertip down the sub's spine.

A tiny shudder of pleasure quaked through Lei's body. Her pussy clamped tight against an aching emptiness. She licked her dry lips and curled her fingers into fists.

What would he do next?

The submissive settled on his knees on the floor, butt lifted high, rather than resting on his heels. He tipped his head down. Waiting. Patiently.

Lei had been forced into that position too many times to count. She'd never voluntarily kneeled before a man. She couldn't now. But that didn't stop her from imagining herself in the submissive's place at this moment. If she closed her eyes, she could feel Malek's gaze sweeping up and down her body. Her skin burning. Her nerves prickling.

It was anxiety and anticipation both. A touch of fear coupled with the expectation of good things, wonderful things. Of unimaginable pleasure. And glorious pain.

If only . . . if only . . .

"Is that a smile I see?" Malek's voice was unexpectedly light, playful. His tone both put her at ease and made her that much tighter.

"No," the submissive answered.

"No, *Master,*" Lei whispered to herself as she opened her eyes. Such a show of defiance surely deserved a punishment. She didn't want to miss this.

What would Malek do?

A chill skittered up her spine.

Malek's brow lifted, but he said nothing.

Ah, he was going to let his submissive wait, wonder.

She unclenched her hands and dragged her sweaty palms down the sides of her legs. A huge lump congealed in her throat.

She swallowed hard and squeezed her thighs together. The burning in her pussy was becoming intolerable.

Malek used the tip of his whip to lift his submissive's chin. "I asked you a question, and I expect a proper answer. So I'll ask again, is that a smile I see?"

The submissive's lips twitched. "Maybe."

This was a submissive who liked to push his luck. Lei had scened with more than enough to know the type. They craved the punishment and weren't by nature submissive. They merely took on the role so they would be in a position to get what they wanted. Depending upon the submissive, and the dom, that could be a few lashes, being humiliated in public, or perhaps being paddled to within an inch of their limits.

But what he probably wasn't expecting was what Malek did, even if they had discussed the possibility ahead of time.

Malek walked away.

The submissive's eyes widened. His mouth formed an "O" of shock; then his lips clamped shut.

Damn. Lei couldn't help but smile at the submissive's reaction. She'd put money on him thinking twice about playing Malek like that again. Or maybe he'd make a different choice in a dom, if that was his game. Either way, it was something to watch.

While Lei continued to study Malek's behavior as he prowled around the open dungeon, he turned. His gaze swept the crowd of onlookers gathered around the perimeter of the room. It snapped to her.

Their eyes met.

The air seeped from her lungs.

Her face burned.

He smiled, and she swore her heart skipped a beat. Maybe two.

Dangerous. That's what that man was.

Her body had never reacted this way to any man before, especially since... being rescued. She met his smile with a tiny nod, then forced herself to walk through the throng toward the back hall, toward her private suite, her haven. Her sanctuary.

Lei was here?

Lei had been watching him?

Malek gave himself a mental head shake, but he couldn't throw off the shock of seeing her *here.* Of all places. A dungeon. After everything she'd been through. What the hell?

And what exactly had he felt when their eyes met?

He wanted to go find her, talk to her, ask her what she was doing here. And then he wanted to drag her the hell out of here. She didn't belong in this shithole. No way in hell. Some of the doms would eat her alive.

But he couldn't, dammit. Not until he was through with Chris. An obligation was an obligation.

After one last glance toward the back exit, where she'd disappeared, Malek forced his focus back on his submissive, who was still kneeling right where he'd left him.

Chris wasn't new to the lifestyle, but this was the first time they'd scened. He had one hell of a pain tolerance and virtually no limits. But he was no fucking submissive. He was merely playing the part to get what he wanted. If Malek had known any of the other doms who frequented this dungeon, he probably would have learned that before tonight.

Malek figured he might as well give Chris what he was looking for and then be done with him. Never again. He didn't play those games.

He was about to take up a paddle when the curtains closing off the windows of one of the private suites lining the back wall opened, revealing the scene within to spectators in the main dungeon.

Lei.

And she was the one holding the flogger.

Malek's breath hitched.

She was a domme. Of course. How could he have not guessed?

The crowd that had been gathered around Chris and him shifted, moving in front of Lei's window, cutting off Malek's view. He figured that was probably for the best. He didn't need the distraction.

He strolled toward Chris, who was kneeling with his eyes cast to the floor, and squatted. "You're no more a submissive than I am," he murmured.

"Pain gets me off," Chris admitted, not denying Malek's allegation. "Not the submission."

"You lied."

"Yes, sir."

"You've picked the wrong dom."

"Yes, sir." Chris's eyes shifted up. "Are you through with me?"

"For your own sake, and safety, you need to be honest. With every dom. Every time."

"Yes, sir."

"I don't owe you a thing. Not considering your lie."

"No, sir, you don't. You're right."

Malek stared at the young man, at his handsome face. He was young. Stupid. Vulnerable. Clueless. And desperate. A very dangerous combination.

"I don't know where else to go," Chris said, eyes pleading. "I... need this." He tipped his head toward the paddle.

Malek flipped the handle in his hand. "Okay, I'll give you what you want. No more lying to me."

Chris's eyes lit with excitement. "Yes, sir."

Malek eyed Chris's hard little ass, his target. "Now, on all fours."

* * *

An hour later, Lei wandered back through the main dungeon on her way toward the exit. After that session, she wasn't feeling what she normally did. It had gone well enough. Her submissive had experienced a breakthrough that was quite emotional to watch, but for the first time since her release, Lei felt like she was just going through the motions. She didn't want to admit what she suspected. Not to herself. Not to anyone.

Mildly discontented, she made her way through the unusually crowded spectator area of the dungeon toward the exit. As she wriggled through a dense pack of men, someone grabbed her ass.

A flash of fury blazed through her body.

"Who the fuck just touched me?" she snapped. Her arms flung across her chest. Her hands shook as her fingers curled into fists. Getting no response, she moved toward a gap in the wall of bodies. But the gap narrowed, the suffocating throng closing her in, making her insides twist.

"Lei," a deep voice said behind her.

She didn't turn around. She couldn't. Her whole body was trembling now. Tendrils of dread wound through her, constricting her throat.

She just needed to get the fuck out of there. Now.

When a man moved in front of her, blocking her exit, she frantically searched for a new path. Her skin crawled. Her ass, where whoever had grabbed her, burned. Her stomach was clenching. Sweat dribbled down her hairline. "Dammit," she muttered, recognizing her panic for what it was. "Excuse me," she said to the man standing in her way. He didn't budge. He leered at her instead, and instantly she felt sick. Trapped.

All those old feelings of panic, despair, and powerlessness bubbled to the surface. Frozen in place, her muscles locked up and she stared back at him.

Would she ever escape the ghosts of her past?

A hand cradled hers. The grip was strong but not crushing; insistent but not overbearing. She looked to see who it was.

Malek.

He stepped up beside her and she gave the leering dom a look that would make any man shrink back. "This way." Together, they wove through the thick crowd, finally breaking free at the exit.

Outside, Malek turned to her. "Forgive me. You looked like you needed some help."

"I was fine . . . but thank you." She glanced around. The parking lot was packed. It was never like this. What was going on? "I've been coming here for a while. It's never been like this."

"Yeah, this isn't the usual crowd, is it?" Malek hadn't released her hand.

She wriggled her fingers, sending him a message she'd like him to let go now. "No, it's not."

"Once a month, the owner runs an ad in the *Metro Times.* On those weekends, you get a different crowd in here." Malek set his hand on the small of her back. That was no better. In fact, the intimate contact made her feel far worse.

"I'll have to remember that." Her back arched, her spine stiffening, as her body tried to shrink away from his touch. "I'm okay now." She motioned to her car. "Thanks again."

"Sure."

She tottered on slightly wobbly legs down the row, toward her waiting car, parked beneath a light. Behind her, she heard Malek's footsteps echoing in the dark. He was following her, but that was okay. At least she felt a little safer. It was late, nearly midnight. And although this area—which was more industrial than retail or residential—was generally considered safe, she couldn't be too careful. At this time of night the street and surrounding area were mostly abandoned—the perfect location for a mugging.

Pretending she didn't know Malek was following, she unlocked her car and opened the door. But before she could slide into the driver's seat, Malek caught her hand again, halting her. She whipped her head around and jerked her hand away. "Please don't touch me. I don't like it."

"I'm sorry." He raised his hands, palms out, the universal gesture of surrender. "Of course you don't...I...just wanted to warn you that there was an accident on I-275."

"Thanks." She gave him what she hoped was a reassuring smile. "Are you going home now, too?"

He glanced over his shoulder before answering. "Yeah, I think I'm done for the night."

"I'll see you at home, then." Aware he was watching her, she gave him a little wave, then slid into her seat and started the car. He stepped back when she shifted into reverse, moving aside, out of her way. She noticed he didn't start moving to his vehicle until she was rolling down the aisle toward the road.

As she waited for an opening in the traffic, a little tremor skittered through her body. An aftershock.

Her counselor had told her it would take time to get better. During those long months she'd endured as a prostitute, she'd seen and experienced some horrific things. Nobody got over that kind of stress overnight. But it frustrated her how often those old feelings surged to the surface. And it scared her how overwhelming they were, too. She'd been utterly frozen in panic back there in the dungeon. Unable to move. To speak. And all it had taken was a look from that man.

She was beginning to think she might never get over this bullshit.

Determined to shove her dark thoughts aside, Lei cranked on the stereo, filling the car with the deep base of a Lady Gaga dance tune, and maneuvered onto the road. In her rearview mirror, she watched a pair of headlights follow her. Malek's, no doubt. Those headlights remained behind her as she turned down one road, then another, winding her way home.

A half hour later, however, when she pulled into the driveway leading up to the house she shared with her sister, Rin, Rin's husband, and his brothers, Malek and Talen, the car that had been following slowed but didn't turn. In her mirror, she caught the flash of silver as the vehicle passed under a streetlight.

She'd seen Malek's car plenty of times. He parked it next to hers in the driveway.

It was red.

Had someone else followed her home? Who? And why?

I'm probably just being paranoid. Again.

Maybe she'd *thought* she'd seen silver. It was very dark around there. The road was canopied by dense, snow-covered branches from the mature oaks and maples flanking both sides of the street. If not for the street lamps and her headlights, the shadows would be so thick she wouldn't be able to see her hand in front of her face. So, of course it would be easy to mistake colors.

Even so, her heart started thumping against her breastbone. Her hands were shaking. She white-knuckled the steering wheel and crept up the driveway. Just as she was parking, Malek's red Mercedes prowled up the winding drive and turned into its spot next to hers.

She exited her car, turned to Malek, and asked him, "Did you just pass the driveway for some reason?"

"No. Why?" His gaze flicked toward the road.

It's paranoia. Post-traumatic stress disorder.

How many times had she thought she'd been followed since she'd been freed? How many times had she reported to the police that she was being stalked?

When would it stop?

"Oh, nothing." She *click-clacked* up to the back door.

Perhaps her therapist was right. Maybe it had been too soon to cut back to two sessions a month.

2

In the past few months, Lei had learned a few things about the family she'd been more or less adopted into.

First, men were slobs. She found dirty socks in the oddest places. And used dishes . . . popcorn kernels . . .

Second, residing with three brothers was a lot like living among a pack of rabid wolves. As much as the brothers loved each other, which was often evident, the boys snarled and snapped and growled at each other. Oddly, their behavior made them endearing.

And finally, as they sang a truly wretched rendition of "Happy Birthday" to Rin, she learned the Alexandre brothers were the world's worst singers. From the first eardrum-splitting note to the last, Lei held her hands over her ears.

To her credit, Rin smiled, hands clasped in her lap.

After Rin gave herself a paroxysm by blowing out all the candles blazing on her cake, they all applauded, and her husband, the eldest Alexandre, kissed her and asked, "What did you wish for?"

"If I tell you, it won't come true." Rin beamed up at her

husband, then turned her sparkly eyed gaze on the rest of the family. "Actually, my biggest wish has already come true. I have an announcement to make." Her gaze slid to Drako. Her smile became impossibly bigger. "Drako, you're going to be a father."

The soon-to-be father's face went white, then flared a deep crimson. He stammered, "I . . . I . . . I."

Malek clapped him on the back. "Damn, big brother. You work fast. Congratulations."

Drako hauled his pregnant wife into his arms and kissed the top of her head. "Thank you."

She tipped her head back. "No need to thank me. I'm proud and very happy to be carrying your child, Drako."

Talen smacked his brother's shoulder. "Congrats."

Drako gave both brothers an evil smile. "You two have a lot of catching up to do."

Lei wondered what he meant by that. Surely, they weren't in a competition to see who could get married and get their wife knocked up first. That would be downright barbaric. Then again, the Alexandre brothers were a little old school in some regards, but very much new school in others. And they were competitive. Made a girl wonder, not that it mattered so much. After all, it wasn't like she was planning on marrying one of the younger brothers anytime soon. She had no plans to marry anyone.

Lei shuffled up to her visibly overjoyed sister and gave her a hug. "My sister, soon to be a mother. I'm very happy for you. And I'm sure you'll be a wonderful mom." She intentionally left out the part about how their own mother had failed in that department. It was, after all, that woman who'd sold Lei into slavery. In their books, she'd relinquished the right to call herself a mother when she'd done that.

"Thank you, Lei. Of course I want you to be a big part of my baby's life. Godmother. Surrogate mom."

Lei stepped aside to let Drako get the cake and take it to Talen, who was standing at the opposite end of the long dining table, knife in hand. "Oh, I don't think I'm ready to be any-one's mom, surrogate or otherwise."

Rin's glowy expression dimmed. "Lei, give it more time. It hasn't been very long."

"I know." Lei gave her worried sister a pat as she plopped into the chair next to Rin's. "Don't get all worked up about me. I'm fine."

Rin slitted her eyes. "I'm not sure if I believe that."

"Believe it." Lei nudged Rin, motioning toward the husband who was now waiting patiently with a little gift-wrapped box in his hand. "Now, open your present."

Rin gave her one last glare, then accepted her husband's gift. "Thank you." Like always, she carefully, meticulously peeled the tape away, leaving the gorgeous wrapping paper intact. That practice was a vestige of their past, when there were so few gifts to unwrap during holidays and birthdays, that they'd learned at a young age to draw it out as long as possible.

Eventually, Rin's ministrations revealed the small jeweler's box inside. The top was stamped with Drako's logo. No doubt she'd find another gorgeous piece of jewelry inside. Drako was, after all, a jewelry designer. And she was already, after only a few months of marriage, a walking testament to his talent.

"Drako," Rin said, blinking teary eyes up at him.

"Open it. I have a feeling you're going to be surprised."

She flipped the hinged top up with her thumbs. Her mouth formed a little "O." "You're right. I am surprised."

Lei shifted her position so she could see what was in the box. Was that a . . . seashell?

Rin lifted the item from the box. It was white, round. "What is this?"

"A seashell," Drako answered.

"I see that. But what's it mean?" Rin asked as she scrutinized it.

"It's a very special seashell. From a very special place. I want to take you there." He produced a large envelope that Lei hadn't realized he'd been hiding behind his back.

Rin flipped the flap up and pulled out a photograph of a gorgeous home. The next picture showed an infinity pool that seemed to be feeding into a deep blue sea. Next, she pulled out a piece of paper and read, "Tarragona, Spain? *Spain,* Drako?"

He nodded.

"We're going to Spain?" she repeated.

"I'm hoping we are."

"Ohmygod!" She jumped up, flung her arms around her husband's neck, and kissed him with such enthusiasm Lei felt a little awkward and averted her eyes. For some reason, her gaze met Malek's and locked there. Something weird happened inside of her. And then she jerked her gaze free and decided to risk another look at her sister.

It seemed Rin had stopped shoving her tongue down her husband's throat. A good thing.

Rin grabbed the picture again. "Wow, Drako. I can't believe it. Spain." She glanced at Lei.

"Lei is welcome to join us," Drako said, as if he were reading Rin's mind.

There was no way she was going to be the third wheel on that romantic getaway of a lifetime. "Oh, no. I can't," Lei said. "I have classes starting soon, after the holidays."

Rin didn't get what she was trying to say. "Well, I'm assuming we're not going right away. Right, Drako? We'll be leaving sometime after Christmas. Maybe during spring break?"

Drako cleared his throat. "Actually... our flight leaves tomorrow morning."

Rin's jubilation dimmed. "Oh." Now, instead of looking like a child who'd been told she was getting a pony for Christmas, she was looking like a child who'd been told Santa was dead.

Lei couldn't stand it. She pointed at the picture. "Rin, look at that place. It's paradise. You deserve a vacation. After what you did for me. After all the sacrifices."

"But—"

"If you don't go to Spain with your husband, I'll move out."

Rin's face turned the shade of a slice of Wonder Bread. "You wouldn't."

Lei crossed her arms over her chest. "I would."

"But I can't leave you alone. What if that bastard of a pimp I bought you from decides he wants you back?" Rin turned pleading eyes to her husband.

He glanced at his brothers. Talen was dishing out cake onto plates. Malek was licking some pink icing off his finger. "Talen and Malek will be here. She won't be alone."

"How long will we be gone?" Rin asked.

"The house is ours," Drako said, accepting a plate from Talen and setting it in front of Rin. "We own the property. So there's no set amount of time. We can come home whenever you want."

"See?" Lei said. "You can come home whenever you want. Once you're tired of all that sunshine and sweet ocean breezes. In the meantime, I have my babysitters." Lei slapped Malek's arm as he set a piece of cake in front of her. Talen was out of reach. "I'll be fine."

Rin lowered her head in thought. "I don't know. Maybe we can go later, in a few months."

"You're pregnant, Rin," Lei pointed out. "If you wait too long, you'll be too uncomfortable to travel. I'm guessing the flight's at least ten hours."

"What you mean is, I'll be too fat to enjoy it," Rin said, cringing.

Lei shrugged. "I was trying to be polite." She took her sister's hands in hers. "Listen, I don't need you planning every moment of your life around me. As a matter of fact, I won't be able to live with the guilt if you do. So either you get on with your life, and your marriage, or I will have no choice but to move out. Please don't make me do that. I'm liking the service here." She winked.

Rin's gaze searched hers. "Are you sure?"

"I have two grown men to keep a watch over me. Which is honestly two more than I need, but if it makes you feel better, I'll deal with it. Go. Enjoy. Soon you'll be too busy chasing a toddler around to relax by that gorgeous pool."

Rin looked up at her husband. Gradually her scowl of confusion turned to a gentle smile of decision. "Okay. All right. I'll go. Tomorrow." Then she glared at Malek and Talen. "But I swear to God, if you two let something happen to my little sister—"

"Don't worry," Malek said, sliding a glance at Lei. "We've got her back."

Rin's eyes watered. "Thank you." She clasped Lei in a stranglehold. "I couldn't live with myself if something happened to you while I was lounging by the pool."

"Don't worry. Nothing's going to happen to me. I promise." Of course, after last night, Lei wasn't so sure she could keep that promise. But she wasn't about to tell her worrywart sister that. "Now, can we eat the cake? I'm dying here."

Hours later, Lei woke to the distant cry of a woman. This was no shout of grief or pain. It was a scream of ecstasy, a familiar sound.

This house was worth over a million dollars. Why hadn't the builders insulated the freaking walls better?

Lei lay in bed, listening to her sister's moans and groans and "ohmygod's" for a while. Finally, she got up, used the bathroom, and headed downstairs to get something to drink. In the kitchen, she heard more voices, male voices. Hushed whispers. They were coming from downstairs, the lower level. Her nerves prickled. Had the person who'd followed her from the dungeon broken in?

After grabbing a knife, just in case, she tiptoed down the steep steps leading to the walkout basement and rounded the corner.

The private dungeon on the right—that's where the sounds were coming from.

She hesitated, relaxed. The likelihood of some stalker breaking in and making himself comfortable in the dungeon were slim to none. Had to be one or both of the brothers burning off a little excess stress.

The image of Malek nude, pounding his rod into a woman, flashed through her mind. Her blood simmered.

From her vantage she couldn't see who was in the room. The hallway was dark. The door cracked open, a blade of light from the dungeon cutting across the otherwise dark corridor. She could easily get a little peek without being seen, if she was careful.

She could.

But she shouldn't.

Talen and Malek deserved their privacy.

Then again, they left the door open. If they cared about privacy, wouldn't they have closed it?

Could.

Should not.

What the hell?

Moving very slowly, carefully, she inched toward the door and peered in.

Talen was in there. With him were two other people, a man and a woman. There didn't appear to be a whole lot of bondage going on. Just fucking. The woman was lying on top of the man, on her back, her legs spread wide. Talen was on his knees, ramming into her from above. Based on the motions of the man's hips beneath the reclined woman, Lei was guessing he was fucking her ass from underneath.

Double penetrated.

Lei's pussy clenched.

During her days as a slave, she'd been fucked in the ass lots of times. In some ways, she preferred it over intercourse. In her head, it was less of an invasion. She couldn't really say why. But never had she been double penetrated.

Being that full, feeling two thick rods gliding in and out...

The woman's guttural groan said it all.

Deciding she'd seen enough, Lei turned around and slammed smack dab into Malek. She stumbled. The knife dropped to the floor. He grabbed her waist, steadying her. His eyes flashed in the darkness as he held her.

She jerked away, snapping, "Sorry!"

"Looking for something?" he asked, gaze wandering up and down her body.

Her face couldn't get any hotter. Or her body any tighter. "No, I just...heard a noise, and I thought we might have an intruder." She glanced at the knife, and Malek's gaze dropped to the floor.

He picked up the knife. His gaze slid to the open door. "Hmmm. In the dungeon?"

She folded her arms across her chest. "Sure, you never know. Someone could be in there, waiting for the right moment to come out. After all, there are plenty of handy places to hide in there, with all that equipment."

"I suppose you're right." He flipped the knife in his hand a few times.

"Anyway, now that I know a prowler isn't creeping around, looking for stuff to steal, I can head back up to bed." She stepped a wide circle around Malek or rather, as wide as the narrow corridor allowed.

He almost let her by before stopping her with a touch to the arm. "Lei, I told your sister I'd watch your back. I always keep my word."

"I don't doubt it."

"Now, about the car that was following you—"

"Oh, that was nothing. I was mistaken."

His eyes narrowed a smidge, just enough to let her know he didn't believe her.

She explained, "I wasn't watching the rearview mirror the whole time I was driving home."

"Of course." He raised one eyebrow. "And . . . ?"

"I assumed when I pulled out of the dungeon parking lot that the headlights behind me were yours. So, I think I convinced myself that you were following me, which was wrong. I'm guessing the car that turned out of the lot after mine probably turned somewhere and I didn't even realize it."

"Maybe."

"So, wouldn't you agree it's too soon to be jumping to conclusions?"

His expression said *no*. His mouth said, "Maybe."

"Good. Now I'm going back to bed. Good night."

"You shouldn't go to dungeons by yourself."

How she hated it when someone tried to tell her what to do. Yes, he was looking out for her safety. Yes, his motives were probably good. But after being told where to go, what to do, when to sleep, what to eat, and who to fuck for over a year, even words of well-meaning advice made her teeth clench. She was still working on that with the therapist, along with a bunch of other shit.

"I appreciate the concern, Malek. And I'll keep your *suggestion* in mind." She took a couple more steps.

He stopped her again, this time by grabbing her wrist. She hadn't even turned around before he'd released her, though. "Lei, about the dungeon—"

"I was admiring your flogging technique," she said, cutting

him off before he said anything about her panic attack. "Nothing more. Now, I need to get to bed. Good night."

He lifted his hands, letting her know he wouldn't stop her again. "Good night."

As she rounded the corner, turning back toward the stairs, she heard the dungeon door shut with a *click.*

Malek paused a moment after entering the dungeon to get his bearings and clear his mind. Lately, since seeing Lei scening with that submissive, his thoughts had been almost exclusively focused on one strong, determined, vulnerable, and damaged young woman with a set of dark eyes that made his heart race. He'd tried—how fucking hard he'd tried—to shove those thoughts aside. But he'd failed.

Since that moment in the dungeon, even his dreams were haunted by those dark eyes, precious face, and tight little body. In fact, it was after he'd woken from such a dream, hard and hurting and needing release, that he'd come down to the dungeon to see what Talen was up to.

Finding her here, touching her, had his balls aching now. He needed a wet, tight sheath. A willing partner. Male. Female. Preferably both.

"Malek," his brother yelled, invading his thoughts.

"Yeah?" He gave a mental head shake.

"Get the fuck over here." Talen was standing now, his cock limp, his face flushed a deep crimson. Brent and April, two of his best friends, and closest lovers, were looking at Malek with expectation.

April licked her lips. "Yeah, Malek," she said, her voice a low, silky purr, "Get the fuck over here." She stood, sauntered toward him, curled her fingers into his hair, and sneered.

Malek's nerves electrified. She wasn't Lei. She was nothing like his little Lei. But April was sexy. She was willing. And... she was cupping his balls through his clothes, making his knees weak. He gathered her long silky hair into a fist and pulled, gently easing her head to one side. Then he tasted her neck while fingering one hard nipple.

April's grip on his hair tightened. A little moan slipped between her full lips, the sound igniting tiny sparks of desire through his entire body. His engorged cock pressed painfully against his boxer shorts.

"I've had enough for one night," Talen said, heading for the door. "Night."

Malek tossed a wave at his brother before murmuring, "Suck my cock," to April. With his fist, he eased her head down where it needed to go.

"Oh, yes. Please, may I?" April was an unusual vixen. She was just submissive enough. She loved to suck cock. Loved to fuck, loved to be fucked. But she wasn't Lei. Was she wife material? Her eyes sparkling up at his, she fingered the waistband of his pajama pants. "Please?"

Shoving aside the sobering thought of his duty to marry, Malek gave a little nod and, while April tugged his pants down to free his cock, waved Brent over to play with her hungry little pussy.

Before he knew it, he was ramming his rod into a warm, wet mouth, eliciting little whimpers from April. Brent finger-fucked her pussy and ass.

Oh yeah, that was one decadent sight. A gorgeous, sexy woman on her knees, taking his cock to the hilt, Brent fucking her tight hole with two fingers. A searing wave of need blazed through him.

"Enough. I want that ass." He jerked out of the wet warmth of her mouth, motioning her toward a bench. "There."

"Yes, thank you, Malek."

The three of them went to the bench and arranged themselves. Brent stood at one side, his cock in line with April's mouth, while Malek stood at the other, positioned perfectly to pump in and out of her tight canal. He smoothed some lube around her puckered hole and breached her in one long stroke.

Damn, that was good.

He closed his eyes and let his head fall back as he settled into a steady rhythm of deep strokes. In his head, he imagined it was Lei's hips he was gripping for leverage. It was her ass taking him from tip to root. Her whimpers and moans of ecstasy filling his ears.

He reached around her hip, fingering her clit, and the ring of muscles clamped even tighter around his cock. "Yes, baby, that's it."

"Master, please may I come? Please?" she pleaded.

Beneath his hand, he felt her trembling, felt her muscles coiling into hard knots. She needed release. And he wasn't about to deny her. "Yes, baby. Come now."

She started quaking, and her ass spasmed around his rod as the first pulse of her orgasm ripped through her body. The room filled with the sound of her cries of ecstasy. In his mind, he saw Lei toss her head back, her silken hair cascading down her shoulders and back. He heard her voice echoing in his head. Felt her ass rhythmically clamp his invading cock like a fist.

His orgasm charged through his body like a lightning bolt, setting his cells on fire. His cum surged down his shaft and exploded into her canal, while he pumped harder, slamming his hips against her bottom until the sharp slap of skin meeting skin drowned out her plaintive cries for more.

When he'd spilled his last drop, he opened his eyes to discover Brent was sprawled on some cushions on the floor, looking sated. April was still bent over the bench, eyes closed, a ghost of a smile curling her lips. Her face was still a sexy shade of pink, just the way he liked it. And her skin glittered with a sheen of sweat.

"Damn," she whispered. "What got into you?" She raised

her heavy-lidded eyes to Malek. "I mean, you've always been good, but tonight you were so aggressive. That was hot."

"Glad you enjoyed it." Malek cupped her cheek and brushed a soft kiss across her smooth skin. Then he went to Brent and lay next to him, rolling onto his side to face him, head propped up with a bent arm. He nipped Brent's lower lip, tasting pussy. His semi-flaccid cock sprang to life. "Mmmm. I could go again in a few. What do you think, Brent?" He hooked his fingers, dragging his nails down Brent's thick chest.

April groaned. "I would love to stick around and watch you two boys play, but I gotta get up early."

Brent gave Malek a little taste of his own medicine. Chewing on the lower lip Malek had just nibbled, Brent circled Malek's hard nipple with a forefinger. "I drove. So I guess that means I have to go, too." He lifted himself onto all fours, crawling over Malek, and looking down at him with hungry eyes. "Damn, it's hard leaving you."

"It's hard having you leave." Malek grabbed a fistful of Brent's shaggy brown hair and pulled, forcing his head down. They kissed, their tongues battling, mating, dancing. Malek's body grew hard, hot. The air seemed to thicken. The room filled with the soft echo of their gasps. Malek's hips thrust forward, his cock grinding against Brent's thigh.

"Okay," April said, loudly. "Brent, I have to go."

"Shit," Brent grumbled as he hefted himself off of Malek. "You can't wait twenty minutes?"

April laughed. "Twenty minutes? With you two, an hour is the minimum. No, let's go." She clapped her hands. "Gogogo."

Brent scowled. "She's like my mother."

"What are you talking about?" April asked. "Are you trying to say I'm a nag?"

"Oh no!" Brent waved his hands. "God help me, that's not what I meant." He gave Malek a quick wink.

Laughing, Malek tugged up his boxers and pajama bottoms while April and Brent gathered their clothes and redressed. At the door, he kissed them each, first April, then Brent. April cleared her throat at least three times while he was giving Brent his good-bye kiss.

Ten minutes later, after they'd left, Malek headed up to his room, hoping he'd be able to sleep now. But he hesitated outside of Lei's open door.

Since she'd come to stay with them, she'd never once slept with her door shut. He wondered if it had anything to do with what she'd been through. Maybe someday he'd ask.

When he heard a little murmur, he tiptoed inside the room. Had she spoken to him? Or was she talking in her sleep?

Curious, but battling a serious case of guilt for coming into her room uninvited, he tried to leave. Instead, he ended up standing next to her bed, watching her in the semi-darkness.

"No, please. Not again," she mumbled. Her legs started kicking. Her face twisted into a mask of pain, fear. "No."

He bent low, risking a slug if she started swinging, and whispered, "Shhhh, baby. It's okay."

"Please, make them stop. Get your filthy hands off," she muttered, eyelids clamped tight, her eyes beneath jerking back and forth as she dreamed. "Please."

"Shhhh. You don't have to be afraid anymore," he whispered. "They can't force you anymore. You're safe. You're free."

She inhaled, then exhaled a slow, deep breath and stilled. "Thankkkkk..."

"You're welcome, baby doll." Fighting the urge to kiss her, he left.

3

"I feel like crap." Rin plopped on her butt on her bed and gave Lei a pouty look.

"If you're worried about me..."

Rin visibly swallowed. "No, that's not what I meant." Before Lei could respond, Rin clapped her hand over her mouth and dashed into the bathroom. The sound of retching and heaving followed.

Ah, *that* kind of crap.

Lei hurried after her sister to see what she could do to help. In the bathroom, she gathered her sister's long hair into a ponytail and held it for her. When it seemed Rin was through, she asked, while handing Rin a damp washcloth, "Are you okay? What can I do?"

"Nothing?" Rin dabbed her face, her watery eyes. "That was fun." Slowly, she rose to her feet. "Wow do I feel woozy. Maybe traveling to Spain isn't such a good idea." She staggered out into the bedroom, Lei supporting her. After sitting on the bed, she added, "I mean, I wasn't one hundred percent sure about it, anyway. I don't want to leave you."

"I'll be perfectly safe. So please don't stay home because of me."

Rin narrowed her eyes at Lei. "But what if... that bastard... decides he wants you back?"

"He's not going to go to all that trouble," Lei reasoned, intentionally avoiding speaking his name. They had both agreed it would never be spoken aloud again.

Whatever it took, she had to convince her sister she was safe. Rin had already sacrificed so much for her. Too much. Including her freedom. Granted, after a few months, it was looking like Rin's marriage of convenience had turned out better than she'd hoped.

Lei said, "Not when it's so much simpler to just go buy some other girl from the traffickers. He's not above kidnapping, but generally he lets someone else do the dirty work. He just picks and chooses his girls, pays for them, and puts them to work."

"You make a good point." Rin sighed.

Lei sat beside her, taking her sister's small hand in her own. It was so hard to believe Rin would soon be a mother. "How are you feeling?"

"Better."

"Good." Lei had so little knowledge of pregnancy she wasn't sure what to do. Once there'd been a pregnant girl in the very first brothel she'd worked. She remembered that girl would eat crackers first thing in the morning, before she'd even gotten out of bed. "Maybe you need to get something in your stomach? That might help." Sadly, that girl had disappeared shortly after arriving. Lei had thought about her from time to time, wondered what had happened to her. That girl had vanished, and so many more after her.

That was why Lei had done what she had.

"I am hungry," Rin admitted. "Very hungry."

"Why don't you get back to packing, and I'll run down to the kitchen and make you some toast?"

"Thanks."

Rin looked like she needed a hug, so Lei gave her one. Afterward, she scampered downstairs, whipped up some toast and tea, and headed back upstairs. It seemed Rin hadn't moved since she left. Not a muscle, outside of getting the remote for the TV hanging on the wall opposite the bed and tuning it to the morning news.

Lei set the plate on her nightstand and handed her the tea first. "It's ginger. Ginger is great for woozy stomachs."

"Thanks." Rin sipped.

They watched the weather report in silence.

Then Lei watched the next clip with her heart in her throat.

The news reporter was standing in an alley Lei knew all too well. "The body of a young woman was found in this alley last night. The identity of the victim is unknown at this time, as is the cause of death. The deceased woman was in her twenties, and she had a fairly recognizable tattoo of a cherry tree on her back. If you have any information about the victim, police are asking you to call Crime Stoppers. As always, your identity will remain anonymous."

Lei swallowed hard. A huge lump had wedged in her throat and she needed to clear it. She couldn't breathe.

Rin seemed to key in to her reaction immediately. "What's wrong?"

"Nothing." A lie. There was no way she could tell her sister the truth. Absolutely determined to convince Rin there was no reason for worry, she struggled to hide her anxiety while frantically fighting for air. It wasn't easy, but she had no choice. "I'm just . . . a little choked up about you becoming a mom. You've been such a wonderful sister. I know you'll make an even better mother."

Rin's eyes teared up. "Oh, Lei." Rin hugged her and sniffled. "I love you so much. You deserve to be happy, as happy as I am."

"Are you happy?"

"I am. Very. I wasn't expecting to be, not the way things started out with Drako."

She'd basically sold herself into an arranged marriage to buy Lei's freedom, so her marriage was looking bleak in the beginning. To hear she'd found some measure of happiness was a huge relief. "I'm so glad to hear that."

Rin ran her hand over her flat stomach. "Ironically, it all turned out okay. I have a good husband, and you and I both have a great life now, better than we ever would have..." Rin's eyes widened. "I'm not saying your being sold was a good thing. It wasn't—"

"It's okay," Lei interrupted her backpedaling sister. "You're right. It did turn out well. For both of us."

"Once you've graduated from college, maybe you'll think about getting married and having a family of your own."

"No way. Before I was sold, I'd already decided I'd never be married. My... experience... only solidified that decision for me. Marriage is not for me. Neither is parenthood."

Rin's expression dimmed, but she didn't say a word to try to change Lei's mind. Lei was thankful for that.

Lei grabbed the plate and waved it under Rin's nose. "Come on, eat some of this toast and then let's get you packed. Even a perfect husband has his limits on patience. After all, he went to a lot of trouble to plan this surprise for you. I know you don't have the heart to disappoint him."

"You're right about that." Rin snatched up a slice of bread and nibbled.

Lei spent the rest of the morning getting her sister's suitcases packed for an extended stay in Spain while hiding her shock and upset over what she'd watched on the news.

That girl...with the cherry tree tattoo. Lei had known her very well, back when she'd been working the alleys and back rooms. Eve had been one of the lucky ones. Rumor was she'd been freed by a wealthy relative. Bought and paid for, just like Lei.

Lei, however, knew the truth.

But that didn't explain what Eve was doing in that alley. Nor did it explain for sure who had killed her.

For the sake of her own sanity, as well as possibly her sister's, Drako's, and his brothers' safety, Lei needed to find out what the hell had happened. Was her former pimp behind the murder? If he was, would there be more deaths?

"You're next." Drako clapped Malek on the back, giving him a slant-eyed grin. "Time to bite the bullet and find a wife. I've done my part."

"Yeah, yeah." Malek drained his coffee mug, then stood to refill it. "No need to rub it in."

Talen, looking hung over, stumbled in just as Drako was about to say something else. "Coffee," he grumbled.

"It's hot. And fresh." Setting the carafe back on the burner, Malek stepped aside to give Talen plenty of room. He cautiously took a sip, felt it burn its way down to his gut, then went in search of food.

He was damn hungry this morning.

"You look like shit," Drako said, sitting at the table, digging into a big bowl of granola with milk.

Talen grunted.

"Your time's coming, too," Drako pointed out, waving his spoon at Talen. "And don't think for a minute that your wife will be okay with you fucking everything in sight like you do now."

"I don't fuck everything in sight," Talen said, sounding injured. "I have some standards."

Drako scoffed.

So did Malek.

Drako said around a mouthful of granola and milk, "By the time I get back from Spain, I expect Malek to have a ring on someone's finger."

"How long are you going to be gone?" Malek asked as he pulled some plastic containers out of the refrigerator.

"Only as long as I need to be. You know how I feel about leaving the two of you here by yourselves."

Talen gave a dismissive toss of the hand. "We'll be fine. Uncle Bob's dead. After losing their leader, Chimera has splintered into dozens of little factions again. They won't be any trouble for a long time."

Drako didn't look so sure. "That's what you'd like to think."

Talen refilled his coffee cup. "That's what twenty-something years of experience has told us. It was only when Uncle Bob, pretending to be John Dale Oram, walked out of that hospital that we started having problems with them again." He put the pot back on the burner.

Drako dug another heaping spoonful of granola out of his bowl. "Still, we'd be fools to let our guard down."

"We're not," Talen said. "We're just not going on the offensive like we were. There's a difference."

Drako ceded with a grunt.

Talen, having consumed one full cup of coffee now, turned to Malek, who was loading an empty plate with precooked sausages and scrambled eggs. "Have you come up with any candidates for Mrs. Malek yet?"

Malek didn't answer right away. He wasn't about to tell them whom he'd like to consider for his first and only candidate. Not yet. "No."

"Hmmm..." Talen narrowed his eyes at Malek. "You're lying. Who is it?"

Drako raised one brow. "You keeping a secret from us?"

"No, I'm not keeping any secrets. And I'm not lying. There's no 'candidate' yet." *Not technically.*

"Then there's someone you'd wish to make a candidate," Talen said, striking a little too close to the truth for Malek's comfort.

"No, there isn't."

"Who is it?" Talen was like a hound on a blood trail. He'd always been that way. For once, Malek was not happy about it. "Is it one of the Randall twins?"

"No."

"April?" Talen asked as he refilled the coffee filter with more grounds.

"No."

"Oh, wait." Talen squinted at him. "Is it Lei?"

Lei picked that exact moment to come into the kitchen. Malek's gaze flew to her face. Her eyes had that look about them, the one that said she'd heard Talen say her name.

"Good morning," she said, pretending she hadn't heard them talking about her. Malek wondered how much she'd heard. He sent a warning glare to each of his brothers. Talen responded with a smirk. Drako's response was a sober nod.

"Good morning." Talen filled the empty carafe with water. When Lei turned to reach into the cupboard, the asshole actually had the nerve to leer at her like the classless bastard he was.

Malek fought the urge to knock him upside the head and gritted his teeth. When she turned back around, an empty glass in her hand, he gave her a little friendly tip of the head.

"Why are you holding a sausage?" she asked.

"Uh." Malek glanced down. He'd forgotten he'd been getting some breakfast. "I was just about to warm these up. Want some?"

Talen coughed.

Drako cleared his throat.

"Um..." Lei's cheeks pinked up a bit. He liked that shade on her. "No thanks." She headed for the refrigerator, then opened the door.

"Just thought I'd offer." Malek shot each of his brothers a get-lost look. Of course they didn't leave. Drako munched on his stupid granola, and Talen poured the water into the coffee maker and hit the button, powering it up for round two.

Malek shoved his loaded plate into the microwave.

Looking extremely amused, Talen said, "So, Lei, Malek here was just telling us—"

"That I was thinking about taking a couple of classes at U of M next semester." Malek twisted around, shooting Talen a warning glare. Then he returned to poking the buttons on the appliance to get it started.

A vanilla yogurt in her hand, Lei gave Malek a semi-smile. "Oh, really? What were you thinking of taking?"

"Sewing," Talen said.

"Sewing?" Lei echoed.

Malek's blood boiled. Bastard.

Doing his damned best to hide his irritation, Malek dug back into the refrigerator for something else to eat with his sausages and eggs.

Drako stood, gathered his empty bowl, spoon, and glass, and took them to the sink. "I need to get back to packing."

"Talen can help you," Malek offered as he shut the refrigerator door. "He's got nothing better to do."

"Sure, I could use the help. My wife is packing half the house. Talen." Drako jerked his head toward the hall.

"Yeah, I'd be happy to help." Talen trudged along, trailing behind their eldest brother.

Finally, he was alone with Lei. He had some damage control to do. He started by shoving a cut bagel into the toaster.

"So, are you really thinking about taking a sewing class?" Lei asked as she settled down on a stool at the raised counter.

Sewing wasn't manly.

Sewing wasn't sexy.

Sewing wasn't even enjoyable.

He mumbled, "Well..."

Her eyes turned sparkly. Her lips curled into a sweet little smile that made his heart thump and his cock thicken. "Are you embarrassed to admit the truth?" She spooned some yogurt to her mouth. The utensil slid between her lips, in, then out. The tip of her tongue darted out, licking away a bit of yogurt that had remained on the spoon.

Damn, he could watch her eat yogurt all day long.

His cock twitched. "Maybe."

"I'm taking a sewing class this semester, too. I changed majors."

"You did?" he asked, watching, mesmerized as she ate another spoonful of yogurt. He swore he didn't get this hard watching porn.

"Yeah, I just wasn't enjoying the science classes as much as I thought. When I heard the university was expanding its arts and fibers program to include fashion design, I decided to make a change."

"Fashion design? Sounds interesting." Malek's bagel popped out of the toaster at the same time as the microwave oven chirped. He pulled his plate out, dropped the bagel on it, then pulled a knife out of the block to slice the sausage.

"Sure, I've always had an interest in fashion. I bet there will be plenty of men in my classes. You wouldn't be the only one."

"Maybe." He arranged the sausage on the bagel, added a slice of cheese and the eggs, and plopped the second half on top of the first, creating a healthy (not) sandwich.

"Of course." She tracked him as he made his way around the counter to the side with the stools. "You should go for it."

He sat next to her. "Sewing?" he repeated. He took a bite,

chewed. "If I was able to get in the same class with you, maybe we could drive together?"

"Maybe. It would depend upon our schedules. Were you thinking about taking anything else?"

"I haven't decided yet." Taking a second class, something to help replenish his testosterone levels might be needed. This whole sewing thing was a bad idea. He didn't know a damn thing about sewing. He couldn't even thread a needle. And that was because he'd never wanted to learn how.

If something needed alterations, he paid someone to do them.

If something needed repairing, he generally threw it away or donated it to charity and replaced it.

Why the hell did he need to know how to sew?

Then she ate some more yogurt and that was it. If it took learning how to sew to get closer to Lei, then . . . what the hell?

"So . . . what other classes were you taking this semester?" he asked.

4

The funeral home was gorgeous. But sadly, it was empty.

At the direction of the silver-haired funeral director, Lei reluctantly stepped into room C, where Eve was being displayed for just one day. Rooms A and B were empty. As her gaze scanned the area, the lack of visitors hit her hard. It seemed that nobody cared that Eve had died. Nobody but an elderly woman, sitting in the first row of chairs lined up in front of the casket.

Lei hoped that woman knew something about Eve's death. But how to bring it up . . . ?

Her heart started pounding hard against her breastbone as she slowly approached the casket.

How had this happened? How had a woman who'd escaped the horrid world they'd both been trapped in ended up dead in an alley?

Lei felt a little sick as she stood in front of the casket, looking down at the woman who'd befriended her when she'd first arrived in Detroit. She was the one who'd told her which girls to avoid and which to trust. She was the one who'd talked her through one of the lowest days of her life.

Dead.

When she turned around, the woman in the front row was looking directly at her. Lei took a seat beside her, hands folded in her lap.

The woman placed one heavily wrinkled hand on hers. "Thank you for coming."

At a total loss as to what to say, Lei simply nodded.

"My granddaughter didn't have many friends. I appreciate your being here."

"She was a good person," Lei said.

"Yes, she was. If only she had learned to make better choices. If she had, she might be alive today." The woman's voice wavered.

"I'm very sorry."

Neither Lei nor the woman said anything for several minutes. Lei didn't have the heart to ask any questions. This was not the time or place. The best she could do was hang around the funeral home and see who else, if anyone, showed up.

And so she did.

She sat with Eve's grandmother, Irene, for a couple of hours, went and bought some lunch for them both, and brought it back. As they ate submarine sandwiches and chips, Irene told her stories about the girl she called Evelyn. About how she'd dreamed of being a ballerina when she was eight, after going to see a local production of *The Nutcracker.* About getting the lead in her high-school musical her freshman year. About the mural she'd painted in her high school and the award she'd received for it. And about the eventual plummet into addiction that led to her becoming what Lei had known she was but Irene was too embarrassed to admit.

Lei had known there was something special about Eve from the first moment she'd met her, but she hadn't realized how special she was. Or what might have been if she hadn't become addicted to heroin.

She wasn't sure what saddened her more: Eve's death or the loss of all that potential.

If only. If . . . only.

After lunch, Lei sat with Irene in that front row for another hour before she became too antsy to sit any longer. Feeling like she was wasting her time, but unable to convince herself to leave, she resorted to strolling around the property. The building was a gorgeous Victorian house converted into a funeral home. It was positioned on a main street cutting through a quaint little town on a wide lot. Outside, just beyond the parking lot, there was a small garden with a fountain. It was peaceful. Pretty. Even at this time of year when the shrubbery was bare, the flowers long gone. She sat on a concrete bench at the far end of the garden. From her position, she could watch the parking lot, see who was coming and going.

About one hour before Eve's showing was scheduled to end, Lei watched a car pull into the lot. It was silver. A man who looked very familiar came out of it and strolled around to the front of the building.

Curious, and wracking her brain, trying to remember where she'd seen that man before—*if* she'd seen that man before—she followed at a distance.

He went in, looked at the sign in the entryway, started toward room C, halted at the door, lifted a hand, and a moment later did a one-eighty before Lei could duck out of sight. His gaze snapped to hers, and a tense moment passed. He said, "A message for you." A second later, he charged past her, slamming through the front door.

"What message?" Lei stood frozen for a moment, then scurried out after him. She caught his car skidding out onto the road. As it zoomed past her, she squinted to read the license plate. All she caught were the letters WVM.

Confused, and still unable to remember where she'd seen the man before, she wandered back inside room C. Thinking she'd ask Irene if she knew him, she headed toward the front row of chairs.

Irene was lying on the floor, between the chairs and the casket.

Dead.

Eyes staring blindly. Lips frozen in a grimace.

Deep scarlet blood seeping from the wound in her forehead.

Lei clapped a hand over her mouth, but it did nothing to muffle the scream.

An hour later, Lei was sitting in her car, shaking hands gripping the steering wheel. She hadn't started the engine. She wasn't sure if she was in any condition to drive yet. But by the same token, she'd looked a cold-blooded killer in the eye. He'd not only gotten a good look at her, but he'd actually spoken to her. His words were still echoing in her head.

A message for you. What message?

The police were packing up and leaving. She wasn't feeling very safe sitting around there, waiting for him to come back and kill her, too. That had to be what he was trying to say. Right?

She'd done her part, given a detailed description to the detective. She'd retold her story at least a dozen times. Now she needed—somehow—to push this whole ugly thing out of her head.

Then again, she'd come looking for answers, wondering if Eve's death might have anything to do with their common history. With what she'd done when she was still a slave.

It's too dangerous. Leave the investigating to the professionals.

She turned the key and the car started. Still trembling, she glanced over her shoulder and maneuvered the car out of the parking space. She slowly drove past the line of police cars angled in front of the pretty Victorian house... turned funeral home... turned crime scene.

A chill crept up her spine.

One question kept whirling around in her mind as she drove home. One nagging question.

Why hadn't the killer shot her, too? Why leave a witness alive?

She constantly checked her rearview mirror as she drove home. Was he waiting for her? Was he following her? She wound through twisty-turny subdivision streets along the way, hoping she'd lose him if he was. Not once did she spy a suspicious car following her.

By the time she pulled into the driveway, she was pretty sure she hadn't been followed. But she still had no answer to that nagging question.

Why?

She let herself into the house and went straight to her room. All she wanted to do was curl up and hide. She didn't want to talk to anyone. Because then she'd have to feel that terror again. That horrid, gut-wrenching shock.

She didn't want to think.

She didn't want to feel.

Escape.

She downed a couple of sleeping pills and let the soothing darkness carry her away.

Her scream tore through his body like a jagged-edged cleaver.

Instantly breathless, Malek sprinted up the staircase, following the sound of Lei's voice. Before he made it to her room, another scream echoed through the house, the sound igniting every nerve in his body.

Three seconds later, he stormed into Lei's room. His gaze jerked to her bed. She was sitting upright, eyes wild, hands clutching the front of her clothes, her face the color of milk.

Without saying a word, he ran to her, hauled her into his arms. She was trembling. Her ragged gasps sawed in and out of her chest.

"I'm okay," she repeated over and over.

He didn't let go. She was shaking. She wasn't okay.

"I'm okay, Malek." She pushed against his chest, but he only loosened his hold on her, he didn't release her. "Malek."

He cupped the back of her head and looked down into her eyes. The pupils were still dilated, so wide he could barely see the ring of brown circling them. "I heard what you said, but are you really okay?"

"Yes." Her lip quivered as the corners tilted up into what he assumed was meant to be a smile. Lei was a terrible liar. "It was just a nightmare. That's all."

He searched her eyes. His hand, the one palming her head, began smoothing back the wisps of hair that had been thrown over her face. The other one, the one currently flattened against her side, remained still. She'd given up a little fight when he'd first grabbed her, but she wasn't wriggling anymore. He wasn't ready to let go of her yet. Hell no. "That must've been one hell of a nightmare."

"It was the pills." Shrinking back from his touch now, as if she'd suddenly realized he was holding her, she jerked backward.

Damn.

"Pills?" he echoed.

"I took a couple of sleeping pills."

He glanced at the clock. It was a little after five in the evening. "You're retiring for the night a little early, aren't you?"

"I wasn't feeling well."

"Are you sick?"

"No, I just had a headache. A migraine." She rubbed a temple.

"And now . . . ?"

"It's a little better now."

"I'm glad. Listen, I brought home some dinner. From Antonio's. There's more than enough for me and Talen. So why don't you help us out?"

She flattened her hand over her stomach. "I am a little hungry."

"Excellent." He stood, then offered her a hand as she scooted to the edge of the bed. After flicking a glance at his extended hand, she accepted it, pushed to her feet, and looked up at him with those glorious dark eyes.

"Thanks." She tugged her hand free.

He fought the urge to cup her chin and claim her mouth.

Whether he wanted to admit it to himself or anyone else, his body had decided there was only one woman who could be his wife. And that woman was Lei.

Now all he had to do was convince her to accept his proposal. And that was going to be no easy task.

But he had an idea.

While she headed into the bathroom to freshen up, he went down to the kitchen to dish out the pasta. Talen was standing at the counter, a foam container in one hand, chewing on a mouthful of eggplant parmesan.

"How much would it cost to make you disappear for the next couple of weeks?" Malek asked.

"Two weeks?" Talen shrugged. "Make me an offer."

"One thousand."

"Five," Talen countered.

"Damn, that's not even reasonable." The echo of little footsteps sounded through the foyer. She was coming. "Three thousand."

"Done. You've got two weeks. I'll pack up and head out after I finish eating." Talen took his carton and a bottle of beer, and headed toward Drako's office. Before stepping into the office, he turned around and gave Malek what he could only describe as a pitying look. "Dude, you've got it bad for her."

Malek grunted and shooed him out just before she rounded the bend, coming into the kitchen. He'd set some plates and glasses out on the dining table and was digging out some silverware when she entered the room.

"Smells great," she said, taking in the set table, then him, as he gathered the rest of the things they needed. "Can I help?"

"Nope, I think I have everything." Napkins and utensils in hand, a bottle of wine tucked under an arm, he headed for the table to finish up the preparations. "Go ahead and take a seat."

He set down the bottle, then folded her napkin and set it next to her plate.

"Such service," she said, watching him.

He uncorked the wine and filled her glass, then his. Next, he opened the foam cartons and lifted the first. "What do you think of Alfredo sauce?"

"Love it."

"Good." He spooned a portion onto each of their plates, added some salad, and finally took his seat.

She gave him a sparkly eyed smile. "This looks wonderful. Thanks for sharing." Her brows scrunched slightly. "Where's Talen?"

"Drako's office, I think. He said he had some important things to do tonight. He's heading out of town on a business trip tomorrow." He lifted his glass. "A toast?"

"Sure, but I shouldn't drink too much after taking those sleeping pills."

"Good point. Just a swallow. How about 'to a new life and new beginnings'?"

"I'll drink to that," she said. They tapped glasses, then sipped. He watched her over the rim. Her gaze slid to the side, avoiding his. She set down her glass and poked at her salad. "Have you registered for your class yet?"

"No, not yet." When she started to stand, he jumped to his feet. "What is it?"

"I need some water."

"I'll get it." He headed into the kitchen, filled a glass with ice and water, and brought it back for her.

Chewing, she studied him as he returned to his seat. "You aren't going to take that course, are you? The sewing class. You never were."

"Of course I was." His face was flaming. He wondered if she could tell.

She tipped her head. Her lips quirked. "*Was?*"

"Was? Am. I *am* taking that class. I'll register as soon as we're done eating. Can I register online?"

Her lips twitched. "Only if you're a current student."

"Then I guess that's out. I'll have to go to the registrar's office tomorrow. I will go."

"Sure."

"I will."

He watched her eat for a few minutes. Watched her lips close around her fork. Watched her tongue slide back and forth across her lower lip. Every now and then she'd glance up at him and he'd have to look away.

He was slightly disappointed when she pushed her half-full plate away and groaned. "I am so stuffed. Thanks again for the dinner. It was delicious."

"You're welcome."

She nibbled on her lower lip as she studied him for several seconds. "You're really going to take that class?"

"Sure, I said I was. Why do you keep doubting me? Shouldn't a guy know how to sew?"

"Of course." Her eyes narrowed slightly.

"Then . . . what? Why are you looking at me like I'm lying?"

"You surprise me sometimes. That's all."

"Maybe that's a good thing."

Their gazes snagged and locked. This was good. Very good. The chemistry was sizzling between them.

She jerked her gaze away. Her cheeks pinked. Staring down at her plate, she played with the fettuccine noodles, winding them around her fork. "Rin hasn't called yet. I hope she's okay."

He checked his watch. "They're probably still on the plane. They had a layover in New Jersey. I have no idea why my brother decided to fly commercial. He never flies commercial."

"Cost savings?"

"Maybe. If he leased a private jet it would probably be flying back empty, and he'd have to pay for that. But he usually likes to know who's doing the flying. Plus, there's the added inconvenience of waiting for flights, changing planes."

"I guess you'll have to ask him." She was still staring down at her plate, pushing food around with her fork.

He reached for her, let his fingertips barely brush against the side of her hand, resting on the table. The second they made contact, she yanked her hand back, hiding it in her lap. "I'm sure Rin will be okay."

"Yes, of course she will. I know that. Drako would never let anything happen to her. But it doesn't stop me from worrying." She lifted her eyes to his. "My sister is all I have. She means everything to me."

"I'm sure she does."

"Not that you and Talen and Drako don't mean something to me, too. Since I moved in, you've sort of become my surrogate brothers."

That was hardly what he wanted to hear. "Brothers?" he echoed.

She chuckled. "Don't care for that descriptive? Would you prefer friend?"

"Yes. No. Maybe." At least friends could sleep together. At least friends could be attracted to each other.

She smiled and his heart lurched. "You are so cute when you're not being a bossy brute."

"I'm not 'cute.' "

"That wasn't meant as an insult. I love how you didn't take offense to the bossy brute part, only the cute reference."

"I cede to the bossy comment. No denying that. On the other hand, puppies and kittens are cute. Grown men aren't. I'm not."

"I guess we'll have to agree to disagree, then."

No, he'd have to prove he wasn't cute.

And he wasn't brotherly.

That was going to be fun.

5

"Marry me," Malek blurted.

He instantly regretted it. What the hell was he doing?

You dumbass, do you want to scare the hell out of her?

Lei's eyes widened. Then she started laughing. And she didn't stop. Not for at least five minutes. Or maybe five hours. "Thank you for the laugh. I needed it today. It's been a rough one."

He wasn't sure what kind of reaction he'd been expecting. But this . . . ? Hysterical laughter? His pride was feeling a little bruised. Really, was it that funny? "I wasn't joking."

She started to laugh again, but the guffaw was cut off abruptly. She scrunched her eyebrows and tipped her head. "Why would you ask me that?" Looking confused, dazed, she shook her head. "I don't understand. Did you get the impression I was looking for a husband somehow?"

"No, not 'looking' for a husband."

Now appearing bewildered and maybe a little scared, she studied him. "I'm . . . speechless." She shoved away from the table. Stood. Sat back down. Looked at him. Opened her mouth but didn't say anything. Snapped it shut and stood again. "My sister married your brother because she needed the money. I don't need money. I mean, sure, money is nice, and I don't have much... I don't have any. But... but..." Her face turned the shade of a fish's belly. "Marriage isn't for me. I'm sorry." She turned to walk away, then spun back around. "But thank you." Once again, she turned away. She took one, two, three steps, then did another one-eighty. "Did my sister put you up to this?"

"Nobody 'put me' up to anything."

"Okay." She started toward the stairs once more. This time she made it as far as the hallway before she turned around to face him again. "It's nothing against you. I'm just... not ready, will probably never be ready to get married. To anyone."

"I understand. We're good."

"Good." She gave him a semi-smile. "I'd still like to be friends."

"Sure. Friends." *Friends. Shit.*

"Thanks for dinner."

"You're welcome."

She didn't leave. Instead, she chewed on her lip. Then she took a step in the right direction, toward him. He didn't say anything because he was one hundred percent sure he'd scare her off if he did. Instead, he waited while she returned to the table and picked up her plate. "What am I thinking, making you clean up after me?"

"It's okay." Standing beside her, Malek set his silverware on his empty plate. "How many times have you tidied up after me and Talen?"

Her eyes sparkled as some of the tension left her face. "Good point." Dirty plate in one hand, both wineglasses in the other, she headed for the counter.

He was right behind her. Set his plate down. Then, ignoring

the nagging temptation to linger near her, he went back to the table to finish clearing it. Meanwhile, he watched her rinse her dish and load it in the dishwasher. Her movements were jerky, nervous. And she wouldn't look at him. In an effort to fill the semi-uncomfortable silence hanging over them, Malek remoted on the TV in the nearby family room and turned it to a music station. And while he sang along with one of Blake Shelton's tunes as he wiped down the table and counters, Lei ran water over the dirty dishes and put them in the dishwasher.

When they were finished, Malek dried his hands on a dish-towel. "Now that we've cleaned up, how about some dessert?"

"Dessert?" Lei's eyes lit up.

He reached into the refrigerator and pulled out three foam cartons. "I have tiramisu, cocoa pistachio shortcakes, and a crème brûlée."

Her gaze zigzagged between the cartons and his face. "Wow, that's a lot of dessert."

He flipped the lid off the first one. "I had a weak moment."

"I guess so."

He opened the second and third carton, lining them up on the counter. "No strings attached. Just friends sharing dessert." When she didn't decline, he grabbed a couple of spoons from the drawer and handed her one. "Dig in."

"I'll get a plate and put a little—"

"No, here." He spooned up some vanilla bean custard and held it out for her.

After watching her eat that yogurt, he was aching to feed her some of this decadent dessert.

She hesitated and blushed, then hastily opened her mouth, leaning in to accept the spoonful. The second her lips closed around the utensil, her eyelids drooped. "Mmmmm..." she said, moving back, leaving him with an empty spoon but a warm and heavy groin. "That's insanely delicious."

"Have more, please. I shouldn't eat all of this."

To his surprise, she abandoned her hesitation and helped herself to half the crème brûlée, several bites of the tiramisu, and half the cocoa shortcake. Then she set down her spoon and said, "Okay. I've gorged on enough chocolate for a month. No more."

And he'd just watched enough food porn for a year. He was doing his best to hide his raging hard-on and was practically gritting his teeth, thanks to a severe case of blue balls. "Glad you enjoyed it."

"Who wouldn't?" She dropped her spoon into the dishwasher's silverware rack. As Malek leaned over her to do the same, she wriggled away from him before he'd gotten close enough to touch her.

Damn.

It seemed his idiotic, poorly thought-out marriage proposal might have made things worse, not better. Now she was going to be even more uncomfortable around him. Maybe more than she was with other men. That was bad. Very bad.

What the hell had he been thinking?

"I have some reading to do for a class," she said as she skittered around the granite-topped island. "Thanks again for the dinner. Everything was delicious. I guess I owe you."

If she felt she owed him, then he was all too happy to oblige. "You know, I like Mexican . . . ?"

She laughed and his heart did a little hop in his chest. If only he could spend the rest of his lifetime listening to that laugh. If only he could spend the rest of his lifetime seeing that stunning smile.

There has to be a way.

"Mexican?" she said.

"Sure. How about tomorrow? After I get back from the registrar's office? Say . . . five-ish?"

"What have I gotten myself into?"

"Nothing yet."

She gave him some serious squinty eyes. "Why did you say 'yet'?"

"I didn't mean anything by it. Honest." He held up a hand, as if swearing in a courtroom. "Like you said, we're friends. Only friends."

"But you asked—"

"Yes, but it was one of those insane, stupid things you do when you're not thinking straight. Either that or it might've been the bottle of wine I drank earlier."

Her eyes went squinty. "You are a dangerous, devious man."

He donned his best nondangerous, nondevious mien. "How could you say such a thing? All I did was accept your offer of a meal. Or maybe you hadn't meant to extend an offer to reciprocate. Perhaps that had been one of those insane, stupid things you do when you're not thinking straight? In which case, I have no expectations and you're under no obligation."

"Oh, shut up." She grinned. "You'll have your Mexican dinner tomorrow. Five o'clock."

"I'm looking forward to it."

"Fine." She pointed an index finger at him, then flicked her eyes down to his groin area. Clearly, she'd noticed his boner. "But let me make something perfectly clear. I'm returning a kindness. There is no underlying meaning to the gesture." Her eyes went down *there* again. Now his cock was hard. And his balls were aching. And his face was on fire. "We're friends. Only friends. And that's the way it's going to stay. Got it?"

"Got it."

"Good." She flounced toward the hallway, her step much bouncier than it had ever been.

He hoped it was he who brought on that bounce. Or maybe what she'd glanced at a few times... Nah, couldn't be.

Lei's phone was ringing when she scurried into her bedroom. She shut the door, snatched up her phone, and not bothering to check the screen, hit the button, answering the call before it went to voice mail.

Expecting Rin, she said, "It's about time!"

"You've been expecting my call?" a man asked.

She knew that voice. It filled her with a strange blend of emotions. It had been at least a couple of months since she'd talked to him last. A lot had happened since then. "No, but I'm glad you called. It's about Eve—"

"I know."

"You do?" His quick response took her by surprise, but she quickly dismissed it. Of course he'd heard. It was all over the news. And he was a federal agent—CIA. "I don't suppose you've heard anything about the case?"

"Only what's been on the news."

"Do you think I'm in danger?" she asked, fiddling with her comforter. "Is that why you called me?"

"Not exactly."

"Oh." Confused now, she shook her head. "Do you mean I'm not in danger? I don't understand."

Silence.

"Lei, you received the message."

Her blood turned to ice. What was this man up to? Was he . . . could he be . . . ? "What message?"

"A message for you."

Her heart stopped for a split second. Then it started thumping hard and fast. Her skin instantly slicked with a cold sweat. She remembered now where she'd seen that man—the one from the funeral home. "What are you talking about?"

"I'm worried, Lei," he said. "About the other girls. That they might be found in an alley somewhere, too. You and I both know how dangerous those men are."

What was going on? What was he getting at? "Those men? Or someone else?"

"You owe me, Lei. It's time to pay your debt."

Her debt? What the hell was he talking about? She didn't remember him ever mentioning she'd have to pay him back for his help. She jumped to her feet and paced back and forth in front of her bed. "I don't owe you anything." Her insides were jumpy, skittery. And that dinner she'd just eaten felt like a huge chunk of concrete in her gut. "There was never any talk of my paying you back. We did what we did because it was the right thing. Because it was good. It was just—"

"No, *we* didn't do anything. I did it all. You didn't do a damn thing. I took all the risks. Don't you think that's worth something? Who takes those kinds of risks for nothing?"

He was right. Nobody did anything out of the kindness of their heart. Not in her world. Now, what the hell did he want?

She forced herself to inhale, even though her lungs were squeezing so tight barely anything could seep in. "So...what do you want?"

"The Alexandre brothers have something I need. You're going to get it for me."

She whirled around, her gaze jumping to the closed door. "What?"

"I've seen the way they look at you. They'll tell you anything. Ask them about their secret. Do whatever it takes."

"Secret? Isn't there another—"

"If you fuck me over or tell them, Lei, you'll find yourself on trial for two murders. Eve and her lovely grandmother."

"But...but—"

"We have witnesses who put you at the scene of both crimes. Do you think anyone will believe the testimony of someone like you? An ex-hooker?"

"I can't—"

"And your fingerprints are on the gun. Your gun. Which was found by police."

Her gun? The one he'd given her for her protection after she'd been released? The one she'd left sitting in the trunk of her car all this time because she'd been too afraid to do anything with it? *How could I have been so stupid?* "They've helped me. Been good to me. There's got to be—"

The call cut off.

A shiver of dread quaked through her body.

She hadn't heard the last from Agent Nate Holloway. No doubt about that.

What the hell had she gotten herself into now?

Already knowing what she'd find, or rather, what she wouldn't find in her trunk, she grabbed her car keys and ran down the stairs.

"A second young woman's body was found in Southwest Detroit last night, this one here, behind this gas station..."

Lei's breakfast surged up her throat. She clapped her hand over her mouth and dashed down the hall to the bathroom. She got there just in the nick of time.

After freshening up, she jerked open the bathroom door. Malek was in the hallway, scowling.

"Are you okay?" he asked.

Her hand shook as she smoothed her hair away from her face. "Yes, I guess I ate something that didn't agree with me."

His gaze grew squinty. "You're very pale."

"I'm still not feeling one hundred percent yet."

He grabbed her arm—such a gallant gesture—and helped her back into the kitchen. He steered her toward the breakfast counter. "Here, have a seat. I'll get you something to drink."

"Thanks." She sat, listening to the news broadcast. They'd moved on to the weather. She'd have to go look up the details of that girl's death online.

A second girl she'd known from her former "career." This one had also left the business with her help. In total, there'd been four girls whom she'd helped escape that hellish life. Now two were dead. Two. For the time being, two more were out there somewhere. In danger. And clueless. She had to find them somehow. Warn them.

"Here you go." Malek set a glass of ice water in front of her, then sat on the stool beside her. "Now, tell me, is there something going on?"

"Something, like what?"

His gaze flicked to her stomach. "Like . . . ?" He cleared his throat as he stared at her belly.

"Oh! Am I pregnant? Not a chance."

"Are you sure?"

"Absolutely."

His body visibly relaxed. His smile returned. "Good. I was worried there for a minute that—"

"That one of my Johns had gotten me pregnant? Pregnancy is one of those things my former *employer* took some lengths to avoid. We were given regular Depo injections, whether we wanted them or not. But that's only because having too many girls pregnant would hurt his bottom line." Her hand, she noticed, was still shaking as she lifted the glass to take a drink. She sipped while Malek studied her. She studied him back while silently considering her options.

She was no Nancy Drew. Or Charlie's Angel. She needed to find those two girls and warn them. And she needed to keep herself out of prison, and her sister and her brothers-in-law safe. Maybe it was wise to tell Malek something so he could help her find the other girls?

"Malek," she blurted just as he started to stand.

He sat right back down. "What is it, Lei?"

"Malek, I don't know where to start."

"I'm here." He reached for her hands but pulled away before he'd touched her. "I want you to feel like you can trust me. With anything."

If only she could.

She tried to think things through, to find just the right

words. She couldn't. She was afraid. Frozen. Thoughts tangled into a massive knotted ball. She was terrified. Of Holloway. Of Malek. Of her feelings for Malek.

"Please, baby. Trust me."

She was in way over her head. That much she knew. She needed help. And she didn't want anything to happen to Malek or Talen. They deserved to know something was wrong, that somebody was after something they had. But she couldn't tell them that. Not yet.

She started with, "The girl on the news this morning."

"Which girl?"

"The one that's dead. Someone found her early this morning in Detroit. I knew her. I knew her well. We worked together."

"And . . . ?"

Now what? She sipped some water, forcing it past the huge congealed lump in her throat. "She's the second one to be discovered dead this week. Two girls. Both murdered. And I knew them."

"Are you thinking you might be in danger?"

I want to tell him everything. But dammit, Holloway's in the CIA. If he said my gun was used in the murder, and the police have it, then I have to believe him. If it isn't true, which I have no reason to believe, then it will be. "Both those girls left right before I did. I never got the whole story about either of them, but the rumor was they'd both been bought back by family members. There were five of us that got out of it that way. Two are dead."

"And the others?"

"I don't know. I'm one of them, of course. I don't know where the other two are. Someone needs to warn them."

"Have you received any threats?"

"None." That was a lie, but she couldn't see any way around it. She needed to keep Malek's focus on the other girls. That way Holloway wouldn't have any reason to suspect him. If

Holloway made good on his threat, she might be facing trial for two murders. Maybe three.

Was there any way out of this fucking situation?

"Have you received any strange calls? Noticed anyone following..." His brows scrunched. "Didn't you ask me if I was tailing you the other night?"

"As I said, I was just mistaken."

"It's possible one has nothing to do with the other, but you still need to be careful. We need to find out why those women were killed."

"I thought the same thing. That's why I went to Eve's funeral and talked to her grandmother. One minute I was sitting there, the next, she was shot, too. In the head. Execution style. In the middle of the funeral home. This is too dangerous. It's a matter for the police, not a couple of wannabe detectives. We need to be cautious and let the police do their thing. But maybe we could try to find the other girls and warn them."

Malek grumbled something under his breath. He shoved his fingers through his hair. "Why didn't you tell me this? I gave my word. I promised to keep you safe."

"I haven't left this house since then."

"Good. And you won't leave. Not until I find out what the hell is going on."

"What are you going to do?"

"I don't know yet. But I can't sit around and do nothing."

"The other girls. I think we should focus on finding them."

"Don't worry, Lei. I'll find out who killed those girls and I'll stop him."

"Please don't do that, Malek. I would feel horrible if something happened to you. Look at that nice old lady. She's dead now, and nobody knows why. Maybe she found out something she shouldn't have. Maybe she poked her nose into something she shouldn't have." Lei couldn't sit still for another second. She slid off the bench and went to refill her glass. "All I want is to live a normal life. I want to forget everything that happened then. Put it behind me. Move on. But here I am, cowering in the shadows. That . . . bastard . . . controlling my life. I might as well still be a slave."

"Don't say that." Malek caught her chin and tipped it up so her eyes met his. "Do you hear me? Don't ever say such a thing. You're free. And no one can control you anymore. You. Are. Free."

Her eyes were burning and she blinked. Once. Twice. Three times. Still her vision blurred. "Is this hell ever going to end?"

"Yes, it is. Because I am going to make sure it does. But you've got to trust me. You have to do what I say until we figure out what's going on and who's behind it."

For a fraction of a second, she wanted to believe Malek could beat Holloway at his game. Then she came to her senses. Of course he couldn't. How could he? He was a good man, yes. Strong. Kind. Intelligent. But he didn't have the connections to protect her from someone like Holloway. "We can't figure it out. We don't have all the facts."

"We will. And once we do, you'll be free to do whatever you want, whenever you want. For the rest of your life. You with me?"

Lei's nod wasn't big, but it was a nod of agreement. She wasn't going to convince him to give it up, after she had brought it to his attention in the first place. The best she could hope to do was hold him back a little, steer him in a safer direction.

"You told me about this because you want my help. Well, I'm going to give it to you. And I'm going to make sure you never regret trusting me."

She was already regretting trusting him as little as she had. "What's next?"

"I want to go to the school and see about registering for classes. After that . . . I don't know. I should call Drako—"

"No, please don't do that," she cut him off, grabbing his

arm. "Don't tell Drako about this." She grappled for a reason to keep this ugly mess from his older brother, knowing that could put her in even hotter water. "He'll tell my sister and she'll worry. She's pregnant. It isn't good for her to worry right now."

"But I need to let him know what's going on." Swiveling the stool to face her, he pulled on the back of hers to swing her around to face him, too. "He won't tell Rin. I promise." Lei was sure she could believe that one. "There are some things you don't know about my brothers and me. Very important things." She wondered if those things were related to what Holloway wanted. "A secret like this could cause serious problems for all of us. I can't keep it from him. No way. But I guarantee Drako will take your sister's health in mind. He can't risk upsetting her."

"Malek, please, can't you just put me on house arrest and look for the other girls?"

"Trust me, Lei. If there's anyone in the world you can trust with a secret, it's me. And Drako and Talen."

6

It was him. Again.

Immediately, Lei's hands started shaking, her heart racing. What now? What?

Her phone, set on vibrate, hummed as it rang a third time. One more ring and it would go to voice mail. One more ring and she wouldn't have to hear his next threat.

She hit the button, but didn't say a word.

"I always knew you were an intelligent woman," he said. "Smart move answering."

"What do you want?" she whispered.

"I don't 'want' anything. I thought I'd let you know that I've been in contact with the lead on a certain murder case, and he tells me they're looking for a woman who fits your description. He called her a 'person of interest.' "

"Well, I had nothing to do with anyone's death. I think you're bluffing."

"Bluffing? Are you sure about that?"

"Yes, I'm sure. You're lying. About the gun. About everything. You just want to scare me so I'll do what you say."

"I guess you'd better hope your alibi stands up."

"This is just a scare tactic," she said, her teeth gritted so hard her temples throbbed. "I don't know anything about a murder or about some stupid secret. Leave me alone!" She cut off the call, dropped her phone, and covered her face with her trembling hands.

She was caught in a nightmare, and she couldn't wake up.

A couple of hours later, Malek returned and proudly proclaimed he was now a registered student at the University of Michigan. He added, somewhat sheepishly, that he'd invited a guest over.

Malek's "guest" was attractive, if you like them skinny, blond, and stupid. Lei didn't. She was actually very surprised Malek did. Upon entering the house, Jodi gushed nonstop about how gorgeous the decor was. Malek played host, giving her the grand tour and introducing her to Lei.

Then Jodi discovered the pool. At the proclamation, "Ohmygod, look at this pool. We should go skinny dipping," Lei headed upstairs to do some research online. She was not in the mood to watch that little tramp throw her skinny little ass at Malek.

What was he thinking?

The echo of that woman's grating laughter followed her all the way up to the second floor. Lei was almost glad when she stopped laughing. Then she considered the most likely reason for her silence.

Lei's blood burned in her veins.

She was freaking jealous.

This was so bad.

After staring at her computer screen for an hour, she was sleepy, her neck was stiff, and she needed to get off her butt and move around. She layered on some warm clothes and, listening for the sound of Malek and his *friend,* headed out the back door for a walk.

The air was crisp and smelled like frozen earth. The crunchy leaves crackled underfoot as she made her way through the wooded part of the property to her favorite spot.

She realized, unfortunately, that the little wood gazebo sitting next to the river was inhabited. It seemed Malek had brought his guest outside. And that was why they'd become so quiet.

Lei slumped against a nearby tree and tried to pretend they weren't there. The river was gray and sluggish. Thin ice formed a crust that reached out a couple of feet from the banks. And the breeze gusting across its surface sent the smell of water and life to her nose. Winter was here—dull, gray, dreary winter. There wasn't a thing about the season she liked. And with Rin gone for at least the next month or so, she'd like it even less than normal.

The sound of Jodi's chuckle filled the silence.

Lei hoped Jodi wouldn't become a repeat houseguest. Keeping her word that she wouldn't leave the house without a bodyguard would be almost impossible.

For some reason, her gaze kept sliding along the river's edge and inching toward the stupid gazebo. It didn't help that she was in a bad spot. From her vantage, she could see Malek and his new friend cozied up on the big, fluffy, built-for-two chaise lounger. They had a pile of blankets on themselves, but she could see enough to know what they were doing. At the moment, they were lying on their sides, facing each other. Jodi's hand was resting on Malek's cheek. And he was kissing her. They were both oblivious to the fact that they had an audience.

Then again, considering Malek's leanings, he probably didn't give a damn who was watching. He had no qualms about fucking in public. She'd learned that after attending a private party hosted by a mutual acquaintance a few weeks ago.

Jodi moaned, and once again, Lei jerked her gaze away.

She should just leave. Why was she standing there, spying, anyway? It was pretty creepy, when she thought about it.

She moved on, following the river's bank as it meandered through the Alexandre brothers' acreage. Occasionally, a rabbit would scamper out of a hiding spot, or a bird would flap its wings and take flight, the sudden sounds startling her. Otherwise, the natural world around her was quiet. The longer she stayed out here, the safer she felt. Safe and completely at peace.

If only she could live out here, away from the noise and distraction of the brothers and all their *friends.* And away from that bastard Holloway and his stupid threats. All she needed was a small space, something cozy and comfortable and private. Nothing like that ridiculous house up on the hill.

Before long, the blustery wind got the better of her, and her fingers went numb. She shoved her hands in her pockets, shrugged her shoulders against the cold, and turned back. When she rounded the bend that passed by the gazebo, she realized there was only one person sitting on the chaise now.

Malek waved her over.

She went.

He flipped the cover back and patted the seat. "You look cold."

"It's a bit brisk out here." She reluctantly sat—on the edge of the cushion. She pulled the cover over her shoulders. "Where's your friend Jodi?"

"She had to leave."

"Ah, that's too bad." She tried to take the sarcastic edge off her voice. She failed.

He chuckled. "Not a fan of Jodi?"

She shrugged. "She seems all right."

"She's more Talen's taste than mine." He patted the cushion again. "Why don't you scoot over a bit? You can warm up better over here."

She felt her nose crinkling. There was something strange about settling in, right where another woman had been a few minutes ago. Lei had a feeling the seat was still warm from her body heat. *Ugh, what is with the jealousy?* "I'm good right where I am. Thanks."

"Lei, I promise I won't try anything. I know how sensitive you are."

"I'm . . ." She turned and looked at him. He had such a sweet expression on his face, somewhat pleading. She scooted a little closer. No more than an inch or two. "There. That's as far as I go."

Malek flung the cover over her and inched closer still. "At least it's a little better."

Silence.

Lei stared out at the smooth water and sighed. "I love this spot. It's so peaceful out here. Quiet. Removed from all the traffic and noise."

"It is nice."

"Did you and your brothers buy the house?" she asked, struggling to find a safe topic, a distraction so she wouldn't think about Holloway. Or Jodi. Or how close Malek was, how good he smelled. How warm he was. "Or did you have it built?"

"We built it."

"Why didn't you build back here?"

"I don't remember. Might've had something to do with the water table being too high to lay a solid foundation."

"I guess that makes sense, sort of." Lei pointed at the houses dotting the landscape on the opposite side of the river. "Though those people seem to have found a way around the problem."

Malek cleared his throat. "It seems they have." Being this close to Lei was killing him. But that was nothing new. His balls were so tight he was gritting his teeth. And his blood was simmering so hotly in his veins he was sweating. But there was no way in hell he was putting an end to his suffering. It would be her choice, not his.

After his short visit with Jodi—a total waste of time—he'd come to one conclusion. He couldn't give up on Lei yet. He was going to keep pushing her, keep winding those little threads between them. That was the way he'd win her: one delicate silken thread at a time.

He said, "You know, my brothers and I have always planned to build three houses on this property, one for each of us. I'm about to meet with the architect to begin work on mine. Maybe I should talk to him about building back here?"

"You should." Lei made a small frame with her hands. "You should put a huge wall of windows facing the water. It's a million-dollar view. Especially in the fall, when all the trees have changed."

"That sounds like a good idea. Do you have any other suggestions? I don't know anything about designing houses. That's why I've put it off for so long."

"I have plenty of ideas. I love to read books about home design. It's another hobby of mine."

This could definitely work for him. From the sparkly eyes he could tell it was more than a hobby for her. It was a genuine passion. He hoped someday her eyes would sparkle like that for him, about him.

"Would you do me a favor, then, and meet with my architect? I'm afraid if I don't have someone help me, I'm bound to design the ugliest house on the street."

The sparkles dimmed a little. "Oh, I don't know. You should build the house of your dreams. Not mine. But I could loan you some books for inspiration."

He was inspired already. He didn't need any damn books. "I've looked at plenty of books. But those are just pictures. I don't know what I want, what I like." He turned on the charm. "Please, Lei."

She met his gaze, then huffed out a little sigh. "You are a hard man to say no to."

He hoped that statement would apply to lots of other things in the future. He amped up the wattage on his grin. It was getting easier and easier to be this way with Lei, to relax and let down his guard and have fun. He liked the man he became when he was with her, even if he was a little softer, a little more pliant.

Brittle things cracked under pressure. They broke. Like concrete. In contrast, elastic, flexible things stretched and held better, depending upon the situation.

This situation called for flexibility. And patience. Lots of patience.

"I'll meet with him I guess," she said.

"Thank you." He took her hand in his and gave it a small squeeze.

She didn't flinch.

His gaze hopped from their hands to her face several times before he whispered, "Lei, I want you to let me touch you."

Her hand moved a tiny bit, but she didn't pull it completely away. "Malek, you know that's hard for me."

"I do know. But that's why I think it's important for you to work through this. I want to help you."

"Why?"

Malek shrugged. He couldn't tell her the truth, that he might be falling for her and wanted to heal her pain, to make her whole again. If he so much as uttered those words, she'd run. "I feel it's what you want. You do want to feel comfortable being around people, being intimate, don't you?"

"Maybe."

"And you do trust me."

"More than anyone else... except Rin."

"And you know, as a dom, that I do have some experience helping people push through certain limits. You do the same thing for your submissives, too."

"Sure."

"Then please let me help you."

Lei thought about it for longer than he would've liked. The entire time, he sat breathless, hoping she'd say the word he ached to hear. And then she nodded, "Okay, but only touch. Nothing more. And not anywhere inappropriate."

"I can deal with that." He gave her no time to change her mind. Because he knew she would if he didn't take action right then and there. "If you want me to stop, say the word *red.*"

"Red. Got it."

Her lip caught his attention. It was quivering. It was a relatively warm day for that time of year, but it was still pretty damn chilly. "Are you cold?"

"A little."

Malek lit a fire in the outdoor fireplace to warm them. When he returned to the chaise, Lei sat relatively stiffly beside him and stared at the flame.

"Are you okay?" he asked.

She nodded and flicked her eyes at him. "Smart move, bringing this up when we're down here."

"I'm not trying to seduce you. I'm not hiding an ulterior motive."

"Right, I know that." She didn't sound so sure.

He fluffed some cushions behind her so she could lean back, semi-reclined. As he worked, he angled over her. She was close enough to touch, to kiss. It was agony. Never had he been so aware of a woman before. His skin sizzled whenever she was near. She didn't even have to touch him and he was warm all over. Warm and hard and eager to take her.

After prolonging the inevitable and abandoning his pillow fluffing, he sat back on his heels. "Better?"

"Um, sure." Her eyes sparkled a little as she looked up at him. At least, he was convinced they were sparkling. "I was fine before, but thanks."

"You're welcome." He settled in beside her and lifted one arm up. "Now, could you sit forward for a second?"

She caught on to what he was doing and eased forward to allow him to rest his arm behind her. Then she settled back in place.

"How's that?"

"It's . . . okay."

They sat like that, silent and slightly uncomfortable (actually, he was very uncomfortable, thanks to a raging erection) for a while. Finally, he shifted slightly, pulling her into his side. As expected, she stiffened.

He asked, "Are you okay?"

"Yes."

Moving slowly, he cupped her chin, turning her head until she faced him. "I've been waiting for this for a long time."

Her lips parted slightly. Those were lips that he would taste. Soon. Very soon. And it would only be him. For now, he would be content to brush his thumb over their plump fullness.

She gave a little shudder as his finger grazed her lower lip, but she didn't move away. Her pupils dilated. That was a good sign. "Malek."

He shifted toward her, aiming for her jaw. He kissed a line from her chin to her neck. "Yes, Lei?" he asked, nuzzling her, drawing in her scent. Deep. Deeper.

"Malek," she repeated, sounding a little out of breath.

This time, he didn't respond. He doubted she expected him to. Instead, he nibbled and nipped his way down her neck. And while he did that, she gathered his shirt in her fists, digging her fingernails into his upper arms. The pain only amped up his body's response. His blood pounded through his veins now, beating a steady but swift thrum from his head to his cock.

"Malek," she whispered as she tilted her head to one side to give him better access to the crook of her neck. "I thought you were going to just touch me."

He glanced up at her face, noted the flush staining her cheeks, then went back to tormenting her with his lips, teeth, and tongue.

Her skin was salty-sweet. Delicious. And her scent was clean and pure and intoxicating. The little whimpers and sighs that slipped between her lips were like the sweetest music he'd ever heard. They made his heart soar.

She was doing it. She was submitting to his touch. And he couldn't be happier.

He would be the one to heal her scars. Only he.

"Let me show you how much pleasure a touch can give," he murmured as he eased his hand under her shirt. He wanted to explore every inch of her body. But not today. No. Not yet.

"I...I..." She shivered, released his arms, and then flung her arms around his neck. "Oh, God."

Malek checked her face again. That pink shade had deepened. Her eyes were closed, thick, sooty lashes fanned over the translucent skin beneath her eyes. "Look at me, Lei."

Her lids lifted. Her eyes focused first on his mouth, then his eyes.

He said, keeping his voice low, soft, "I'm going to touch you on the stomach."

She nodded and closed her eyes, stiffening slightly.

His hand crept up a little, after hovering over the heat at the juncture of her thighs. Rather than tease her with little shy touches and tickles, he set his hand firmly on her stomach.

She gasped. Her eyelids jerked up. Her expression changed from one of desire to one of fear and confusion. "Rrrrreee."

"You know what you need to say if you want me to stop. Do you need to say it? Do you need me to stop?" He didn't move his hand, not a finger. It killed him, but he did it. He kept it still.

Something else had been still, too. Much too still. Lei's stomach. She wasn't breathing.

She whispered, "I..."

"Breathe, baby. Inhale." He inhaled with her, slowly drawing air in through his nose. "Good, now exhale." He blew a steady stream out through his mouth. "Yes, that's the way. Again."

She breathed with him, in and out, in and out. It didn't take long for her anxiety to ease.

"We can stay like this as long as you need," he whispered. "Until you're so comfortable you don't even realize my hand is there anymore."

The corners of her mouth twitched. "If we do that, we may be here until springtime. Maybe longer."

Lei was dying. Her insides were a mixed-up jumble of conflicting emotions. Her nerves were blazing, overloaded by sensations. She wanted it all to stop. And yet she didn't.

Here she was, reclined against Malek, his hand resting softly on her stomach, and you would think she was in a torture chamber. She hated that such a simple thing, such a simple, common pleasure, caused her so much agony. And she was determined to get past it with Malek's help.

The icy wall she'd erected around herself was beginning to feel more like a prison than a cocoon.

His chuckle reverberated through her body, sending little pleasant tremors quaking up and down her spine. Yes, there were good emotions in there, but they were overshadowed by the bad. Happiness and fear. Anticipation and uncertainty. Thrill and anxiety. If only it could be the other way around, and the good could start to overtake the bad. If only she didn't immediately flash back to those awful ugly days the minute a man laid a hand on her.

She jolted as a particularly horrific memory surged to the surface and she scrambled away from him. Then, frustrated and angry, she dropped her face into her cupped hands.

"Give it time," Malek said.

"Dammit, I just want to forget. Why can't I forget?"

"The memories will fade."

"That's what my therapist keeps telling me. But will they ever fade enough?" She uncovered her face to meet his gaze. Through watery eyes, she took in the sight of his worry-riddled expression. "You're no more sure I'll get past this than I am."

"If there's any hope, you will. And I'll help you however I can."

She wrapped her arms around herself. "I wish there was a pill I could take to make it all go away forever."

"I wish there was one, too." Moving slowly, he adjusted the blankets to help her stay warm. "I have a memory or two I wouldn't mind erasing."

"Will you tell me?" Malek didn't respond right away, and Lei immediately regretted having asked him. How could she be so stupid? She'd just asked him to rehash a memory he was as desperate to forget as she. He'd never once asked her to talk about what happened to her. "I'm sorry. I shouldn't have—"

"I was young at the time. I don't know exactly how old, maybe four or five. I don't think anyone realizes I saw what I did." Malek was staring into the fire now, as if the scene were playing out in the flames. "I watched my mother die."

"Ohmygod." Lei clapped her hands over her mouth.

His gaze slid to hers. "I still see her sometimes, looking at me, her eyes full of pain. Some of the details have faded, but not all. And every once in a while something will stir those memories back to the surface. A sound. A scent. And I'll feel all those emotions again, the terror and confusion."

"I'm so sorry you saw that. You were so young."

"This might seem weird, but I think that experience made me a better man. A stronger man."

"Really? How?"

"I understand what other people are feeling, I think. More than I would have if I hadn't gone through what I did so long ago. And forgive me for saying this, but I believe your experience, as horrible as it was for you, will also make you a better person, too. If nothing else, you can look at a sex worker and not see something less than human like so many people do. You see the woman who is trapped in a life she didn't choose."

"I wish I could help them all."

"Maybe someday you'll help one get out."

She had. She'd helped four. But look how that had turned out.

He added, "Maybe you'll help more than one."

"I don't know. I think it's a lot harder than anyone realizes." *Including me.* "It's not just a matter of getting them freed. They need help afterward, too. Help finding new jobs, safe homes, medical help breaking addictions. Look what's happening now. The girls who got out, like me, are turning up dead. I'm just one woman. One. I can't do all that for them. The problem is too big for just one person, too complicated."

"Maybe it is too big. Maybe not. But that's not the point. You will eventually reach a crossroads and you'll have to make a choice. You'll either let your past cripple you or inspire you to do something good." He reached for her face, and her whole body clenched. But she didn't back away. She refused to let herself shrink back from him. Malek was a good man, flawed but kind. And he cared a hell of a lot about her. He cupped her cheeks and eased her head down. Then he kissed her forehead and released her. "It's late. And I'm hungry. I believe someone promised me a Mexican dinner."

"Sure, but it'll have to be delivery. Someone has put me under house arrest."

"Delivery's fine." He flipped back the covers, stood, and offered her a hand. "Ready to head inside?"

"Sure, but one last question. I never see you go to work. Do you work?"

"I do." He sat, grinning. It was an I-have-a-naughty-secret kind of grin. "I write."

"What do you write?"

His grin turned more wicked. "Novels."

"What kind? Can I read one?"

"Maybe." He smoothed the cover over her legs. Her heart skittered in her chest.

" 'Maybe.' Why not? Are you being secretive?"

"No, I'm not being secretive. I'm just not sure you're ready to read my books."

"Why? Are they violent?"

"No."

"Then...?"

"Let's just say I live by the cliché. I write what I know."

She connected the dots and nodded. "Ah, let me guess, is there perhaps bondage in your books?"

"Yes, there is."

"Got it. And you're probably right. I might not be ready to read something like that, especially written by a male dom."

"When you're ready, let me know." He stood again. After dousing the fire in the fireplace, he offered her a hand up.

She accepted it. "Thanks, will do. By the way, I'm a little short on cash this week...."

"No problem. Dinner's on me tonight." His fingers wove between hers. Giving her a sideways glance as they walked up to the house, he added, "I'll take a rain check."

7

After calling Drako to talk about his potential choices in a wife, filling him in on the local deaths, and then spending the next half hour convincing his older brother that he didn't need to come rushing home—he could handle this situation without him—Malek went to the kitchen.

He was on edge. He was hungry. But more than that, he was frustrated, irritated. And it was all because of that damn conversation about his upcoming marriage.

He was close to Drako. He respected him because he was the oldest, the leader of the Black Gryffons. But a very small part of him felt slightly irritated when Drako tried to bust in and take over all the time. That was how he'd always been. This was especially true when it came to talking to Drako about anything personal, especially women.

Drako was really pushing him toward marrying April. But the more they talked about it, the more Malek wanted to dig in his heels and tell him no.

It wasn't that Drako didn't present some good arguments for going with April. He had. Drako had talked about how much more sense it meant to pick someone who was ready to be married, who didn't have a shitload of baggage hanging around her neck.

But... April? Even the thought of marrying April made his gut twist.

It wasn't that April was a bad person. Or that he disliked her for any reason. Rather, it was the thought of giving up Lei that made his stomach coil into a painful knot.

Of holding her at arm's length.

Of treating her as a sister, instead of a lover.

Of being close to her, within reach, and never being able to touch her again.

But... but...

As Drako had said, he had chosen a woman he had thought he couldn't love. It had turned out okay for him. Although things had been a little rough for a while.

Should he listen to Drako's advice? Go with April?

Or should he go for Lei and keep busting his head against the walls she'd built around her heart?

Drako's words echoed in his head, *Give it up. Lei doesn't want you. And you don't have enough time to make her want you. In the end, you'll only hurt her.*

He saw her now, in the family room, sitting in a chair in front of the fireplace. Her legs were curled up. A quilt hid her body from him. She was reading, head tipped down. Her glossy black hair shielded part of her lovely face.

As if she sensed he was staring, she looked up. The corners of her lips curled. It was a shy, sexy, mind-numbing smile.

"I ordered dinner. It'll be here in about forty minutes."

She glanced at the clock hanging on the wall. "Did you talk to Drako?"

"I did. That's why I just got around to ordering the food."

The smile faded. Worry darkened her eyes. "And...?"

"He insisted on coming home."

"Will he tell Rin?" she asked, closing her book.

"I talked him into staying in Spain."

The relief on her face couldn't be clearer. She visibly inhaled, then exhaled. "They're not coming?"

"No."

She bit her lip. It was quivering. And Malek could imagine cupping her chin and kissing her until she wasn't shaking anymore. "Thank you."

"Don't thank me yet."

"Why's that?" she asked, chuckling softly, misreading his threat as a joke.

"Because I'm going to be the biggest pain in your ass until this is over. You won't step a foot outside that door without me."

She stopped laughing. "You know, I was thinking about that. Is it really necessary?"

"Drako said it is. And I agree."

Her lips thinned. She stared at her book, sitting in her lap. She blinked several times. "Okay." She sighed heavily. "Fine."

He hadn't expected Lei to jump for joy over having him be her shadow. But after that moment they'd shared out in the gazebo, he'd hoped for a better reaction than this. He could appreciate the fact that her life had been fucked up by those bastards. And she was trying hard to put it all behind her. But was it really so bad that he was going to be her bodyguard?

I should call fucking Talen and let him babysit her.

Nursing his bruised ego, Malek went to the kitchen, grabbed a few beers, took them up to his room, and turned on the TV, hoping it would distract him. He slumped onto the couch.

Three beers, a pleasant but slightly awkward Mexican dinner with Lei, and several hours later, he forced himself to make the call he'd been avoiding for days. He called Brent and asked him to come over.

He'd put off this conversation long enough.

Immediately, Brent could tell something was up. The minute he walked into the house, he asked, "What's wrong?"

"Let's go upstairs." Not sure where Lei was, and afraid he'd be overheard, he took Brent up to his room. He closed the door.

Brent took in the collection of empty beer bottles, the plate and napkins, and the reality show playing on the TV and gave Malek a worried look. "What the hell is going on with you?"

"I don't know."

Brent slanted a look that said *bullshit.*

Malek flopped into the chair nearby and kicked an ankle up on the opposite knee. Then he dropped it back down, leaned forward to rest his elbows on his knees, and rubbed his temples. This was going to be a hellish talk, and he wasn't sure where to start.

Better to talk about something safe first. "I'm fucked in the head."

Brent nodded. "It's a woman."

"Yeah."

Brent sat in the chair next to his, draped his arms over the armrests, and rested an ankle on the opposite knee. "They always fuck you in the head. Who is it this time? April?"

"No."

"Then who? Jodi?"

"Not her either."

"Well, damn, dude, you have a lot of women in your life. Want to give me a clue?"

Malek couldn't help chuckling at that statement. "I haven't fucked this one. That should narrow down the list."

"Sure it does. Now I'm confused." Brent looked confused, too. Not that Malek could blame him. "Who haven't you fucked?"

"It's Lei."

"Who's Lei?"

"My sister-in-law."

"Have I met her?"

"Not yet."

"Okay." Brent leaned forward, giving Malek the nonverbal go-ahead to tell his story.

"It's complicated."

"Isn't it always when it comes to women?"

"But in this case, it's even more complicated. Lei is my brother's wife's sister. She was a sex slave, sold by her mother. Her sister hunted her down, and with my brother's help, bought her freedom."

Brent's eyes went wide. "What kind of fucking mother sells her daughter into slavery?"

"A fucked-up one, that's what kind."

"Yeah," Brent nodded. "So, this Lei is hot?"

An image of Lei flashed through his mind, and he felt his lips tipping up into a semi-smile. In his imagination, he saw her gorgeous, expressive almond-shaped eyes. Her smooth porcelain skin. Her lush lips. "She's the most beautiful woman I've ever seen. But she's got problems."

"Who wouldn't, if their mother sold them to slave traffickers?"

"Yeah."

Brent shrugged. "So, you give her time, take it easy, right?"

"Right." If only he could give her time. If only. *This is it. Time to tell him about getting married.* "Except there's a problem. Our family has some . . . unusual traditions. And I need to get married. Soon. That's what I really needed to talk to you about tonight."

Brent's face paled. "You? Married? How soon?"

"By January first."

"January first? That's fucked up." Several emotions seemed to play over Brent's face, including shock, disbelief, and maybe pain. He stared down at the floor for several long, excruciating seconds. "What happens if you don't want to get married?"

"My wife will be picked for me."

"Fuck. Who does that anymore? I mean, nobody arranges marriages anymore."

"Some do."

Brent scrubbed his face with his palms. Malek could tell he was struggling to hide his feelings, but he was failing. And Malek's heart ached, seeing Brent like this. "Married," he repeated, shaking his head. "Do you want to get married?"

"It depends." Malek reached for him and set his hand on Brent's. "It doesn't have to change what we have."

Brent didn't respond right away. He stared at the floor. And Malek stared at him, studying every inch of his face. Damn. He'd known this would be hard. That was why he'd put this conversation off for as long as he had. But he didn't think it would be this bad. For one, he'd assumed—stupidly—that Brent wouldn't care whether he was married or not. So many of their friends lived in open marriages, it was almost expected. Finally, Brent said, "How long have you known?"

"I've known I'd be expected to marry eventually for a while, since before Drako's wedding. But I just found out about my deadline a few days ago."

"Before I came over last?"

Malek nodded. "I didn't know how to tell you."

"Shit."

He hated to see his friend, his partner, his confidant and lover suffering like this. He longed to embrace him, kiss him, tell him nothing would change. But the truth was, he didn't know now if that was possible, as much as he wanted it.

He loved Brent. His heart ached when Brent hurt. His heart leaped when Brent was happy. He couldn't imagine life without Brent.

"Let's get back to Lei," Brent said, avoiding the topic of

their relationship for now. Malek had a feeling it was too painful for him to discuss at the moment. But sooner or later they would have to talk about their future. After this, Malek wasn't looking forward to that conversation. Absolutely, Malek wanted to continue being lovers. But in the long run, what Malek wanted didn't matter. Malek had to focus on Brent's happiness, not his own.

As a dom, that was his obligation.

As a lover, that was his commitment.

Malek said, "I have feelings for Lei. Complicated, confusing feelings for her. And when I try to imagine myself married to another woman, I get this empty, hollow sensation inside."

"So, marry her."

"She's not ready for marriage yet. She's not even close to ready."

"Can't you put it off for a while?"

"No."

Brent surged to his feet. "Dammit, this is fucked up." After shooting Malek a glare, he began pacing back and forth. "I don't get it. What difference would a few months, or a year make?"

Of course Brent didn't get it. Not many people, outside of his own brothers, would. "There are reasons for my family's traditions."

Brent stopped pacing and locked an angry stare on Malek. "Yeah? Like what?"

"I can't get into it."

Instantly, Brent closed up. Malek watched him emotionally shut down. His eyes became cold; his expression blank. Brent was a generous, giving lover, and his best friend. But whenever something came up that Malek couldn't discuss with him, Brent became extremely hurt. More than once, the issue had almost cost them their relationship. "I don't know what you want me to tell you, then. You've got to marry someone. You pick or your wife is picked for you." Brent checked his watch, then smoothed his palms down his legs. "I gotta go. I'm meeting someone in a half hour."

"Brent, I'm sorry. I wish I could tell you everything."

"I wish you could trust me."

Brent left.

8

Lei was so nervous her hands were shaking. She'd snuck out of the house—like a teenager who'd been grounded. But Malek had given her no choice. And here she'd thought it would be better for him to embrace the whole bodyguard thing than to go Dirty Harry vigilante on the bad guy.

Everything will be okay.

Yes, she'd taken a chance by leaving the house tonight. But there was a good reason for it. After spending hours upon hours on the Internet, trying to track down those two girls, all she'd found was a Facebook page for one of them, Kate. Naturally, she tried sending a private message. And another. No response. But she had learned something useful. They shared an acquaintance in common. And that acquaintance was having a party tonight.

The plan was simple. Go in. Find Kate. Tell her to change her name and leave town. And then go home.

Easy peasy.

After slamming her car door, Lei smoothed her sweaty palms down her skirt and *click-clacked* up the front walk of the upper-middle-class suburban brick colonial. She rang the bell, and listened to the echo of laughter and music inside.

Outside of the whole sneaking out thing, this was what she needed. Interaction. With people. More than just Malek. For more than one reason. Outside of trying to hunt down Kate, being cooped up with Malek was messing with her mind. He was becoming the center of her world. She couldn't stop thinking about him. Finding ways to be around him. It was getting bad.

The door swung open and the acquaintance, Gwen, holding a glass of champagne beamed a greeting. "Lei! So glad you could make it. Come in." Gwen stepped to the side, closing the door behind Lei. In the foyer, she motioned to the small room to the left. "You can throw your coat in there. Then come on back." Gwen handed her the glass of champagne. "Here, this'll get you started."

"Thanks. Is Kate O'Shea here?" Lei took a little sip of the sparkling wine—delicious.

"Kate O'Shea? I haven't seen her yet. But I did invite her. I didn't realize you two knew each other."

"Yeah." She didn't elaborate, not knowing how much about Kate's background Gwen had been told.

"Okay. Well, I'd better get back in there." Gwen flounced off and Lei clacked across the stone foyer to the small but cozy office turned coatroom. After setting down the glass, she shrugged out of her coat and draped it over the back of a leather chair in the corner. Then she followed the sound of voices toward the heart of the house.

The open kitchen/great room area was packed with chatting, drinking, laughing guests. After doing a visual sweep of the room, searching for familiar faces—both good and bad—Lei spotted Gwen standing at the far end of the great room, next to the fireplace. She was talking to a man who looked a little familiar—good looking, tall, with dark, shaggy hair.

As she walked toward them, she remembered where she'd seen him. He was the one who'd been at Malek's—her—house the other night. In the dungeon with Talen. Feeling a little uneasy, especially when a couple of men standing close by gave her an appraising up-and-down look, she took a slight detour, heading into the kitchen to avoid passing directly in front of them.

Just as she was helping herself to a fresh glass of champagne from the tray sitting on the kitchen island, Gwen came bouncing up to her. The man she'd been speaking with was behind her. "Lei, this is Brent. Brent, this is my friend Lei. You two know at least one person in common." Off she flounced, before Lei and Brent had even exchanged hellos.

Lei gave him a friendly smile as she offered her right hand. "Brent, it's nice to meet you."

"Yes, it's nice to meet you, too. Malek has told me a lot about you." His handshake was firm and strong and brief, thank goodness. His voice was masculine, a deep baritone. His face was traffic-stopping gorgeous. And his expression was not the least bit creepy.

"Malek has talked about me?"

"Sure. Malek and I are good friends. Close friends." His gaze flicked around the room. "Is he here with you?"

"No, I came alone."

"Oh, really?" At her nod, he asked, "So, how do you know Gwen?"

"School. You?"

"I met her through a mutual friend. She's—"

"Lei!" the object of the conversation cut in, grabbed Lei's hand, and started tugging on her arm. "Sorry," she apologized to Brent. "There's someone who wants to meet her. Lei, this way."

"Okay, sure." Lei glanced over her shoulder. Brent had already found someone else to talk to.

"I met these guys last weekend," Gwen jabbered. "They are both super hot and have great jobs. They'd like to go on a double date." She whispered, "The tall one's mine," before halting directly in front of the two men Lei had noticed earlier.

Once again, they gave her *that* look, the kind her Johns used to give her. Creepy. A little shiver of unease quaked up her spine. Then she felt even more uncomfortable when she realized one of them looked familiar, too. And this one wasn't a friend of Malek's.

"Pete, Rob, this is my friend Lei."

"Nice to meet you, Lei," the shorter of the two, Rob, said. He wasn't the one she thought she recognized. It was the other one. Pete. Judging by the way they were both staring at her, she was pretty certain she had been right about Pete; he had been one of her Johns. And he'd told Rob about her former career—that term used loosely.

Gwen chattered, "Rob here was telling me about an artist friend of theirs who was having an event at—"

"Excuse me," a woman interrupted, stepping up to Gwen. "We're out of champagne. Gwen, did you have some more somewhere?"

"Oh, sure, I'll get it." Gwen gave Lei a raised index finger. "Be back in a minute." Off she trotted, leaving Lei with two men who gave her a serious case of the icks.

Lei decided a hasty retreat was in order. "Excuse me, but I see a friend—"

"Don't I know you from somewhere?" Pete asked, a semi-sneer pulling at his mouth.

"Oh, I doubt it." She took a couple of steps away. But one of them grabbed her arm, snapping her back around. She shot the offender, Pete, a warning glare. "What the hell? Let me go."

"I do know you," Pete said, a cruel smile taking the place of the sneer. His grip tightened. "How about we go upstairs and get more comfortable? Or maybe we should hit a hotel, where we can have some privacy?"

Lei jerked her arm. Her heart rate kicked into high gear and her face started burning. The air was getting thick. She couldn't breathe. "Let go. Now. Before I—"

"What? Scream? Call the police?" Pete leaned closer, too close. "You're a hooker. Do you want everyone here knowing that?" With his free hand, Pete reached for her breast.

She slapped his hand away before it reached its target. "I am *not* a hooker."

"I saw you. At a party. You were one of the girls there. Fucked my friend. He said you were good with your mouth." Pete dragged his thumb over her lower lip.

About to gag, she jerked back and smacked his hand away. "I don't know what you're talking about. You're wrong. That wasn't me."

"So...what? You've retired? What's one more time?" Pete said coolly as he started walking through the kitchen, hauling her along. "Come on, Rob. You in? She can handle us both."

"Sure." Rob stepped up on her other side, looped his arm around her waist, and gave her a nudge.

"I said no," she shouted, her gaze jumping from one cluster of party attendees to another. Nobody was looking at her. Nobody was noticing she was being half-dragged out of the room. Not one person.

Where was Gwen?

In the kitchen? No. The living area? No. No Gwen. No Brent.

She was on her own. Standing in a crowd, but alone. Defenseless.

Rob and Pete hauled her forward another several feet.

Going into full panic, she started fighting back, trying to break free from her would-be rapists before they got her outside. But Pete had a strong grip on her arm, and Rob grabbed her other arm as they dragged her toward the foyer.

"Dammit, somebody help me! You bastards!" she shouted, desperate now. If they raped her. Oh, God, if they got that far, she didn't think she could make it through that.

"Shut the hell up," Pete growled. "It isn't like we're doing something you don't do every day. You'll like it. I promise."

"Gwen!" she shrieked as they shoved her toward the front door. If they got her outside, it was over.

Pete opened the door. "Shut up, bitch. Sheesh. Quit making such a fucking scene."

"Excuse me," someone said behind her. That someone was a male.

Tears started blurring Lei's eyes. She was relieved. Petrified. Desperate. Embarrassed. All she wanted to do was get the hell out of this place. Go home. With Malek. Where she was safe.

Dammit, all she'd wanted to do was find Kate and warn her that she might be in danger. She'd never in a million years thought she'd run into one of the agency's Johns at this party.

How many more times would this happen? When? Where? Would the nightmare ever be over?

Pete snarled. "Fuck off, she's ours."

"What the hell are you talking about, yours?" the man behind her said.

"This cunt is a whore. Here to do a job. Don't worry. We'll pay her." With his free hand, Pete grabbed a wad of bills from his wallet, waved them in front of her savior's face, whom she still hadn't seen because he was standing directly behind her, and shoved them down the front of her dress. The unmistakable *rip* of the fabric echoed through the foyer.

"I'm not a whore," Lei said, teeth gritted. Humiliated, furious, and just plain freaked out, she threw her hands over her chest, closing her fists around the shredded material.

"Yes, you are," Pete said, as he cupped her mound.

Bile surged up her throat and she gagged. She twisted, trying to break free. She kicked. She tried to shove him away. But between Pete and Rob, her arms were absolutely no use.

"Let her go," the man behind her said in a low but even tone. That tone, and the energy she felt buzzing through the air, reminded her of a dog that was about to attack.

"Fuck off." Pete pinched Lei's nipple and she screeched in pain and smacked her hands over her breasts. "Go find your own whore. I paid her. She's mine. I can do anything I want."

"I don't want your fucking money," Lei growled. "Just let me go."

Pete's hand skimmed down her body. "Isn't that sweet? She's willing to give me a freebie."

"That's not what I meant." Her lungs were burning for air. Her knees were soft, rubbery. "I'm not willing to give you anything."

"Last chance, asshole," the man behind her said. "Let the lady go."

"Lady. That's a good one." Pete laughed. The hollow sound echoed across the foyer. "Let's go, Rob." He opened the door.

"No!" Lei shrieked as she dug in her heels.

One second, she was about to be hauled through the door, and the next, all hell broke loose and she was caught in the middle of a melee. She was jostled, then shoved off her feet. She landed on the hard tile floor, ankle throbbing, eyes blurred with unshed tears. Clutching the torn front of her dress, she scooted back against the wall and watched the three men throw punches at each other, waiting for a chance to make her getaway.

"What the hell?" Gwen shouted.

"They tried to rape me." Lei's hand trembled as she pointed.

"What?" Gwen scurried to the three men, tried to break up

the fight, was thrown aside, then raced back to the party. A few moments later, she returned with several other men. They had better luck getting the brawl broken up.

"What the hell is going on?" Hands on hips, Gwen looked from one man to the other.

Lei climbed to her feet, hands gripping the torn pieces of her dress. "I need to go home. Now."

Gwen ran to her side, gaze zooming up and down. "Ohmygosh. Your dress. What happened?"

Pete dabbed at his bloody mouth with one hand and pointed at Lei with the other. "It was the whore's fault."

Everyone looked at Lei.

"I told you, Gwen." She closed her eyes and wished for the floor to swallow her up and make her disappear. "They tried to rape me."

Rob piped in, pointing at Brent. "We weren't going to rape anyone. The cunt's a whore. She took my money, but that asshole thought he'd play hero."

Lei saw red. She grabbed the bills that had been smashed into her bra and threw them on the floor. "The hell I did. I didn't 'take' anything. You rammed that money down my bra. And you ripped my dress doing it." Humiliated beyond words, she charged for the door, staggered outside, and teetered on wobbly legs toward her car. She buckled herself in and was cranking the key when someone knocked on her window.

Fearing the worst, she ducked, glancing up through the glass.

It was Brent.

"Can we talk?" he asked.

She did owe him a thanks for what he'd done. After making sure Pete and Rob were nowhere in sight, she hit the button, powering down the window.

He motioned to her passenger seat.

"Um, okay." She hit the unlock button as she watched him circle the front of the car. Feeling self-conscious, she fussed with the torn dress, doing her best to hide herself.

He ducked inside and shut the door.

She hit the button, locking them in.

"First, are you okay?" Brent asked.

"Yeah." She fisted the front of her dress. "I'm humiliated. Embarrassed. But I'm not hurt. I guess it was a mistake, coming here by myself. But I never imagined... Anyway, thanks. For what you did back there." With her free hand, she pointed at his bloodied lip. Even in the dark car she could see it was swelling up pretty bad. "I should be asking you, are you all right?"

"I'm fine."

Waiting, curious to find out why he'd followed her, she nodded, hoping it would encourage him to continue. It did. Sort of.

He said, "To be honest, I don't know what I'm doing here."

She wasn't sure what he meant by that.

He continued, "I mean, if you and Malek get married, I should be happy for you. Obviously, you've lived through hell. Are still living through hell. You deserve happiness, someone who will protect—"

"Wait," she blurted, cutting him off. "Where did you get the idea that I was marrying Malek?"

"He told me you were. I think. Maybe we didn't get that far. The conversation veered off on a tangent."

"I'm not marrying Malek," she stated.

"He's marrying someone."

"It won't be me."

Silence.

Lei waited, wondering why Brent was still sitting in her car, staring at the windshield. "I need to go."

He turned to her. "Can you explain to me why he has to get married by January first? I don't understand."

"I didn't know... January first? Really?" That explained the silly, impulsive, crazy marriage proposal.

"That's what he said."

"All I know is my sister married Malek's older brother, Drako. Their marriage started out as kind of a business arrangement. I thought it was more for her benefit than his. But they love each other now. Rin never told me that Drako was told he had to get married. Maybe it was written into a trust or a will that the brothers have to marry by a certain age?"

Brent's face scrunched up. The expression was a little charming. "That's so Hollywood."

"Yeah, you're right." She chuckled. It was an empty, hollow laugh. Humorless. "But you know what they say about truth being stranger than fiction."

"If you had to marry someone you didn't love in order to inherit a billion dollars, would you do it?"

"That's a tough one." Lei thought about the question for a moment. Would she? For a billion dollars? After everything she'd been through? "I don't ever want to be married, not to anyone, so my first inclination is to say no, absolutely not. But a billion dollars is a lot of money. I could do a lot of good with that much."

"What if you loved someone else?"

"Malek loves someone else?" she asked.

"Malek says he loves me." Looking absolutely heartbroken now, Brent shoved his fingers through his hair. "I believed he loved me until he told me about this. Now, I'm not so sure. Shouldn't he be willing to give up everything for love?"

"Now *that* is Hollywood," she said softly.

"I hear you."

More silence. Lei wanted to go home. She couldn't wait to

go home. But she couldn't tell this man, who had helped her—and more importantly, who was clearly upset—to get out of her car.

"I'm sorry," she said.

"For what? You didn't do anything."

"I'm sorry Malek is hurting you. You seem like a good man."

It was Brent's turn to laugh now. And his chuckle was just as flat and emotionless as hers had been. "As the old cliché goes, the good always finish last."

"You know, when Rin and Drako were first married, they agreed to allow Drako to continue certain relationships with people. Maybe that's what Malek is thinking—"

"It wouldn't be the same. Right now, there are three of us: me, April, Malek. The relationship is balanced. That balance would be thrown all to hell if Malek had a *wife.* Wives are not lovers. They expect more."

"I understand."

A heavy silence fell over them once again. This time it stretched on much longer. It seemed Brent had said what he'd come to tell her, and yet he didn't leave. He sat in her passenger seat, staring through the windshield, his expression completely unreadable.

Lei didn't have the heart to shove the poor guy out, but it was getting late and the echo of voices approaching was making her anxious. All she needed was for Pete and Rob to come find her and finish what they'd started....

She fiddled with her keys, hoping the sound would bring him out of his trance. "You mentioned a woman named April. What if Malek married her? There isn't any chance the three of you could continue as you have been?"

"No, she's been in love with Malek for months. If he marries her, she'll change. She'll do her damned best to push me out for good. It would be better if he married someone else. Someone who can't love him, who never would love him." Brent slid her a look.

She didn't like that look he was giving her.

Was he thinking she might be that someone?

"Oh, no. No. Like I said, I'm not marrying Malek. I'm not in my sister's position, so desperate for money I'd do anything to get it."

"Forgive me for butting in where I probably have no right to, but it looks like you could use some protection. Stability." He tipped his head toward Gwen's house. "Nothing would have to change for you. You could agree to keep things as they are. You would be married in name only—"

"That sounds just fine and dandy, since I'm not interested in starting a relationship with any man, anyway. Being married might not be such a bad thing if that kind of arrangement could be made. But Rin told me she must bear her husband a child. At least one. I can't do that. There's no way in hell. None."

"Are you . . . ?"

"What? Infertile? Not that I'm aware of. But I just couldn't . . ." The image of Malek lying on top of her, thrusting his thick rod into her flashed through her mind. She felt instantly nauseous and a tiny bit warm at the same time. Heat crept up her neck. She cranked the key. "I need to go."

"I'm sorry," he said. "I'm such an ass. Who asks someone they hardly know a question like that?"

"It's okay," she lied, glancing in the rearview mirror. Anxiety was pulling her insides into tight knots. "But I do need to go, really."

He opened the car door. Before he left, he said, "It was good talking to you, Lei. I hope we get the chance to talk again."

She smiled, but didn't repeat the sentiment. To be honest, she wasn't sure she ever wanted to talk to Brent again. What would they say? Would he try to talk her into marrying Malek just so he could keep Malek to himself?

Lei's phone rang just as she was pulling into her driveway. She glanced at the screen.

It was him. Holloway. And she knew what he wanted. The problem was, she wasn't ready to give him an answer yet.

She hit the button, cutting off the call, and dropped her phone into her purse.

9

The doorbell ring caught Lei off guard. Because the Alexandre brothers' house was situated on a winding private road, a good quarter mile from any other home, they didn't get unexpected visitors very often. No solicitors. No Mormons. Not even any Girl Scouts hawking cookies. Most of the time, the visitors they did have didn't ring the bell. They called whichever Alexandre brother they were coming to see as they pulled up, letting them know they'd arrived.

"Malek?" she shouted, wondering if perhaps he'd invited someone over, and they had tried calling his cell, but he hadn't answered. She climbed the steps, knocked on his bedroom door, then pressed an ear to it.

Was that the sound of running water?

He's probably in the shower.

The bell rang a second time, so she dashed back down the stairs and barefooted it across the foyer's stone floor to the door. She opened it, discovering two men were standing outside on the front porch. They were facing their backs toward the door, but at the sound of it opening, one of them spun around.

It took her too long to recognize him. By the time she realized who he was, Holloway was half inside.

"Well, hello there," Holloway said. He pulled aside his jacket, flashing his gun.

Reacting out of pure instinct, Lei tried to slam the door. But right away, she knew that wasn't going to work. She took off, sprinting through the house, thinking she'd grab the phone off the kitchen counter and lock herself in the bathroom to call the police.

She didn't make it that far.

About halfway down the hall, she felt something heavy slam her in the back. The world became a blur. She hit something hard. The air left her lungs, and she struggled to re-inflate them.

"I'm getting really tired of this," Holloway whispered in her ear. "You owe me."

"Wait!" She couldn't see. Blackness and blinking white lights obscured her vision. She knew she was lying on the floor. The tile felt cool beneath her. She was squirming, kicking, swinging her arms, trying to fight.

I'm going to die. And Malek is just upstairs. And then what? Would Malek be next?

"Malek!" she said, her voice a hoarse rasp.

Something smashed into her mouth, a gag. A nasty taste filled her mouth, muffled her voice.

Completely overcome with panic, she thrashed harder. She was throwing herself around so violently the world was a blur, even though the blackness had faded. She felt like she was in the middle of a car accident, being tossed back and forth, left and right.

"You will do what I say," Holloway hissed, again in her ear.

"Yes, sure." Pain exploded in her head. Before she'd recovered, a second blow hit her in the rib cage. Excruciating heat knifed through her body.

"You can't play me," Holloway murmured. He was too close. Right in her face. "Don't you think others have tried? Nobody plays me."

Suddenly, there was the sound of scuffling. Holloway jerked backward. Male grunts followed, the sharp smack of skin striking skin. The second attacker dashed around her. They were fighting someone else. Malek?

Moving slowly—every twitch of a muscle was painful—she scooted around to see what was happening.

Sure enough, Malek had heard her. But at the moment, it wasn't looking good for him.

She heard herself scream. A sob tore up her throat.

Holloway held Malek's arms behind his back, had a knife to his throat. The other guy kicked him in the belly.

Malek's face went white.

"No!" she yelled. They were going to kill him. She had to do something.

What?

She pushed herself to her hands and feet, and bear-walked toward the kitchen. Then she dragged herself upright, using the kitchen island's counter as leverage, and groped for the phone lying in the center. The stretching, reaching, was painful, but nowhere near as bad as hearing the bangs and bumps and thuds behind her. Sagged against a stool, she dialed 9-1-1 and did her best to hold it together and answer the operator's questions.

Watching Malek get kicked and punched was killing her.

Then, much to her surprise, the men stopped and dashed out the front door.

"They're gone!" she yelled into the phone, right before she dropped it. Sprinting, despite the pain, she raced to Malek's side, rolled him onto his back, and prayed he was still breathing.

He looked pale.

He was still. Too still.

Was he . . . ?

She pressed her ear to his chest. She searched for a pulse. Nothing. No movement. No *thump-whump* of a heartbeat. No soft whoosh of air.

"No," she whispered, her shaking hands reaching, searching, feeling. "No, dammit." She choked on a sob. Thinking—hoping—she was too frantic to feel a pulse or hear anything but the heavy pounding of her own heartbeat. She pressed her head to his chest again and prayed for a miracle. But she heard absolutely nothing. He was too still. It was too quiet. She searched his face. Was he turning blue-gray? Or was that the light?

"Where the hell is the ambulance?" she screamed. To Malek, she yelled, "Come on, Malek. Please don't die. Please."

He didn't move.

He didn't freaking breathe.

He just lay there, looking dead. Too still.

Breathe, dammit.

She had no idea how to do CPR, but she decided she could do him no harm by trying. She pinched his nose, inhaled a deep breath, and exhaled into his mouth. She did it again. And again. Then she started pushing down on his chest like she'd watched in movies and hoped the damn ambulance would get there soon.

With every compression, her panic escalated. She kept staring out the open door, wondering why it was taking so long for help to get there.

She breathed a couple more times, then went back to pressing on his chest. "Okay, you win. If he doesn't die, I'll do anything. Absolutely anything." She stopped pushing and blowing to see if he'd started breathing on his own.

Nothing.

"Did you hear me?" she shouted at him. "Is it too late? Malek, please don't die. Please." Tears were blurring her vision. She couldn't see. She couldn't breathe. She couldn't think. She went back to pushing on his chest, blind and desperate and terrified. And she went back to praying.

Finally, a police officer knocked on the door.

"He's not breathing," she screamed, her voice so hoarse it was barely above a whisper. "Help me! Please!"

The officer stooped down. "What happened?"

She didn't have time to tell him what happened. She had no words either. She could only think about blowing and pushing and praying. And where the hell was EMS?

"Miss, please stop," the officer said, pulling on her arm.

"I can't stop. He'll die."

"Let's see if that's true." When it was clear enough for him to get close, he bent over Malek's face, listening for breath. He felt for a pulse on his neck. "There's a pulse. He's not dead."

"Ohthankgod!" To her eyes, he still looked dead, or nearly dead. But she wasn't trained. She cupped her hands over her mouth as a hard, gut-wrenching sob tore up her throat.

"Here's the ambulance." The officer helped her to her feet. "Are you injured, too?"

"I think I bumped my head." Just now realizing her head was throbbing, she fingered her scalp. Blood. She was bleeding.

"We'll get you checked out, too." He waved the EMS technicians over, pointing at Malek. "Loss of consciousness. Maybe loss of pulse and respirations there." He pointed at Lei. "Head injury here."

One technician went to work on Malek.

The other approached her.

She waved him away. "I'm okay. Take care of him."

"My partner's handling him. Where did you hit your head?"

"Back here." She indicated the spot with her finger. He parted her hair to check it. "Looks like you might need some stitches." He then went about checking her over from head to toe, asking what hurt, flashing lights in her eyes.

In the meantime, the officer shot questions at her as quickly as she'd answer them.

"What happened?"

"Did you know the men?"

"Do you think Mr. Alexandre knew them?"

"Why do you think they attacked you?"

"Did they take anything from the house?"

She answered as best she could, knowing she couldn't tell them the whole truth. She was absolutely certain the CIA agent she was dealing with had ways of hiding the truth, or covering things up. Most of the time, her response was, "I don't know." Finally, she was helped into an ambulance, not the one with Malek, and ferried to the hospital.

She sat for hours, waiting for a doctor to stitch her scalp back together. During those long hours, she became more and more worried about Malek. She kept asking for an update, but nobody could give her one. It was frustrating; she wanted to cry, and she just knew someone had to know something. Why weren't they telling her anything?

When a young female doctor came in and patched her back together, Lei basically begged her for help getting an update on Malek's condition. The doctor seemed as genuinely determined as all the nurses and other hospital folk who had promised to help her before.

But unlike them, this doctor actually came back with news.

"Your friend was just taken into surgery," the doctor informed her.

Lei sat speechless for several moments. Her tongue wouldn't work. Her mouth wouldn't move. Inside her head, a million questions bounced around, but she couldn't utter a word.

The doctor, sensing her shock, sat on the stool next to the

bed. "He has some internal bleeding, but there's no reason to think he won't come out of surgery okay."

"I need a phone. I need to call my sister. I need to call his brother. I'm alone. There's nobody..."

The doctor nodded. "Let me see what I can do."

"They're in Spain. It'll be an international call."

The doctor grimaced. She slid her hand into her pocket and offered Lei her BlackBerry. "You can use mine." A sob blocked Lei's throat before she could say thank you, but the doctor seemed to understand. She smiled and stood. "I'll be back in a few minutes. If it rings, just ignore it."

A tear dribbled down Lei's cheek. "Thank you."

Once the doctor had left her partitioned area, Lei dialed. She held her breath as the phone rang once, twice, three times, four. "Pick up, Rin. Answer the phone." After the sixth ring, the call clicked over to voice mail. Lei dialed again and waited, hoping Rin would answer this time.

She didn't.

Lei left an urgent message, telling her as few details as possible, and hung up.

Shortly afterward, the doctor returned to accept the phone. "I've written your discharge orders. You'll be free to go in just a little bit."

"I can't leave," Lei said. "I can't leave until I know he's going to be okay."

The doctor glanced at her chart, then smiled. "You know, that bump was pretty bad. You have a concussion. Maybe we should keep you for a few more hours?" Lei finally exhaled. The doctor patted Lei's knee. "Get some rest. As soon as there's word about your...?"

"Brother-in-law," Lei provided.

"Brother-in-law, I'll let you know."

"Thank you again, doctor."

The doctor pulled the curtain shut.

Lei settled back on the bed and closed her eyes.

Sometime later, someone nudged her. She jerked upright, heart in her throat. Her hands flew to her face, to block the blows.

Had that been a dream? Or had someone been beating her?

Lei's gaze jerked around the darkened room. The hospital. She was in the hospital. Safe.

"Are you okay?" It was the doctor. She was standing next to the bed, brows furrowed.

Lei sucked in a deep breath and let it out. "I'm fine. My head hurts a little."

"You were yelling," the doctor said.

"I was?"

The doctor pulled out a light and flashed it in Lei's eyes. "Are you feeling nauseated? Dizzy?"

"No."

"I want you to lie down." She tucked her light back in her pocket as Lei reclined back down. "Okay. Anyway, I came to tell you your brother-in-law is out of surgery. He's stable."

A sob tore up Lei's throat. She clapped a hand over her mouth. Malek was stable. Alive. "Can I see him?"

"Not yet. He's still in recovery. I'll let you know when he's moved to a room. In the meantime, I'm going to write a prescription for some pain medication. The nurse will bring it in shortly."

"Okay. Thank you again. For everything."

"Not a problem." The doctor left.

A little while later, the nurse came in with a paper cup of juice and a smaller cup with some pills in it. She handed both to Lei. "This is just a mild pain medication."

Lei swallowed the tablets, washed them down with some

juice, and lay back down. She didn't realize she'd fallen asleep again until she was being gently shaken awake.

"You were shouting again," the doctor said.

"I'm sorry."

"Is it normal for you?" she asked, checking Lei's eyes with the light for the second time.

"Not that I'm aware of."

"Hmmm." The doctor looked concerned and slightly confused. "You're checking out okay neurologically. I'm going to go ahead and discharge you. Your brother-in-law has been moved to a room on the surgical floor. So far, things are looking very good. The injuries weren't as extensive as they'd appeared."

"He's going to be okay?"

"He's going to be okay."

That was the best news Lei had ever heard. "Ohthankgod," she blurted.

The doctor wrote something on a scrap of paper. "Here's his room number. The nurse will be in to go over your discharge instructions soon, and then you're free to go."

Lei clutched the paper in her hand and scrambled from the bed. She paced the floor until the nurse came in. She tried to pay attention to the instructions she was given, folded the written discharge documents, stuffed them in her pocket, and headed for the closest elevator up to the third floor. She followed the signs to room 315, pushed open the ajar door, and stepped inside.

It was a private room. The lights were dim but illuminated enough for Lei to see Malek's handsome face. His eyes were closed. He was resting. She approached as quietly as possible, slid her hand over his, and cupped her hand over her mouth.

This man had almost died while fighting to protect her. Nobody had ever done anything so selfless, other than her sister.

Rin had more or less sold herself to buy Lei's freedom, and no doubt she'd put her own life and safety at risk plenty of times before that while trying to hunt Lei down. She would forever be grateful for what Rin had done—the risk, the sacrifice, the courage she'd shown.

And she would forever be grateful for what Malek had done, too.

Especially since the attack had been her fault.

He would never ask for any kind of payback, but Lei had to find a way to show him exactly how grateful she was.

His hand stirred under hers.

Was he awake? Her gaze shot to it, then jumped to his face.

His eyelids slowly lifted. "Lei? You're safe," he murmured.

"I'm safe. You're safe."

He visibly exhaled. "Need to call Drako."

"I've already tried calling Rin. She isn't answering."

"My phone?"

"I don't know."

"Pocket." He started to move, as if he were trying to sit up. He winced, then wrapped one arm around his waist. "Shit."

Lei gently pressed on his shoulders. "I'll look for your phone. You can't move. You just had surgery."

He didn't fight her. "Dammit, there's nobody at home."

"It's okay. You have to stay here, in the hospital. You need to give yourself time to heal."

His eyelids closed. "But you don't know..."

"Don't know what, Malek?"

"Phone," he said, his voice weaker.

"I'll find it and I'll call Drako. I promise."

She went on a full search for his phone. She found a plastic bag in a cupboard. In it were his clothes, his shoes, and his phone. It was off.

Respecting the hospital's cell phone policy, she went downstairs to the lobby before powering it up.

It didn't turn on.

She hit the buttons a few more times and said more than a handful of curse words. Even though she whispered, she caught the attention of a man sitting nearby. He glanced at her, then went back to reading the two-year-old issue of *Time* he was holding.

Now what?

She glanced outside.

The first light of morning was touching the eastern sky. She was exhausted, despite the bit of sleep she'd managed to get down in the emergency room. She felt grungy, a little hungry, very foggy headed, and achy all over. She wanted, more than anything, to have a hot shower, a meal, and about twelve hours more sleep. She needed to charge Malek's phone and call his brother.

But she was absolutely petrified of going back to the house alone.

What if those men came back? What if they were waiting for her to return?

She was alone. Scared beyond words. With no phone. No car.

Her life had spiraled out of her control yet again. Her head was spinning. She felt faint. She plopped down on a bench, lowered her head, closed her eyes, and tried to think her way through this.

"Excuse me, miss. Are you all right?" It was a man's voice.

She glanced at him.

A police officer.

A quiver of distrust snaked through her.

Since her sister bought her back from the traffickers, she'd been reluctant to trust anyone. Cops. Men. People in general. And now, after Holloway's attack, she was even more petrified. But she had to get home somehow. It was at least twenty miles.

She couldn't walk. There were no buses. With no money, no credit or debit card, she couldn't hire a cab.

"I need . . . help."

The officer glanced at his watch. "What's the problem?"

"Is there any way you'd be willing to help me get a cab? I was attacked, brought into the hospital in an ambulance. I have no way to get home."

"Where do you live?" he asked.

She rattled off her address.

"Ah, yes. I heard the call about your home invasion on the radio. Glad you're okay."

She was okay physically. But mentally, emotionally . . . ? She had a feeling it would be a long, long time before she'd be emotionally okay. If ever.

He motioned for her to follow him. "I can give you a ride. I'm off the clock."

Praying she had stumbled upon an honest, trustworthy cop, she reluctantly followed him.

10

"The house is clear, miss," the officer said, standing outside the patrol car. He'd left Lei in the car to wait while he checked the house from top to bottom. "You have a top-rate security system. And no sign of forced entry. Did the responding officer say how the assailants got in?"

"They didn't have to tell me," she confessed. "I let them in."

"Ah." He didn't sound all that surprised by her confession.

"I never would have guessed a bad guy would knock on the front door."

"Generally, if they do that, the victim doesn't live to give a description. You're damn lucky."

"Wow." Lei felt her face pale. Lucky? Not hardly. Little did this policeman know that the attacker was—more or less—one of his own. And there'd been a reason why she'd been left alive. Luck had nothing to do with it. She couldn't very well help the bastard if she was dead.

The officer checked his wristwatch. "I need to get going. Gotta get the kids off to school soon."

"Sure." Lei eased out of the car, muscles screaming in protest. "Thank you for the ride. And for checking the house."

"You're welcome. Here's my card." He pulled a white business card out of his pocket and handed it to her. "Call me if you have any more trouble. When you get inside, activate that alarm system. And don't open the door for strangers."

"Will do." Thinking she might be able to trust the officer, but still very afraid, Lei followed him out onto the front porch. He made it as far as the first step before something inside her snapped, and she called out, "Wait!"

He turned around and gave her a raised brow "What now?" look.

Lei opened her mouth, moved her lips, but no words came out. Her throat was blocked, even though she was desperate for help. She sucked in a deep breath and tried again. Tears burned in her eyes. But still nothing.

Dammit. Not again.

This wasn't the first time she'd been frozen with fear. Unable to speak. Unable to reach out for the help that was mere inches away.

If only she knew for certain she could trust him.

"You should get inside, miss," the officer said.

She nodded and stepped back through the doorway. The officer rounded the front of his patrol car, gave a little wave, and drove off.

Now she was alone.

In an empty house.

She shut herself in, locked the door, set the alarm, and flipped on every light switch she passed as she made her way through the first floor. She checked each and every window and door, even though the police officer had already done it. Then she went upstairs, turned on all the lights up there, checked every window, every closet, and under every bed.

There was nobody hiding under a bed.

Nobody hiding in a closet.

Nobody waiting for her.

Somewhat satisfied she was safe—there was still that niggling doubt—she plugged in Malek's phone, found her cell phone, dropped the officer's card on her dresser, and plopped down on the bed. She checked for messages.

Ten. All from Rin. The last one: *Lei, call me the minute you get this message. If I don't hear from you soon, I'm going to call the police!*

Lei wasted no time dialing.

This time Rin answered on the first ring. "Ohmygod! I was scared to death! What's going on?"

Lei gave Rin the slightly abridged version of the story, trying to underplay the danger, and the longer—but still edited—version to Drako, after Rin handed over the phone to him.

Once she'd wrapped up her long-winded summary, he told her, "I'm sending over two men to keep an eye on you until Talen is home. He's on a plane now. The security guards I've hired will call you on this phone when they arrive on the front porch. Wait until you get the call before you open the door. Do you understand?"

"Yes."

"Good. They will be there within the hour."

Rin came back on. "Lei, don't blame this on yourself."

"I'm not," she lied.

"I know you a helluva lot better than that, brat."

Lei smiled to herself, despite all the terror and anxiety and guilt she was still swamped in. "I'm going to hop in the shower, before your husband's bodyguards show up."

"Okay. I love you, Lei."

"I love you, too. Bye."

Lei took the phone into the bathroom with her, cranked on the shower, and scalded herself until she felt semi-human again.

Then she toweled off and threw on a pair of sweats and a T-shirt. Her phone rang as she was combing her wet hair. She shuffled downstairs, then peered through the peephole to make sure the men who were talking to her on her cell were the ones standing on the porch. Then she opened the door.

"I'm Tim," the first one said as he strolled past her, thumbing over his shoulder. "And this is Steve."

"Glad you're here." When Steve stepped inside, Lei slammed the door shut behind him and hurried to reactivate the alarm.

"It's okay, miss. We'll take care of everything from here," Steve said as he punched a security code into the alarm.

"Sure, okay." Not sure how she felt about her two new housemates-slash-security guards, she headed upstairs to her room, locked the door, pulled out her computer, and tried to get back to researching Kate and Heather. Her eyelids became heavier with each page she viewed until she could do nothing to keep them open.

Giving in to the overwhelming exhaustion, she slid under the covers, cut off the light, and went to sleep.

"It's okay, baby doll. You're safe. I'm here."

The voice was a low rumble, distant, but getting closer. She felt instantly at ease, the terror fading away by the second.

"Yes, that's it. Relax. Rest."

Was that . . . ?

She opened her eyes. "Malek?"

"I'm home now. I'm here."

"But you should be in the hospital." She pushed upright and blinked at him. It was him all right. In the flesh. Sitting on the edge of her bed. In the darkness, he looked just as handsome and strong and healthy as ever.

"I couldn't rest. Not knowing you were here by yourself."

"But that's insane! You just had major surgery."

"I'm okay." He moved his arm and she realized there was an

IV pole standing at the head of her bed. "See? I have medicine. And a nurse will be by later to change my bandages."

"Are you in pain?"

"It's tolerable." He leaned slightly to the right, favoring that side.

"Please get in bed."

"Okay." He pulled the covers back.

"I didn't mean . . ." She watched him slide under the covers.

He settled on his back, smiling. "Better?"

It wasn't what she'd had in mind, but he was in bed. And maybe it was better if he was nearby, in case he needed anything. "Better." She lay back beside him, making sure she left a good-sized gap between them.

"You know," Malek said, rocking his head to the side to look at her, "I remember you saying something just after the attack."

She couldn't remember what she'd said then. Who would? She'd probably said a lot of things, since she was pretty damn terrified. "Yeah? Like what?"

"Like . . . you promised to do anything I asked if I didn't leave you."

"I said that?" A hazy memory flashed through her mind. She had said something like that.

"You sure did."

"Are you certain?"

"Positive. And I'm holding you to it."

Silence.

She had a feeling she knew what he was going to ask her to do. At least, if what Brent had told her was true. "I was trying to keep you alive."

"It worked."

"Yes, it did." And she was so, so grateful for that fact.

"You said you would do anything. And now I want you to keep your word."

And now she was in another man's debt. All in the interest of keeping herself out of prison and two ex-prostitutes . . . and Malek . . . alive. "Which means . . . ? Are you going to tell me to marry you?"

"No, my brother might have played that way with your sister, but I'm not Drako. I won't marry you until *you* ask *me*."

She couldn't help laughing at that one. "You expect me to propose?"

He eased his arms up, crossing them behind his head. "It'll happen."

"You're way too confident for your own good."

"Nah." His hand found hers. He squeezed, then released it. "Now, both of us need rest. So shhhh."

"But you didn't tell me what you're expecting from me if it isn't marrying you."

"We'll talk about it later. After you've had some rest."

"But—"

"Sleep. Or I may be inspired to do something else that people tend to do when they're *in bed.*"

Lei crossed her arms over her chest, then squeezed her eyelids shut.

Within seconds, Malek's breathing was slow and even, and he was still. And gradually the reassuring sound of his steady inhalations and exhalations lulled her back to sleep, too.

Lei woke up sometime later, draped over Malek like a big heavy sandbag. That couldn't be comfortable for him. Or safe, considering his injuries. Moving carefully, she shifted her position, easing off of him.

He groaned, started to roll over, stopped, winced, and exhaled a long, deep breath.

Clearly, he was in pain.

Clearly, he should have stayed in the hospital.

Lei glanced at the plastic bag hanging from the pole. Empty.

It was no wonder. She checked his brow. He was sweating, but didn't feel feverish.

"Stubborn man," she grumbled. "You should be in the hospital. I hope you have some more of that medicine here." After a fairly thorough search, she realized he didn't. She hoped the nurse he mentioned was on her way.

Unsure what to do, she ran downstairs to grab some coffee and look for his discharge papers, to see if there was a phone number for the nurse. Coming up empty-handed, she went back up to check on Malek.

He was looking worse, and she was starting to panic.

Sitting on the bed, next to him, she leaned down and concentrated on breathing. "Malek," she said, "where is your nurse?"

"Coming" was his answer. His teeth were gritted, his pale face a mask of agony, his features drawn tight.

How she longed to take away his pain. "How much longer? Do you know?"

He shook his head.

"Phone number?"

"Don't have one."

Her fingers curled into fists, fingernails digging into her palms. She couldn't stand seeing him this way. He was suffering. And here she was, just sitting there, watching. Powerless to do anything to stop it. "Tell me what to do." Her gaze kept jerking back to that withered bag on the pole.

"Nothing."

"I can't do 'nothing.' Can I call a doctor? Get a prescription for something?"

Again, he shook his head. "I'm fine."

"You're not 'fine.' And I'm giving that nurse ten minutes to get here." A fat tear dropped from her lashes, landing on her cheekbone. She dragged the back of her hand across her face. "This is insane. There's no reason for you to be suffering like this. If she isn't here by"—she checked the clock—"eleven-thirty, I'm calling 9-1-1 and having your ass hauled back to the hospital."

"No."

"Yes, you're in no condition to stop me."

Malek grabbed her arm. His grip was like a vice, stronger than she would have expected. "I said no."

"Malek." A sob ripped through her chest so hard it hurt. She cupped her hand over her mouth. "Please."

"Won't leave you."

"Why? What's the point? You can't help me when you're like this. You can't protect me."

"Yes, I can." As if to prove his point, he jerked upright, hauled her into his arms, and slammed her down onto the bed. He levered over her, breathing heavily, and stared into her eyes. "I can. And I will."

"But Drako hired security guards."

"I don't trust them. I don't trust anyone but my brothers. And they're not here."

Lei reached up and cupped his cheek. Even when he was in horrific pain, he was strong and protective. She couldn't respect him more for what he was trying to do. And yet, she feared that protective instinct would get him hurt again...or worse. "Please, Malek. You're going to hurt yourself. If something happens to you because of me—"

"Nothing is going to happen to me. I'm fine. It's just a little pain." He closed his eyes and leaned into her hand. And just like that, the pain left his face. It was weird. "When you touch me, I feel a little better." He bent his arms, lowering himself onto his side. "Don't leave me and I'll be okay."

If she didn't see it, she wouldn't have believed it. But it sure did appear that her touch was making him feel better.

It wasn't that she didn't believe in the power of touch. Many years ago, she'd studied Reiki, what was considered by many to be an alternative form of medicine. But her studies had been cut short, when her mother had sold her, and she hadn't even achieved the level of First Degree.

"O-okay." She rolled onto her side to face him and stroked his cheek.

He sighed. "Damn, that's better than sex."

She flinched.

"Sorry," he snapped. "I didn't mean it like that."

"I know," she said, although she didn't really know anything. "It's okay." She concentrated, trying to recall what she'd learned from her Reiki master. She started to sit up so she could actually focus.

Malek stopped her. "Do you remember what we talked about last night? Your promise?"

She closed her eyes, trying to concentrate on sending healing energy, qi, through her palms and into Malek's body. "Sure, but we don't have to discuss that right now. It can wait." She shifted positions as much as Malek would allow, so she could reach his stomach. Oh so gently, she placed her hand on his abdomen.

"I want to talk about it now."

The doorbell rang.

Lei jumped, yanked her hands away, and started to sit up.

"The security guards will get the door," Malek said, doing his best to keep her where she was. He failed.

"I thought you didn't trust them." She scooted to the edge of the bed. From this position, she could reach him better.

"It's the nurse."

A couple minutes later, a heavyset man came lumbering into the room, carrying a bag. He took a look at Malek, then the IV pole and frowned. "I'm sorry I'm late. I got a flat tire."

"It's okay," Malek said.

Figuring she'd give Malek and his nurse some privacy, Lei tried to leave. Malek stopped her by grabbing her hand in that iron grip and refusing to let go.

So she did her best to stay out of the way while the nurse went about his duties, checking Malek's heart rate, temperature, blood pressure, and bandages. He changed the IV bag, then handed over a couple more and showed Lei how to replace the old one once it was empty.

A half hour later, Malek was looking much more comfortable and the nurse was on his way out.

"This is insanity, Malek. What doctor would let a patient leave—"

"He didn't *let* me leave. Now, back to that conversation we started." Malek pulled on her arm until she settled on the bed next to him. But to her relief, he didn't touch her. He simply insisted she lie with him.

"Can I just say, I am absolutely stunned that you heard me. You were unconscious. You were...I don't think you were breathing."

"Some people describe an out-of-body experience when they die," he reasoned.

"Was that what you had? Did you see yourself? Were you hovering over your body, watching me?"

"You could say that." He smirked.

Lei knew that smirk. He was lying.

But if he hadn't experienced some kind of out-of-body episode, how could he have heard...? "Wait a minute. Are there security cameras in this house?"

He laughed.

"When did you have time to watch the video footage?" She swung, as if she was going to smack him, but she intentionally missed.

A second later, a sickening thought zipped through her mind. A video tape. What else had he heard?

He caught her arm, pulled, and before she realized it, she was lying on top of him. "That was the first thing I did when I got home." He grabbed her other arm and lifted them both over her head.

A blast of panic shot through her system and she froze.

"Breathe, baby," he said, his voice low and soothing, smooth and rich and reassuring.

She sucked in a lungful of air and slowly released it.

"Yes, that's better. We're going to work on this little problem of yours. Because I like to touch you. I want to touch you." He gathered both her wrists into one big fist and cupped her face with his free hand. "I have to touch you."

He hadn't heard Holloway? *Ohthankgod!*

"Malek, please. I can't be what you want. I can't be a wife to you. I'm too fucked up."

"Shhhh. I won't let you say that. You're not 'fucked up.' You're afraid. You're scarred. But isn't everyone? Doesn't everyone have their hang-ups? Their irrational fears and issues?"

"But—"

He pressed his index finger to her lips and her throat closed up. The words she'd been about to speak got lodged somewhere between her gut and her mouth. And she could do nothing but lie on top of him and feel his chest rise and fall beneath her. She felt his breath fan over her face. And she felt something else—a prominent, hard *something* poking her in the belly. If he was in pain from her lying on top of him—as he should be—it wasn't putting a stop to certain bodily functions.

"Why? Why are you doing this? Why wouldn't you just let me be, leave me to work out my problems with my therapist?"

"Lei, I could say that I'm just trying to be a good friend like

I did before. But the cold hard facts are, I've never wanted a woman like I want you. I know you don't want to hear that, but it's the truth, and I'm not going to fucking lie or hide it or pretend I don't anymore. I want to touch you, stroke you, kiss you from head to toe. I want to make you ache for my touch when I'm not there."

Lei sniffled. Tears were burning in her eyes. Malek meant every word he said. She could see it in his eyes. She was overwhelmed with emotion, so lost she didn't really know how she felt or what she wanted or what she should say. "It's the drugs," she said.

"Kiss me, Lei."

She couldn't remember the last time she'd kissed a man. It had been so long ago. In another life. Before she'd been taken from home and dragged to hell.

"Kiss me," he demanded. Showing a little impatience, he hooked his hand behind her head and pulled until her mouth touched his. At the intimate contact, her breath left her lungs in a huff. Her body stiffened.

His lips were soft beneath hers. The kiss was a gentle, patient tease. A little brush this way and then another the opposite. It wasn't chaste. But neither was it a cruel possession.

His fingers tangled in her hair, massaged her scalp, as his lips slowly seduced her. Her initial shock and panic faded, and gradually a simmering heat gathered between her legs.

Seeming to sense her reaction, Malek pushed to deepen the kiss. His tongue traced the seam of her mouth. And when she parted her lips to pull in a much-needed lungful of air, it slid inside, filling her mouth with an intoxicatingly sweet flavor.

She couldn't help but respond now. Her blood was warm, rushing through her system, pulsing and beating through her body in waves. She was getting breathless again, but not because she was petrified. No, she was becoming aroused for the first time in years. She wanted Malek's kiss. Was enjoying Malek's kiss. Could think of nothing but Malek's kiss and what it was doing to her body.

When the kiss ended, she gazed down into his eyes and whispered, "Wow. I didn't think . . . I honestly believed . . ."

"What, baby? That you'd never want a man again? That you'd never tremble in a man's arms, overwhelmed by need, rather than fear?"

"Yeah."

"You can. You will. And when the time is right and you're ready, I'll make you forget you ever feared my touch." He waved his hands, both of them.

She realized, belatedly, that he had released her sometime during the kiss. She'd lain there, kissing him, and enjoyed it.

Worried about what her weight might be doing to his wounds, she climbed off of him.

"You're going to keep your word, Lei. Regardless of how I heard what you said, a promise is a promise."

"What does that mean, Malek?"

"It means you'll come to me every night, an hour before bedtime. You'll sleep with me. But that's all. Only sleep."

She could do that. And there was more than one reason for it. "I think you're making a big mistake."

"Let me worry about that. And there's one other part to our arrangement. During that hour before we go to sleep, you will do as I say, even if it makes you uncomfortable."

She felt her body go cold. Do as he says? Did he realize how those words would strike her?

"Oh, hell. I didn't mean it like that." Malek's eyes widened. "Don't shut down on me now, Lei. I'm not going to force you to fuck me. I'm not going to force you to do anything. What you do, you'll do with me, for me, you'll do because you want to."

"Do I have a choice?"

"Sure, Lei. You always have a choice. But you'll agree to this because you want it as much as I do."

She glanced at the clock on the nightstand. "I need to get some things done."

"Sure. Go ahead." He smiled. It was a devious grin. Wicked. And sexy as hell. But in his eyes, she saw something else. A softness. Need. Hope. "You know where to find me later."

11

"You got what you wanted, you bastard," Lei snapped, her fingers clutching her phone so tightly it hurt. She was in her bathroom, crouched in the corner. She figured that was one place there shouldn't be a security camera. "I'll do it. Whatever you say." The son of a bitch had made his point. He'd pushed her to the breaking point. And she was tired of fighting him. Tired of looking over her shoulder.

"I knew you'd do the right thing, given the right motivation," the caller said.

She had nothing to say about that. "What do you want me to do?" she grumbled.

"Whatever it takes to find out where the Alexandre brothers are hiding a certain valuable artifact. It's going to be cylindrical in shape. Very old—"

"What makes you think he'll tell me, assuming they're actually hiding an artifact?"

"History tells me," Holloway said, voice sharp. "Men are weak. A beautiful woman can own us, bring us to our knees just by spreading her legs."

Spreading her legs.

No. Not that.

Her blood turned to ice. Here she thought she'd escaped from that hell, and now she was right back in it—being prostituted, basically. Only this time, the pimp had a badge.

"Don't tell me you've got a problem with that," he said smoothly. "At least Malek Alexandre isn't a seventy-year-old man with arthritis, BO, a limp dick."

No, he wasn't a nasty seventy-year-old man who grabbed and clawed at her like she was a hunk of meat. He was a man who'd laid his life on the line for her. And despite the whole *sleep with me* thing, he wasn't asking her to pay him back.

She closed her eyes and tried to imagine having sex with him. At first, the image was not at all unpleasant. But it turned to a nightmare as she imagined the hurt of her betrayal shadowing his eyes when he eventually found out why she'd been fucking with him.

She couldn't do it. God help her, she just couldn't. Malek was the one human being, besides Rin, who hadn't used her in one way or another. She didn't want to betray him, even if it was some stupid, crusty old chunk of metal. Terrified, she said, "I can't. I . . . can't. Why don't you hire someone else? I'll help you find someone—"

"No."

"But it's just a dumb old piece of junk. Anyone can do a job like that."

"You'd think, but no. It's gotta be you."

"Why? Why me?"

"You know the consequences," his voice was cold, menacing. She knew all right. Dammit, she needed to find a way to protect Malek. And then she needed to locate Heather and Kate—if it wasn't too late already. "I'm done playing games, Lei."

The call ended.

Lei tossed her phone on the counter and cranked the shower on full blast. She felt so fucking dirty. Her skin was crawling. Wearing her pajamas, she dashed in, hoping the almost scalding water would wash away the guilt. While she stood there, hot water pounding on her head, she closed her eyes and tried to come up with a plan. She knew she needed to protect Malek. That was her first priority. Next, she needed to find those girls and warn them.

How? So far, she'd accomplished absolutely nothing but nearly getting herself raped and killed, and Malek almost beaten to death.

Dammit, if only she had some help. If only she could tell Malek the truth.

Don't do that. Look what happened to him already. Tell him what's going on and God only knows what will happen to him next.

No, she needed the help of someone who was more objective. Who would want to help because it was the right thing to do but wouldn't want to get too involved.

The cop who'd driven her home from the hospital popped into her mind.

Trustworthy or not? How could she know? Was she able to even discern that? After all, she'd been so sure, not that long ago, that Holloway was trustworthy, and look how that had turned out.

Still undecided, she found his card, and with her heartbeat pounding in her head, she dialed the number. Her finger hovered over the red button, the one that would end the call, as she listened to the line ring. It rang eight times, then clicked over to another line.

"Ann Arbor Police Department, Sergeant Wallace speaking."

"Hello, I'm trying to reach an officer named Vasquez."

"Hold, please."

Lei's finger lowered, resting on the red button. Cut off the call? Or not?

"Vasquez," he said.

"H-hello. This is Lei Mitchell. You drove me home from the hospital."

"Yes, Miss Mitchell. How can I help you?"

Once again, her eyes started burning and a sob bubbled up her throat, threatening to cut off her voice. She swallowed a few times, struggling to fight back the tears.

"Miss Mitchell?"

"I need help."

"Are you in danger?"

"Yes."

"Where are you?" he asked.

"At home."

"Hang on, I'll get dispatch—"

"No, wait," she cut him off. "I'm safe for the moment, but I need help. I need to meet with you."

"Can you come down to the station?"

"No." Her hand shook as she smoothed a strand of hair back from her face. "Can we meet somewhere else? I can't risk going there." She imagined herself being cuffed and hauled to a jail cell. For all she knew, she was a person of interest in a murder case.

"What about the coffee shop on Fourth?"

"Too public."

"You're not making this easy."

"Sorry. I need somewhere safe, private. Where we won't be overheard, can't be followed."

"Okay. The Hanford Inn in Plymouth. I'll call you with a room number in a bit."

"Okay, bye." She hit the button, tossed her phone into her purse, and dug out her car keys.

Twenty minutes later, she was dashing into the Hanford Inn,

head in constant motion as she looked to see if she'd been followed. Inside, as she rode the elevator to the fourth floor, she suffered through one wave of doubt after another.

Could she trust this man?

What if he was working with Holloway? What if he didn't believe her?

What if he called Holloway and told him she'd reported him?

Oh, God, she felt sick.

By the time she reached room 402, she was about ready to say to hell with it and make a run for it.

She lifted her hand to knock.

Last chance. Trust this man or go back and tell Malek everything?

She knocked, and a split second later, the door swung open.

"Hello, Miss Mitchell," he said, stepping to one side to let her pass.

Her legs literally wobbled as she shuffled into the room.

He shut them in and motioned to a chair. "Have a seat. Do you want some coffee? Water?"

"No thanks," she said, as she swallowed hard. She was pretty sure anything that went into her stomach would come right back up. She sat in one of the two chairs crowded around the small round table in the very back of the room. He sat opposite her, dropped a yellow legal pad on the table between them, and said, "Okay, what's going on?"

"Is there any chance you can keep this just between you and me?"

"It depends."

In other words, she had to assume he couldn't.

"What would you say if I told you that the person who attacked me was..." Her throat closed up. She coughed. She swallowed.

Vasquez leaned forward. "Do you need some water?"

She shook her head, inhaled, exhaled. Again. Her gaze dropped to the yellow paper. "He's in the CIA," she blurted.

"Who? The man who broke into your home?"

She nodded.

"What makes you think that?"

She told him, "He had a badge."

"He showed it to you?"

She nodded. "This past summer, I was . . . working as a call girl. Agent Holloway was working undercover, pretended to hire me a couple of times. But we never . . . you know. He just kept asking me questions about my pimp, the other girls. I had no reason to believe he wasn't legit. He even helped me get some of the girls freed."

"Okay."

Lei couldn't tell from his expression whether he was believing her story or not.

"What happened next?" he asked.

"My sister had been searching for me for months, and she was able to . . . compensate my 'employer' in exchange for my freedom," she explained, making quotes in the air with her fingers. "I didn't hear from the agent again. Until recently. He called me, asking me to do something terrible, something illegal, and when I refused, one of the girls we had worked together to get freed was found dead."

"You think he did it?"

"He pretty much admitted it when he called me shortly afterward. I refused to help him again, and not only did he threaten to have me framed for the girl's murder, but he told me if I continued to refuse, all the girls we helped would be killed."

Vasquez shook his head. "Hmmm."

"When I refused him a third time, that's when I was attacked."

"Whose death is he supposedly framing you for?"

"Eve, Evelyn Barket. Have you heard anything about a person of interest who fits my description?"

"No, we get regular updates on the case. Haven't heard about a person of interest at all. I can check with the lead on the case, see if there's been any recent activity."

For the first time in days, Lei actually felt like she could breathe freely. "That's a relief. I was so scared."

Vasquez scrawled Eve's name on his paper. "What is it this guy, Holloway, wants you to do?"

"Steal something. From someone very close to me."

The officer jotted down some notes. "This doesn't sound like the MO of a CIA agent. For one thing, the CIA wouldn't be involved in sex trades."

"Not even human trafficking?"

"No, the CIA's focus is intelligence. I'm guessing he lied and the badge is a fake. But I'll see what I can do to find out for sure. In the meantime, if he's still threatening you, you should go stay somewhere safe. He knows where you live. Do you have any friends or family you could stay with for a while?"

"I don't know." She motioned to his pen. And when he handed it to her, she wrote down the names of the two remaining girls. "I'm worried about these girls. If I don't agree to help him, they could be on tomorrow's six o'clock news. I've tried everything to track them down, but I can't find them. They should be warned." Next she wrote down Gwen's name and address. "This person knows Kate, but I don't know if she's been in touch with her recently."

"I'll see what I can do."

"Thank you." Feeling a shudder building deep inside, she wrapped her arms around her body. "It all sounds so crazy, I know."

"I believe you." He stood. "Do you have a phone number where I can reach you, in case I come up with anything on Holloway or the girls?"

"Sure." She wrote her cell phone number on the top of the page. "I guess I'll get going."

"Whether this guy's for real or not, he sounds dangerous. Don't take any chances."

"I won't." She dug her car keys out of her purse and stood.

He led her to the room's door. Before he opened it, he said, "I'll call you when I have something."

"Thank you."

Aware of everyone around her, she scurried out of the building and to her car. She raced home and spent the rest of the day alternating between preparing meals for Malek and researching the CIA, as well as digging around the Internet for information on Kate and Heather and Nate Holloway. She found absolutely nothing on the girls. But she did locate a couple of excellent sites on the CIA. Vasquez was right. It seemed human trafficking would be outside the scope of the CIA. If that was true, was he also right about Holloway being a fake? In one sense, that possibility almost made her feel better. If he wasn't an agent, he might not have access to the resources an agent would possess, like computer programs to track down her cell phone calls or credit card purchases. And he might not be able to make good on his threat to frame her for Eve's murder.

But if he wasn't a CIA agent, what was he? And why, exactly, would he be trying to get his hands on some mysterious artifact?

She Googled for hours, through the afternoon, through the evening, into the dark hours of the night. Her eyes barely able to focus, she dragged her sore body up the stairs and into her room. She changed, brushed her teeth, and was about to fall into bed when she remembered her promise to Malek.

Hoping he was sleeping, she tiptoed down the hall to his room and pushed open the door. The soft buzz of his snoring greeted her the instant she stepped inside.

It seemed tonight he wouldn't be tormenting her. After settling into bed, she closed her eyes and prayed.

Once again, Lei woke up the next morning sprawled on top of Malek. She hadn't realized before how much she moved around while sleeping. Evidently she wasn't so sensitive to touch when she was unconscious.

As she shifted positions, she became aware of something else.

Malek was aroused.

Being careful, she eased her weight off of him.

He groaned, slapped an arm over her back, and pinned her down.

A little jolt of discomfort zipped through her. She wriggled. His hold tightened.

He had to be awake.

"Malek," she whispered.

"Hmmm?" he responded. His voice was low. The vibrations hummed through her body. It was a pleasant sensation. Very pleasant.

"I need to go . . . if you get my drift."

"Hmmm," he said again.

"Malek, doesn't it hurt, with me lying on top of you?"

"No." He lifted his arm, freeing her. "Not at all. Come back when you're done."

"Come back? I need to get moving. I don't recall lounging in bed until noon being part of our agreement."

"It wasn't. But you cheated me out of my time last night."

"I'm sorry. Something important came up. I promise I'll come to bed earlier tonight." Not waiting for his response, she scampered down the hall to her bathroom and took care of all the basics, including a shower. She was feeling pretty good by the time she got out. Clean. Well rested. Just overall less stressed. She dressed and combed her hair. As she was heading down the hall, toward the stairs, she heard male voices in Malek's room. His nurse had arrived.

She barefooted it downstairs, got the coffee going, and shoved a couple of bagels in the toaster. She made a tray for Malek, and before she ate her own food, took it up to him.

He was sitting up, smiling. He motioned to the IV pole. "I'm free."

"Isn't it a little soon?" She shot the nurse a worried look.

The nurse wrapped the plastic tubing into a ball. "I wouldn't have taken him off the IV if I didn't think he was okay. His pain level is low enough now that he can take oral medications. And he can eat and drink."

"But he had major surgery just two days ago."

The nurse shrugged. "We all heal at our own rate. He's doing well." To Malek, he said, "Now, that doesn't mean you shouldn't be resting. You don't want to do too much yet."

Malek lifted his hand as if taking a vow. "I promise, I'll take it easy."

The nurse motioned to Lei as he gathered his things and placed them back in his bag. "I have a feeling she will make sure of that."

"You bet I will." Lei set the tray on the bed.

"Okay, Mr. Alexandre, I'm through here, unless you wanted me to help with your shower." He motioned to the plastic and metal bench sitting next to the door.

"Nope, I'm good," Malek said.

"Okay. I'll be back tomorrow. Remember, you don't want to soak your incision, but it's okay to wash it with soap and water." The nurse left the room, leaving the bench where it sat.

Lei slid Malek a raised brow look. "No shower?"

"I thought you'd help me."

She tried to imagine how that was going to work. "Um..."

"Just kidding. I can handle a shower on my own. Now that

I'm off the IV, maybe I should cancel the nurse altogether," Malek said, grabbing the bagel off the plate. He took a big bite and chewed.

"I don't think that's a good idea at all."

"Hmmm." He swallowed. "Why not?"

"What if you get an infection? What if you get sicker? Doesn't that wound need to be checked at least once a day?" Looking extremely unconcerned, he continued to munch. Meanwhile, she had a mini panic attack. "I'm not a nurse, Malek. I don't know anything about wound care."

"Okay, *maybe* I'll keep him for a couple more days, if it would make you feel better." He slurped his coffee, lifting his cup. "Thanks for the breakfast."

"You're welcome. And, yes, it would make me feel better. A lot."

"Did you eat already?" Grimacing a little, he reached for the TV remote sitting on the nightstand.

"You're in pain." She grabbed the remote for him, hit the POWER button to turn on the TV, then handed it back.

"It's fine. Just a little ache. I can handle it. Why don't you bring your breakfast up here and join me? We can watch the news."

"Sure, okay." She went down, grabbed her plate and coffee, and brought it up.

As she entered the room, she heard the news anchor speaking, "Another woman's body was found this morning—"

Click. The TV went dead.

12

Malek, still holding the remote, dropped it on the mattress and pretended nothing was wrong. "There you are. After you eat, I think we should—"

"Why did you do that?" Lei plunked her tray on his bed and grabbed for the remote. "Why'd you turn off the news?"

He held the remote out of her reach. Damn him for his long arms. "I didn't think you needed to hear about another murdered woman right now. Especially after our attack."

"I'm an adult. I get to decide what I do and don't need to hear, thank you." She lunged for his hand and tried to pull the remote free.

He refused to give it up, stubborn man.

Praying the victim wasn't either Kate or Heather, she sprinted down the stairs, zoomed through the kitchen, and remoted on the family room TV.

"The body was found behind this hardware store," the reporter said, motioning to the dilapidated concrete building behind her. "An autopsy will be performed today, but it's fairly apparent the unidentified victim died of a gunshot to the head. There is nothing linking this murder to the other two from earlier this week, but people in the area are convinced the three are related." She paused for a moment, then smiled. "And now, back to you, Meredith."

No photograph of the victim had been shown. No sketch. Nothing.

"Dammit." Lei hit the CHANNEL button, hoping to catch more details, a police sketch of the victim, or a description. But the other channels weren't broadcasting the news. She killed the TV and headed back upstairs. When she stepped into Malek's room, she gave him a glare. "I missed most of the report."

"The police don't have anything yet."

"Did you know about that murder?"

"I did. It was on last night's news."

"Why didn't you tell me?"

"Because I was sleeping—"

"This morning."

"There's nothing to tell yet."

"Bullshit. Three women are dead. I personally knew two of them. And we were attacked."

"And at this point there's no reason to assume this third one had anything to do with the other two, or with our attack." He tipped his head and narrowed his eyes. "Unless there's something you're not telling me . . . ?"

"No, of course not." She wanted to fiddle. Or look away. But he was studying her, trying to decide if she was lying. She didn't need him thinking she was.

"Do you know who attacked us?" he asked.

"No." She pointed at the TV. "Do you know who that dead woman is?"

"No. Do you?"

"How would I know?"

Malek's gaze sharpened slightly. "I can't shake the feeling that you're keeping something from me."

"I'm not." Lei sat on the edge of the bed. "I'm not hiding anything. I'm just scared. I don't know what to do."

"You're safe as long as you stay in this house."

"How can you be so sure? Someone attacked us. Here. In this house."

"Which is why we'll be going on a little trip as soon as Talen returns."

She needed to get to her phone and call Vasquez. Find out what he knew about the dead woman.

"Drako and Talen are working on this. Hopefully it'll all be over soon and things will be back to normal."

Normal. How she longed for that. She slumped onto the bed and cupped her hands over her face. "When is this nightmare going to end?"

"Soon, baby. I promise." He eased one of her hands from her face, wove his fingers through hers, and squeezed. "I'm going to take care of you."

"You shouldn't have to."

"I don't mind."

"But—"

"Hellloooo!" a male voice echoed through the house. Lei recognized it. Talen.

"Damn," Malek mumbled.

Lei jumped up off the bed and scrambled back away from it. She didn't need Talen getting the wrong idea.

Talen thudded up the steps and into the room. His gaze jerked from Lei's face to Malek's, then back again. "Am I interrupting something?"

"Nope," Lei said.

Malek didn't respond.

It took all of two long strides for Talen to reach the bed. "What the hell happened to you?" he asked Malek.

"I fell," Malek said.

The brothers laughed.

Lei failed to see the humor in the situation. But she did see an opportunity, and she was going to take it. If she could get Malek out of town, hidden away somewhere safe, that would be one less person to worry about. Then she could focus her energy on locating those two—or was it one now?—girls.

"Two men attacked us. Right here. In the house. Your brother almost died trying to protect me," Lei explained.

Two sets of male eyes landed on her.

"Is that so?" Talen asked, his tone not at all light or joking.

"Yes, that's so," she said. "And it's no laughing matter."

"Sure." Talen's mien was serious now, as it should be.

"And I'm wondering if the attack was my fault," she added.

One set of eyes widened—Talen's. Malek didn't look surprised.

"It's not your fault, Lei," Malek said.

Talen asked, "Why's that? Why do you think it's your fault?"

She explained, "Because two girls I used to... work with... were killed recently."

"And you think you were supposed to be next?" Talen asked.

"Sure." Lei pointed at the television, which was now off. "I think someone's going around killing all the girls who've recently left that bastard. A third woman was found dead this morning."

"We don't know yet if that one is related to the others," Malek reminded her. "She hasn't been identified yet."

"Were the police involved in your situation here?" Talen asked.

"I called them, of course." Catching the hint of something negative in Talen's reaction, she added, "If I hadn't called for help, Malek would be dead. As a matter of fact, I believe he was dead when EMS arrived."

Talen's expression soured even more.

"Obviously, we need to go stay somewhere else for a while," Malek said.

"Already taken care of. Drako's made all the arrangements. But you're not in any condition to drive, and I need to stay here and take care of some things."

"I can drive," Lei said.

"No," the guys said in unison.

Now she was insulted. "There's nothing wrong with my driving."

"That's not the problem," Malek said. "If we're followed, things could get a little dicey."

"I can handle 'dicey' better than you can right now. After all, you've recently had surgery. You're not in tip-top shape. Not to say you didn't give those two guys a run for their money, Malek, but you're a writer, not Special Ops . . ."

Malek and Talen exchanged looks.

Malek blurted, "Talen is—was."

"What?" she asked.

"Navy SEALs," Malek told her.

Talen looked mighty surprised. Either he wasn't Navy SEALs, or he was but didn't want anyone to know.

"He should drive us." Malek motioned to the stairs. "Lei, go get packing." He acted as if he might give her fanny a smack, but a don't-you-dare glare stopped him before he made contact. She noticed, as she scurried away, that she wasn't the only one glaring at him.

"Okay, if you think it's necessary." She headed for the door. "I'm not sure how much to pack. How long do you think we'll have to stay away? A few days? A week?"

"Oh, I don't know," Malek said. "Maybe a month."

"A month?" she repeated. Yes, she wanted to get Malek out

of town and away from Holloway. But she was hoping they wouldn't have to stay in hiding that long. Her whole life was crumbling apart. "Classes start right after the New Year. I hope we can make it back by then."

"Me, too, Lei. Bring everything you'll need for one month, just in case."

"Okay." Feeling a sense of urgency, and hoping his estimate was way off, that they'd be back home long before the first day of classes, and this whole hellish thing would be over, she scampered upstairs to gather a month's worth of clothing, personal items, and her school books and supplies. A half hour later, she had a mountain of things sitting in the middle of her room, including her sewing machine and laptop. After putting in a call to Vasquez and leaving a message on his voice mail letting him know she was leaving town, she shuffled downstairs to find the brothers had locked themselves in Drako's office. She jiggled the handle, then knocked.

Talen opened the door and she peered inside, finding Malek sitting in the room's corner, looking a little pale.

"I'm ready to go whenever you are," Lei said.

Talen said, "Good. We'll get going shortly."

Angling her body half in the room and half out in the hall, she told him, "My stuff is sitting in the middle of my floor."

Talen headed through the door. "I'll load up the truck."

Lei followed him up the stairs.

His expression, when he saw the mountain, was more than a little comical.

"All this?" He sounded breathless, and he hadn't lifted a single thing yet.

"Yes, 'all this.' I need everything here. Malek said I should pack for a month."

Talen grumbled something under his breath. Lei had some notion of what he might have said. In all fairness, she couldn't blame him for being a little cranky. She'd packed a ton of things.

To appease her guilt for making him work so hard, she helped Talen haul her stuff out, despite his repeated attempts to convince her he could do it by himself. It didn't escape her notice that Malek had packed absolutely nothing. Not even a pair of underwear.

"Where are Malek's things?" she asked.

"Doesn't need anything. We're taking you to another of our properties. He has clothes there."

"Another property? Sheesh. How many houses do you guys own?"

Talen merely shrugged and smiled.

"Did you three inherit—" She cut herself off. "Sorry, that's none of my business."

"Yes," Talen said as he wedged the last bag in the back of his Navigator. He turned to face her. "We did inherit a crapload of money." He waved her toward the door. "Now, let's get you two somewhere safe."

She hesitated. "One thing we haven't thought about, what about Malek's nurse?"

"What about her?"

"Him," she corrected.

"Him," he echoed. "My mistake."

"Well, if we're in hiding, how will the nurse find us? Will you tell him?"

"Hmmm." Talen visibly considered the situation for a moment. "It's probably better if we don't tell anyone where you're staying."

"But Malek still needs medical care." She didn't like the way Talen was looking at her. She held her hands palms out. "If you're thinking I can handle the job, you're wrong. Malek and I already discussed it."

"Okay. We'll figure it out later. If you can help Malek with the basics in the meantime, I'd appreciate it."

"The basics I can do."

Together, they went inside the house. Lei headed up to her room to make one final sweep. She didn't want to forget anything. Once she was sure she had everything she'd need, she headed back down. Malek and Talen were at the door. Talen had an arm around Malek's waist and was supporting him as he slowly crossed the threshold. Lei watched, wincing, as he struggled to get down the front steps.

He'd been acting pretty spunky when he was stationary, but now that he was up and moving around, she could see he still had a lot of recovering to do. She owed Malek all the help she could give him until he was one hundred percent back to health. Being in hiding for at least the next couple of weeks meant she'd have plenty of opportunity to give him her undivided attention.

Malek insisted he ride in the backseat, with Lei beside him. Talen helped him into the vehicle, leaving him to fasten himself into his seat belt, so he could climb behind the steering wheel. Off they drove, heading west.

Malek looked at her as they zoomed around the tight curve of the freeway entrance ramp, blinked slowly, and said, "Sorry, but I doubt I'll be much company."

"It's okay. Rest."

His lips curled into a hint of a smile. "Talen, make sure nobody's following us." Then he leaned his head back and closed his eyes. Within minutes, his breathing was slow and even. In his sleep, he slumped a little, leaning against her. Eventually, his head flopped onto her shoulder.

Talen's eyes flicked to hers in the rearview mirror. "How's he doing?"

"Sleeping," she said as quietly as possible.

"Good. Don't let the act fool you. He's in a lot of pain. He just doesn't want you to know."

"I figured as much."

"Listen, while you're out here, by yourselves, don't let him do anything stupid."

"I won't. Then again, the man can be rather bullheaded."

"We all can be. It's a family trait."

"I feel for Rin, then."

"Drako's the worst. But your sister seems to know how to handle him." Talen chuckled. "She's got him wrapped around her little finger right now. Especially with the baby coming."

Lei couldn't help smiling. "I can't wait to be an aunt."

"And I can't wait to be an uncle."

"So, once Malek gets married, will it be your turn?"

Talen grunted. She took that as a yes.

"What's the deal? Why do you *have* to be married?" she asked, gently repositioning Malek's head.

"It's a condition of our inheritance." Talen's gaze met hers in the mirror again. "Don't tell my brothers I said this, but it's probably a good thing we have to get married. I didn't feel that way a few months ago. But now, seeing Drako and your sister... I'm not dreading it as much as I was."

"Malek seems to be one hundred percent on board with the idea."

"That doesn't surprise me."

She almost told Talen about Malek's proposal, but she didn't. She could imagine Talen giving Malek a hard time about her refusal. She didn't want to be responsible for that kind of humiliation.

Instead, she sat back and closed her eyes. "How long will we be on the road?"

"A couple hours."

She glanced at the truck's clock, then shut her eyes again. Two hours. If she could fall asleep, the time would fly by.

13

She woke up with her head inclined to one side, resting on top of Malek's tipped head. Blinking, she checked the window. The truck had stopped. They were parked in a wooded area. The view out the window revealed a thick forest and snow as far as the eye could see. The view from the other side of the vehicle was quite different. A house. Contemporary. Boxy. With lots of windows. A parking area, shoveled, front walk, shoveled.

"Okay," Talen said. He cut off the engine. "We're here. Wake up, you two."

"I'm awake," Malek grumbled, sounding like he was far from awake.

Lei unfastened her seat belt, and after Malek removed his head from her shoulder, she scooted toward the door and opened it. A blast of arctic air whooshed into the car, taking her breath away for a moment. She wrapped her arms around herself and hurried around the front of the truck.

Talen was already helping Malek out by the time she had circled around the side. "Trunk's open," he said.

She slip-slided around to the back, lifted the hatch, and

pulled out a couple of bags. Luggage dragging behind her, she followed the men up the front walk to the door.

Talen let them inside.

Lei stepped into a wide, open living area, inhaled the earthy scents of pine and lemon polish and a wood-burning fire, and looked up. The ceiling above soared at least two stories up. And the sun shone through the expansive windows, warming her face. It looked like a mountain lodge, all wood-paneled and rustic—a very large, expensively furnished mountain lodge.

"This place is gorgeous." She parked the luggage in a safe spot where nobody would trip over it.

"Glad you like it." Malek gritted his teeth as he bent to lower himself onto a nearby couch.

Lei rushed to his side and offered some help. He grabbed one of her hands, but didn't use her for support. Once he was sitting, she tried to back away, but he wouldn't let go.

"Sit with me for a few," he said.

She pointed at the door. "But the luggage."

"Talen can get it." Malek pulled on her hand, forcing her to bend at the waist. His gaze wandered a little south of her face, halting at about boob level. His lips curled into a sexy smile. "Hmmm. Nice view."

Lei glanced down, realized her V-neck T-shirt was gaping, and clapped her free hand against her chest. "You are a—"

"Hungry man," he finished for her.

Glaring at him, she yanked her other hand out of his grasp. "If you're hungry, then I suggest you let me go help your brother. I'm not going to make Talen carry all my crap in by himself." Sporting a burning face, she hurried outside.

Talen seemed to be trying to hide a laugh as he passed her on the front porch. "Everything okay?" he asked.

"Your brother is a brat."

"That's not news to me."

She grabbed as much stuff as she could carry and hauled it to the house, passing Talen on the way inside. He gave her a glittery-eyed grin.

When she dumped her load, Malek called her name.

"I'm not done yet," she said, making a one-eighty to head back outside.

It took another five trips to the car before everything was inside. Talen sighed as he dropped the last piece of luggage. "Whew. I never realized traveling with a woman could be so exhausting. There's a car in the garage, in case you need to run to the store for supplies. The refrigerator, freezer, and cupboards should be stocked. . . ." He headed for the kitchen, which was open to the living area, pulled open the stainless-steel refrigerator door, and peered inside. "Looks like you're set for at least a week."

"Wow, what service," Lei said. "Does this place come with a full-time cook, too?"

"No, you're on your own there." Talen headed over to his brother. "I kept a close eye on traffic, and I'm sure nobody followed us. Nobody knows you're here but me and Drako. I'd better head back. Do you need anything else?"

"Nope. All set. Thanks."

Talen gave Malek a thump on the shoulder and then beamed at Lei. "Okay, you two. Stay safe. I'll keep you posted, let you know when it's safe to come back."

"The sooner the better," Lei said.

Talen slid Malek a glance. "Of course."

He left.

Once again, she was alone with Malek. But now she was alone, alone. Out in the middle of nowhere. In this . . . gorgeous, cozy, romantic place.

If she didn't know better, she'd wonder if he'd arranged to have those thugs beat him up so they'd have to go into hiding.

"Lei?" he said.

"What is it?"

He let his head fall back and closed his eyes. "I'm sorry, Lei."

She hadn't seen that coming. Why would he apologize to her? "Sorry? For what?"

"If I'd taken care of those two assholes when I had the chance, we wouldn't have to be out here hiding like a couple of moles."

Lei's heart swelled. "Ohmygod, Malek. This isn't your fault. You fought hard. You fought damn hard. When I made that comment about you not being Special Ops, I didn't mean you weren't brave and strong. There were two of them and only one of you. You could have been the biggest, baddest Army Ranger alive and still they might have kicked your ass."

"It shouldn't have mattered. I should've been able to take care of them. There's no excuse. None." He was staring straight up at the ceiling, but still Lei could see the anger and frustration in his eyes. "I fucked up. I am a fuckup."

"No." She knelt in front of him and placed her hands on his knee. "I respect you so much for what you did. Nobody has ever put their life on the line for me the way you did. And I will forever be grateful to you for that. Who knows what might have happened if you hadn't. I might've been the next woman lying dead in an alley."

He slammed his fists down into the couch seat. "I hate that I can't do a damn thing right now."

"You have to give yourself time to heal."

His gaze slid to hers at last. Now his eyes were cold and hard. She'd never seen him look like that before. It was as if she were looking into the eyes of a stranger, and that frightened her a little. Correction, it frightened her a lot. "When I find those bastards, I'm going to kill them."

"Those guys deserve it, after what they did to you. But you can't do that, stoop to their level. It's wrong."

"I won't be caught," he snapped. "I'll make sure of it."

"Malek, I've known you for months. That's not a long time. But I'd like to think it's long enough to know that you aren't a cold-blooded killer."

He didn't speak. She wanted him to. She needed him to.

She continued, "Since I've come to live with you, you've been the only man I've been able to even remotely trust. Look at how close we've become, in such a short time. I never thought that was possible."

His expression softened slightly.

"The reason I've been able to trust you is because I believe you are a good man, honorable, trustworthy, honest, self-sacrificing."

He shook his head. "I'm just a man. Not perfect. Not a god."

"I don't need you to be perfect or a god. I just need you to be the man you've been the past few weeks."

Silence.

"Malek, up until now, you've been trying to help me learn to trust. You've been focused on healing me. Those assholes nearly took your life. That was a horrible thing. And they deserve to be caught, to spend the rest of their lives in prison. At least this will give me a chance to help you, too. To help you heal."

He blinked. His lips thinned and he sniffled. "You are a remarkable woman. I've never met anyone like you before."

She smiled. "You're pretty damn remarkable yourself." When he set a hand on her head, she laid it on his knees and closed her eyes. Sitting there, with him sweetly stroking her hair, she realized something surprising.

Malek needed her.

Needing was a lot different than wanting. Definitely different from lusting.

Well, if he needed her, he could have her. The broken, imperfect woman she was. For as long as necessary.

But only as a friend.

Not a wife.

Not a lover.

She could have sat like that for hours. But the rumble of his stomach inspired her to finally get going. He grumbled a little when she lifted her head, but when she told him, "I'm going to get you some lunch," he didn't complain.

While she made them some sandwiches, he watched her, silent, but not quite so brooding. She hoped he'd somewhat accepted the fact that their hiding wasn't his fault, that it was just an inconvenience. And maybe, just maybe, they could make the best of it.

That was exactly what she planned on doing, now that she felt somewhat confident that she'd done all she could to help Kate and Heather. It was up to Vasquez now. She hoped he'd have better luck than she had.

After they finished eating, she took care of the dishes, then threw some more logs on the fire and settled on the couch next to Malek.

"It's so quiet and peaceful here," she said.

"Too quiet."

"Is there such a thing as too quiet for a writer?"

He grunted and shrugged.

"Would you like me to get your computer? Would you like to get some writing done?"

Another grunt.

She took that as a yes and went in search of his computer. She found a laptop in the first bedroom she checked. After making sure he had everything he needed, she excused herself to do some reading, figuring he'd be less distracted if she left the room.

But an hour later, she was tired of being alone. She'd unpacked and done some snooping, and now she was craving some company. His company. She tiptoed out to the living room and discovered he was asleep, his computer in his lap, his body slightly slumped to one side.

So much for getting some work done.

Chuckling softly, she admired him for a moment.

He really was a remarkable man. Not just drop-dead gorgeous, but patient and strong and sexy, too.

And also determined. Stubborn.

If she had any notion of marrying, he was the only one who'd come even close to being a potential husband. He'd even worked long and hard at gaining her trust. That right there earned him a second thought.

But . . . marriage?

He saved my life. Obviously he cares a lot about me. And he needs me.

Marriage.

Maybe it won't be as bad as I thought? Maybe I won't fail him.

Her phone rang, and recognizing the ring tone, she scurried off to find it. She caught it on the third ring.

"Lei, are you okay?" Rin asked, sounding extremely worried.

"Of course. Why wouldn't I be?"

"Well . . . I heard Drako talking to Talen . . ."

"And what? Talen brought us out to a gorgeous place out in the middle of nowhere so we'd be safe. Was there another murder? Or did Talen find something? Was there a threat?"

"No, it's nothing about that."

"Then what?"

Rin hesitated.

"Rin, what the hell is going on?"

"Okay, okay." Rin sighed. "I heard Drako talking to Talen about Malek's wedding. He's chosen his wife. It isn't you."

Lei's heart stopped. Literally. She stopped breathing, too. Rin's words had slammed her harder than any kick or punch ever had. Mostly because they'd come out of nowhere.

Moments ago, Lei had thought—assumed—he was waiting for her to change her mind about his proposal.

"Lei?" Rin said weakly. "Are you still there?"

"Yeah."

"I thought he would have told you by now."

"Maybe he just hasn't gotten around to it yet."

"Yeah, maybe." Rin sighed again.

Lei echoed her. "Don't worry. It's for the better if he marries someone else. I'm a train wreck. Speaking of which, how are you feeling?"

"Better, I guess. I'm not so tired, but I throw up a lot. Especially in the morning. The doctor said that's normal."

"I'm glad you're doing okay."

"Yeah."

Lei couldn't help hearing the guilt in Rin's voice. "Rin, don't worry. I'm fine. I mean, I don't want to be anyone's wife. I've always felt that way."

"I've heard you say that, but I just thought—"

"That I'd changed my mind?" Lei finished for her sister.

"Maybe."

"No, I haven't. I don't ever want to be married. I won't be any man's possession again." Lei forced a smile, knowing it would lift the tone of her voice. "Really, this comes as a huge relief. I didn't know how I was going to tell him he needed to find someone else."

"I guess that's good, then."

"Sure." After a beat, she asked, "Did you hear who he was marrying?"

"Her name's April. Have you met her?"

Lei's heart lurched. "Not formally."

"And . . . ?"

"She's a safe choice for him. I guess that's what he wanted, safe. I heard she and Brent and Malek have had this ongoing threesome thing for a while. If he marries April, things can pretty much stay as they were."

"Oh, I didn't realize that. What would you have done if he'd married you?"

She thought the answer to that question would be to let him make the choice for himself, but that wasn't what came out of her mouth. Instead, she said, "I don't know."

"Yeah, it's tough. Oh, darn. Drako's getting impatient. I have to go. We're heading into town to do some shopping for the baby."

"Have fun."

"Stay safe, little sister."

"I will."

The instant the call ended, Lei's eyes filled with tears.

14

Malek hit the button on his cell phone a little harder than necessary. He couldn't help it. He was irritated.

Drako was being an ass.

Normally, he could handle Drako's surly, overbearing personality. But not when it came to this. He had every right to choose whom he married. And he had every right to take as long as he needed to convince his chosen bride to marry him.

Drako didn't like it, but he could kiss his ass.

Malek closed his eyes and gritted his teeth.

It wouldn't take much longer. He'd already made some great headway with Lei. She was tolerating his touch much better now. And he was feeling more comfortable with her, too.

But Drako was insisting he pick someone else. Someone easy.

He wasn't ready to give up on Lei yet. She was special. She was The One. She was the woman who made all the other women in the world disappear.

His heart sank at the thought of waking up every morning without her by his side. The last two nights had been absolute heaven. Granted, he'd gotten very little sleep. Between the thrill of holding her, freely touching her when she was asleep, and the wild thrashing and kicking and screaming she did periodically, he was catching maybe a couple of hours of sleep total. But he didn't care. There was plenty of time for that later.

Already, he was looking forward to tonight.

He was also eager for Lei to come out of her room. She'd been in there a long time. Too long.

Moving cautiously, he eased himself up off the couch. The pain in his gut was still excruciating. But he'd done his best to hide it from Lei. He felt like shit because they'd been forced to go into hiding after the attack. That was his fault. He couldn't handle seeing his pain reflected on her face, too. She was too delicate, too fragile right now. She needed to be protected and cherished.

Forcing himself to walk with as much fluidity as he could, he ambled across the great room and headed toward the bedrooms. Just before he made it to her room, her door swung open.

Their gazes met for an instant; then she jerked hers away.

Her lips thinned. Her face paled.

The sparkle in her eyes was gone.

Something was wrong.

"Lei?" he said.

"Are you hungry?" Her voice was flat. And her face was a little puffy. Dark circles stained the thin skin under her eyes.

"No. What's wrong?"

She smiled. Or rather, she tried to produce an expression that would pass for a smile. It didn't. "Nothing."

"Tell me."

"Nothing's wrong." She inched past him, avoiding any contact with him. "Nothing at all."

He grabbed her arm and instantly regretted it.

She lurched around, yanked it free, and hissed, "Don't ever touch me again."

What the fuck?

"Lei, tell me what's wrong."

She shook her head. "I said nothing. Nothing's wrong." She sighed. "I'm sorry for being so snappy. I just... I heard some news and I'm kind of cranky."

"News about what?"

"Nothing important." She waved away his concern, not that it worked. "Don't worry. I'm fine."

She was a horrible liar. But he was glad for that.

This time when she started to walk away, he didn't stop her. She went one way, toward the kitchen. He went the other way, to his room. After closing the door, he pressed an ear to the door connecting to hers, and when he was sure the coast was clear, he snuck inside.

He felt like shit for snooping, but he needed to find out what the hell had happened. If she was upset with him, and he couldn't get to the bottom of it immediately, there was absolutely no way he'd be marrying her. As much as she wanted to convince him she didn't want to marry him, he knew she wanted it, too—as much, if not more, than he did.

He glanced around her room. There were some school books lying on the bed. A notebook filled with her loopy handwriting. He skimmed the contents, flipping pages. Notes from a class, it seemed. On the front page was a listing of friends or classmates. Names. Phone numbers.

News. She'd said she'd received some news.

There wasn't a TV in the room, so she couldn't be referring to that sort of news.

Computer?

It was sitting on her dresser. He felt the cover. Cool, not hot. It hadn't been powered on for a while, if at all today.

He turned back toward the bed. Phone. It was lying next to the notebook.

After taking a moment to listen for her, he shuffled over to the bed, snatched up the phone, and checked the call log. She'd been talking to her sister just a few minutes ago.

"What the hell are you doing?" Lei. Pissed.

Shit. Think quick. "My phone's dead. I was hoping I could borrow yours?"

"Ever heard of asking first?" she snapped, her voice chilly. Her eyes were slits. Her mouth was a hard slash. She'd never looked at him like that. He had to find out what the hell was wrong.

"I'm sorry." He put down the phone and lifted his hands in surrender. "I wasn't going to use it without talking to you first. I . . . assumed you'd be back in a moment and then I'd ask."

"Why not ask when we were out in the hallway?"

"I got distracted."

She gave a little humph and glared at the open door, the one connecting the two rooms. "I didn't realize that door led to another bedroom. I thought it was a bathroom."

"There's a third bedroom upstairs, if you'd rather take that one. But it's a loft, over the kitchen, with no door."

"I guess I'll stick with this one." She squinted at the door. He guessed she was looking for a lock.

She wanted to lock him out?

Whatever the fuck her sister had told her had set him back in a big way.

He left through the door she had been leering at, making a point to lock it from her side before shutting it. Then he jerked his phone out of his pocket and dialed his brother.

Drako answered on the fucking tenth ring. "What's wrong?" he asked.

"What the fuck is going on?" Malek growled, trying hard to keep his voice low.

"What do you mean?"

"I meant what I said. What the fuck are you up to?"

"First, I'm not 'up to' anything. And second, what the hell are you talking about?"

"Lei."

"What about her?"

"She's upset." He pressed his ear to the connecting door, listening for her.

"And . . . ?"

Satisfied she wasn't eavesdropping, Malek moved to the other end of the room. "It's gotta be your fault. What did you say?"

"Nothing. I haven't talked to her."

"Then you had your wife say something to her. I want to know what the hell she said."

"Hang on." Drako muffled the phone with his palm while he talked to his wife. Malek couldn't make out what they were saying. All he could hear was a low-pitched male's voice and a higher female's. This back and forth went on for a long time, so long that Malek was tempted to hang up.

"It's not good news," Drako said finally. "But nobody is to blame."

"What? Tell me."

"Rin overheard me talking to Talen."

"What did she hear?" he hissed, biting back a handful of curse words.

"Me talking about you marrying April."

A wave of white-hot rage charged through his system. His fist clenched. His jaw clenched. His gut clenched, too. Dammit, Drako had gone too far this time. Too fucking far. "I told you, I'm not marrying that woman. Dammit!"

"I didn't know she was listening."

"Fuck." He needed to pound something. To hurl something . . . at Drako's head. This wasn't fair. It wasn't right. Nobody had interfered with Drako's marriage. He had no right. "I don't want to marry April. Got it?"

"I hear you, Malek. But you may have no choice now."

"I'll straighten it out."

"There's another problem."

Something else? What the hell was it now? "What's that?"

The doorbell rang.

"Who's at the door?" Malek asked.

"The other problem," Drako said, sounding slightly apologetic.

Malek jerked the curtains aside. His room faced the front of the house. Thus, from his vantage, he could see who was standing on the porch. "What the hell is April doing here?" he yelled.

"Talen gave her the address. That's what we were talking about when Rin overheard me."

"Fuck!" He jerked the curtain shut and stomped toward the door. "It's a good thing you're not here right now."

"Look, I know you have the right to choose your wife."

"Shut the hell up." He jerked open his bedroom door.

"Bro, Lei's got problems. She's nowhere near ready to get married to anyone. Rin said so, said Lei told her she was feeling pressured. By you. Is that what you want?"

His heart jerked. He closed the door. "I... don't know."

"Think about it."

"But look at your wife. She married you for money. It didn't bother you that she was feeling pressured."

"That's different."

"How?"

"It just is. She didn't have any feelings for me. It was just a deal we struck. I wouldn't have married her if she'd felt obligated for emotional reasons. That's a surefire way to start trouble."

"Maybe." Malek went back to the window. "But things with

April aren't all that simple either." He peered out and watched April totter back to her car.

"Talk to her. See if you can work something out. In the end, I think April is more capable of setting aside her emotions and making a solid decision than Lei. Lei's just too damaged right now."

Malek rammed his fingers through his hair. This situation was so fucked up, and he couldn't think straight. How the hell was he supposed to make the right decision? "If only I had more time. A few weeks, even."

"You know what the contract says."

The contract. The fucking contract.

Malek pulled the curtain aside again. April hadn't gone back to the porch yet. With any luck, she was headed for the freeway. "And so what if I don't get married by January first? What's going to happen? Is someone going to fire me? Are you going to report me to the trustee?"

"No, but... you saw what happened when Rin was kidnapped. We know a little about the gifts now. We know what that clause means. If you aren't married, maybe you won't get one?"

Malek's phone beeped, indicating he had another call. He glanced at the screen. It was April. He hit the button, sending her call to voice mail.

"Maybe I won't get a 'gift,' anyway," he said. "Could have been just you, since you're the oldest, the leader. Maybe I don't need some fucking supernatural gift."

"What if you do? What if it's the difference between saving our lives or dying? Losing The Secret or keeping it safe? Like it or not, this is our life, our reality, our obligation. You have less than two weeks to be married."

"Fuck."

"Good luck, bro. As your oldest brother, I want you to be happy. But as the leader of the Black Gryffons, I need you to do the right thing. You might not be able to have both . . . at least not right away."

"I get it." The doorbell rang again. "I gotta go let April in. Later."

"Bye."

Knowing he was in for a shit storm, Malek hobbled to the door. He arrived there at precisely the same moment as Lei. She glanced out the sidelight, saw who was ringing the bell, turned a one-eighty, and avoiding eye contact with Malek, headed toward her room.

As he was opening the front door, Lei's bedroom door slammed, the sound echoing through the entire house. He flinched, sucked in a deep breath, and welcomed April inside with a tip of his head.

"Malek!" April dropped her bag at her feet and flung herself at him, taking him off guard. "I was so worried about you."

He steadied himself before she knocked him on his ass. He was holding her stiffly, trying to handle the pain.

She clued in right away. She unwrapped her arms from around his neck and stepped back. "Oh, darn. Did I hurt you? I didn't mean to. Here." She took his hand in hers and started dragging him toward the couch. "You just had surgery. You should be lying down."

Malek couldn't help pressing a flattened hand against his wound. When she'd thrown herself at him, he'd clenched his abdominals. Now they were burning like a son of a bitch. "I'm okay." He eased onto the couch.

She dragged an ottoman over, knelt in front of him, grabbed his feet, and plopped them on top of it. "How's that?"

"Fine."

"Good. I'm going to get my stuff. Then I'm going to make you something to eat."

"I'm not hungry."

"That's okay. It's going to take me a while to get everything." She blew him a kiss, then bounced away.

All Malek could do was close his eyes, let his head fall back, and say to himself, over and over, *Oh shit, oh shit, oh shit.*

How the hell was he going to get this straightened out? He couldn't stomach the thought of hurting Lei more than she already had been. He knew she was locked in her room, thinking the worst and wondering what kind of game he'd been playing.

Somehow, he had to clear this up. And quickly. Or he would face an impossible choice.

"Where should I put my stuff?" April asked when she *click-clacked* in with her first load. Clearly, she'd packed to stay for a long time.

"Just leave it there by the door for now."

She scrunched up her face. "Why would I leave everything sitting by the door? Am I leaving soon? Don't you want me to stay?"

Shit! Women.

He was tiptoeing through not one but two emotional minefields. The chances of him being blown to hell were pretty much one hundred percent.

"First room on the left. I'll show you." Walking slowly, he led her back to the bedrooms. She would stay in the room farthest from his for now. He motioned to the door. "This one."

"Thanks." She wobbled past on her platform stilettos, stopped in the middle of the room, and glanced around. "Where's your stuff? Aren't we sharing a room?"

"Not right now." He pulled her closer, lowering his voice. "Look, Lei's here. She has to stay here with us. And I don't want her feeling uncomfortable."

"Your sister-in-law? Why would she feel uncomfortable?"

"Just . . . please, April."

"Fine." She shook her head, sighed, and dropped her bags

on the floor. "Sheesh." She gave him an up-and-down look. "You're acting funny, strange. Is everything okay?"

"I was beat to within an inch of my life. I just had surgery. Tell me, would you act strange if that had happened to you?"

"Sure." Her eyebrows scrunched. "But I have the feeling it isn't that. Anyway, I'd better get the rest of my stuff inside. It's starting to snow again." She pulled off her shoes—a smart move—rummaged in a bag, and produced a pair of boots. "I guess I can forget about being sexy and go with these." She dropped the boots on the floor and stuffed her feet into them.

"Yeah, probably wouldn't be so sexy if you slid and broke your ankle."

"Good point." Now stomping, she headed out of the room. "Be back in a few." Off she went.

Malek made a beeline for Lei's door. He knocked.

"Yeah?" she shouted through it.

"Can I talk to you for a minute?"

"I'm busy."

"Please, Lei. It's important."

"Fine." A few seconds later, the lock *clicked.* "You can come in now."

He entered and closed the door behind himself.

"Leave the door open, please." Lei was sitting at a table positioned in front of a wide window. Her laptop was on, the screen displaying a Web site for a clothing store, from what he could tell.

He cracked the door open just an inch.

"What is it?" Her voice was as sharp as a razor.

"I know what Rin told you. She was wrong."

"Rin told me 'bout what?"

"About my marrying April."

Lei's gaze jerked away.

Malek moved closer, reached for her, but when she glared a

warning, he pulled his hand back. "I'm trying to tell you I don't want to marry April, Lei."

"Yeah, well." Lei stood, took a couple of steps away, and folded her arms over her chest. "I told you before, it's better if you do marry someone else."

Fuck, that hurt. "But, Lei—"

"I'm not wife material. I can't trust. I can barely tolerate being touched. It was hard enough before. Now it's impossible."

"Why? I'm telling you that conversation was just a misunderstanding. What your sister heard had nothing to do with what I want, what I have decided."

"So are you telling me you 'decided' I would marry you?" Her eyes narrowed to sharp little slits. "Don't I have any say in this?"

"Of course you do." He didn't like the way she'd phrased that. "It isn't like that."

She lifted one perfectly arched brow.

"Lei, I care about you. I need you."

"Yeah, and I'm grateful to you for what you did for me. You took a beating to save me." She tipped up her chin and looked him straight in the eye. There was no pain in her eyes now. No confusion. Only determination. "If I married you now, it would be because I felt obligated to you because you'd nearly died. Not because I feel the same way for you as you feel for me. I told you—from the start—I'm damaged goods." She thumped her chest with her fist. "I just can't let myself be vulnerable. I can't let anyone in. Nobody."

"But—"

"Do yourself a favor. Give it up. You don't have much time and you're wasting it on a lost cause. I won't ever love you, Malek. Not the way you want me to. Not the way you should have a wife love you." She pointed at the door. "That woman out there, maybe she's not perfect, but who is? Ask yourself this: Is she one hundred percent committed to making you happy? If the answer is yes, then you've found the right woman. She'll give, give, give. She'll submit, submit, submit." She went back to the desk and rested a hand on the chair. "All I would do is take, take, take until you're drained and empty and dead inside." In a clear effort to end the conversation, she sat and turned toward her computer and started poking the keys.

Malek felt as if all the air had been sucked from the room and he couldn't breathe. "But—"

"Go on, Malek, find your bride and spend some time with her. You'll make her a very happy woman."

He didn't want to walk away now. Not with things being like this between them. But what else could he say to change her mind? It seemed she'd made a decision. And it was final.

The woman he loved didn't want him.

Frustrated, angry, he charged toward her, yanked her out of that damned chair, and crushed his mouth over hers.

15

Lei fought like a little hellcat at first. But he just kept on kissing her. She even nipped at his lip a little. But he didn't release her. With lips, teeth, tongue, he claimed, he seduced, he conquered. Until she was breathless, clinging to him instead of clawing at him.

Just as he'd hoped.

As she softened, the kiss became less urgent. Now it was a patient exploration on both sides. Tongues stroking, tasting. Hands gliding up and down, mapping new terrain. Malek's body was growing hard, tight. His mind foggy. His nerves electrified. A pounding ache erupted between his legs, and he rocked his hips forward to grind away the burn.

"Malek," she said into their joined mouths. "Please."

"Please, what, baby?" He angled back. One hand had found a breast. The other was cupping the back of her neck. He looked into her heavy-lidded eyes. They were watery. "Are you crying?" In response, one fat tear dripped from the corner of her eye. "Why?"

"Because I can't do this." She shrank away from him. Wrapped her arms protectively around herself. "Please don't force me."

"I don't want to force you to do anything."

"Good. Then you'll go marry April."

"But what about us? Our feelings for each other?"

She dragged her hand across her face. "You want me, like a man wants a woman. It's just lust. Nothing more."

"You don't know that."

"I do. Because if it was more, if you really wanted what was best for me, you'd walk away."

He hated hearing those words. They sliced his insides like razors. Moving slowly, he cupped her cheek and thumbed away a tear. "What do you feel for me?"

She pulled his hand away from her face and took a step back. "Respect. Friendship. Gratitude."

"Desire."

She threw her hands into the air and stomped toward the window. "Okay, sure. Desire. But that's not enough. I'm still not what you want, what you need." Lei pointed at the doorway behind him. "She is. April."

"Malek?" a soft female voice said. It was coming from the doorway. "Is something wrong?"

He turned a one-eighty. "No, nothing's wrong."

April's gaze jumped from Malek to Lei and back to Malek again. "I've interrupted something." Visibly shaken, she stumbled backward. "It was a mistake coming here."

Malek didn't move.

Lei did. "Wait!" She dashed across the room, grabbing April's hand and keeping her from rushing away. "I'm sorry if you've gotten the wrong impression here. There's nothing going on between Malek and me. Absolutely nothing."

"I saw you two." April's lip quivered. "You were kissing."

Shit.

Lei's gaze snapped to Malek's.

Malek shook his head. This was all fucked up. April had walked smack dab into the middle of it. She didn't deserve this. Neither did Lei. If only Drako and Talen had left him to make his own fucking decisions. "I'm sorry," was all he could say.

"That's it? I'm sorry?" April's cheeks pinked. She blinked several times. Her eyes reddened. Dammit, she was going to cry, too. Two women crying, all in the span of maybe ten minutes. He was a fucking asshole. "Is that all you can say?"

"Go talk to her, Malek," Lei said through visibly gritted teeth. To April, she said, "It's not what you think. I was upset and he was trying to—"

"He had his tongue shoved down your throat," April pointed out.

Lei visibly inhaled. Exhaled. "Yes, he did. But it didn't mean anything. Tell her, Malek."

He wasn't going to tell that to anyone. Because that kiss did mean something. It meant a hell of a lot.

Lei glared at him. "You're an idiot."

Maybe he was. Okay, yes, he was. He was an idiot if he married April when he was in love with Lei. Dammit, it wouldn't be fair to April. Or to Lei.

Malek cleared his throat. "I'm sorry you drove all this way to find out you're in the middle of a fucking mess."

April's lips thinned and her face changed from a rosy pink to a deep crimson. "You asshole."

"Malek, what the hell are you doing?" Lei said, hands thrown in the air.

"He's telling me to get lost," April said, her narrowed eyes focused on him.

"No, he's not," Lei told her.

They both looked at him.

Now, he was no pussy. He had never backed away from a

confrontation. But facing two furious women was nothing he'd ever wanted to endure. He'd rather be cornered by a pack of rabid wolverines.

"I'm not going to lie to anyone. It wouldn't be right." He turned his focus on April, who looked like she was ready to disembowel him with her bare hands. "You know my situation, that I have to be married in the next two weeks. We talked about it when you visited me in the hospital."

"Yes," she snapped, "that's why I drove all the way over here, to be with you, to plan *our* wedding."

"I see that now. I wish you'd called me first."

"You don't want to marry me," April said.

"I haven't proposed, April. You misunderstood."

She visibly flinched, and it killed him to hurt her. Absolutely killed him. Before this wedding shit, she'd been a good friend to him. He did care about her.

"It was my brother who was pushing me to marry you."

She folded her arms over her chest, stood silent, staring down at the floor for several long, torturous moments. "I'm glad you told me the truth before it was too late."

"I was hoping you'd see it that way."

She tipped her head toward Lei. "You want to marry her, don't you?"

He nodded.

"But that's the problem," Lei said. "I'm not going to marry him."

The two women stared at each other for several tense moments.

Finally, April started laughing. "Ohmygod, you are so fucked," she said to Malek.

"Yes, I am," he said, his gaze zigzagging between the two women.

"What are you going to do?" April asked.

"I don't know." His gaze went back to Lei. Her body language told him everything he needed to know. Arms crossed. Chin held high. Gaze sharp.

To Lei, she asked, "Why won't you marry him?"

"I don't love him," Lei stated.

April's face scrunched into a grimace. "Damn, that's harsh."

"It's the truth," Lei said.

Malek wasn't buying it. Now, more than ever, he was convinced Lei did love him. She loved him but didn't want to. She was afraid. That was all. Scared. That was actually good news. There was hope for them yet. He shrugged. "Now you know everything."

"So...?" April's brows furrowed. "Should I leave? Should I stay?"

"That's up to you," Malek said. "If I don't choose a wife, one will be chosen for me. Drako's made it clear who his choice would be if it came to that."

April pointed at her chest. "Me."

Malek nodded.

Her shoulders sagged. "Great, I'm the booby prize."

"I feel like shit," Malek admitted. "You deserve better than that. You deserve to be married to a man who worships you." He slid a glance at Lei. She was watching, her expression unreadable. What was she thinking right now? What was she feeling? He didn't believe, not for one minute, that she really wanted him to marry April. She'd merely convinced herself that it was the best thing for both of them.

He'd felt her surrender in that kiss. Was she afraid of how he made her feel? Of what loving him might do to her?

"Do you think you might ever love me?" April asked him.

"It's not that I don't love you, April. There's something there, between us. I'll always love you. But it's not *that* kind of love. Not the love you'd told me once that you were waiting for. I don't want you to go into this with any expectations that I can't fulfill—if it comes down to the two of us being married.

We've been lovers all this time. That was exactly why we didn't marry sooner."

"In other words, you want me to agree to marry you, even though you're in love with another woman." It wasn't a question; it was a statement. One that required no answer. April looked to Lei for an answer, which surprised Malek. "What would you do?"

"Do you love him?" Lei asked.

April glanced at him, then smiled. "God help me, I do."

"He's a good man," Lei said. "Brave. Honest. Honorable."

"Yeah." April crossed her arms over her chest, mirroring Lei. "He's a good man."

"If your marriage isn't what you expected, could you live with your decision?" Lei asked her.

"I don't know." April back-stepped toward the door. "I need some time to think this through."

Lei nodded.

Malek did the same. "Yes, please think it through. I couldn't live with myself if I thought you'd gone into this with any false expectations."

"Sure." April chewed on her lower lip. "Thanks. It's been hell hearing this, seeing it, but I'd still rather have it in my face than to go on blindly thinking everything was perfect. Better to know the truth, even if it's ugly."

She left.

Lei's gaze returned to Malek. "That was . . . unpleasant. You could've made it easier on yourself by keeping your feelings for me out of it. But you didn't." After a beat, she added, "I . . . respect you for not taking the easy way out and lying or sugarcoating the truth."

"I won't do that to her."

"Good for you." Lei inched around the bed until it was between them. "Hopefully she'll still agree to go through with the wedding."

She didn't hope for that. No the hell way.

He asked, "You want me to marry her? Even though she's as doubtful about it as I am?"

Lei stared down at the bed for several long moments. "Yes, it's the best thing for both of you. The love will come later, like it did with Drako and Rin."

She had done one hell of a job convincing herself of that. Obviously. It was going to take a lot to make her see she was fooling herself. The quickest, easiest solution would be to admit that giving her up would break his heart. But he couldn't get himself to stoop to using guilt to manipulate her. No way.

Instead, he did his best to hide how he felt and headed for the door. He'd fought for her, and he'd lost.

For now. He'd give her some time to live with her decision, to think it over. To consider all the consequences. With some luck, she'd realize she'd made a mistake soon, before it was too late.

Well, that was done.

It was a good thing.

A necessity.

The best decision for everyone.

Now everything could go back to normal.

Who the hell am I kidding?

Lei slumped onto her bed and remoted on the television. She needed noise, distraction. Staring at the screen, she channel surfed, but the images didn't really register in her brain. She couldn't help playing back that awful, awkward, painful conversation.

I can't believe I just convinced Malek to marry another woman.

Lei buried her face in her hands. The tears started flowing, and she just let them go. Why couldn't she be normal? Why couldn't she let herself be vulnerable? It was what she wanted.

Malek was what she wanted. But she'd just told him to marry April.

Her stomach knotted as the image of Malek, lying in bed, holding her flashed through her mind. Never again would she wake up to his face in the morning. Never again would her bed smell like him. Never again would she feel the strength of his arms wrapped around her body or the electrifying glide of his hands over her skin.

That all belonged to another woman, or would very soon.

Restless, she paced the floor and tried to remind herself why it had been the right thing to do. She believed it. If she could just keep that in mind, maybe she'd get through this.

Maybe.

Something made her glance at the TV as she stepped in front of it.

Her heart jerked. Her skin went cold.

It was one of the men who'd nearly killed Malek. The man who'd broken into the house with Holloway. He was on the news, and he was wearing a blue uniform. A cop. An Ann Arbor cop. And standing behind him was Holloway. "We would like to encourage anyone with information regarding this woman to step forward. You can remain anonymous. Someone has seen something. Someone knows something."

She scrambled for the remote and clicked the RECORD button. Then she grabbed her phone and dialed Vasquez's phone number. She figured he'd want to know about this.

His answer sounded surprised, "Hello? Lei?"

"Yes, it's me," she said, pacing back and forth in her bedroom. "I just saw one of my attackers on TV."

"When?"

"Just now. On Channel Two news. He's an Ann Arbor police officer."

"Hmmm. You're sure it's him?"

"Yes." She hit the button, pausing the recording. "I'm watching the report right now. He has some bruising on his face from the fight, though it looks like he tried to cover it with makeup."

"Let me see what I can find out."

"He's reporting on another dead woman, found in Detroit. The others have all been tied to my former pimp. I knew them both. But I missed the beginning of tonight's report, and last night when the murder was reported, they didn't identify the victim. So I don't know yet if I knew this victim. Have you found Heather or Kate?"

"No, I haven't. But that could be a good thing. If I'm having such a hard time tracking them down, there's some hope that your CIA agent is having a hard time, too."

"Have you been able to verify whether Holloway is in the CIA?"

"No, I knew it was going to be tough."

She started pacing, her gaze jerking from the TV to the window, back and forth, back and forth. "What should we do?"

"Are you safe? Have you received any more threats?"

"I think I'm safe, and no, no more threats."

"Okay. I'm going to check out the station's Web site. Hopefully they'll have a clip of the report on there and I'll recognize him. And then I'll take it from there. You stay put."

"Okay. Thanks. And be careful. You saw what that man did to Malek."

"Don't worry. I'll be fine. I'll call you if I get something."

"Okay, bye." Her stomach rumbled as she clicked the button, ending the call. Feeling jumpy once again, she headed to the kitchen to scrounge up something to eat. She was in the middle of putting together a sandwich when Malek came into the room. Alone. He was moving stiffly, one hand pressed to his abdomen.

The air between them seemed to crackle, thanks to the tension between them. Even so, she worried at the dark circles under his eyes.

He should be resting, healing.

"You look tired," she said as she put away the deli meat and cheese.

"I'm fine."

Fine? Not.

He eyeballed her sandwich with hungry eyes. "What're you making?"

"Sandwich. Would you like one?" She slid the plate across the counter. "Take this one. I'll make another."

"Thanks." He eased himself onto one of the bar stools at the counter.

She didn't like the way he was wincing. And his face looked pale. "Has Talen figured out the visiting nurse situation yet? You should have someone with medical training checking on you for at least another couple of days."

"We both decided against it. It isn't safe to have anyone here." He focused fully on her, and instantly she felt awkward. "Lei, I don't know if I can stay in this house with you."

"Then don't."

"You aren't safe anywhere else, and I'm not leaving you out here by yourself."

"What about Talen?"

"Someone needs to stay at the house. I can't go back there yet either."

"Then I guess we're stuck. I'll do what I can to make it easier for you." She finished making her sandwich, gathered up a napkin and a glass of cola, and started circling the counter.

"Stay with me," he said, tipping his head toward the stool next to his. "I hate eating alone."

She didn't budge. "Didn't you just tell me you can't be alone with me? Where's April?"

"Sleeping. I guess it was the drive from hell coming out here. Snow the whole way. Her little car isn't the best in bad weather."

If that right there didn't tell Malek something about the woman he was about to marry, Lei didn't know what would. "She drove all the way out here by herself. To be with you."

"You have a point."

"That's a woman who really, really cares about you."

"Would you? Drive three hours in a snowstorm for me?" he asked.

Lei stared at her sandwich as she thought about her answer. Would she drive three hours to take care of a friend who needed her? Yes, especially if it was Malek. But would she drive three hours to be with a man who she knew was looking for a wife?

Probably not.

"Malek, it doesn't matter what I would do. Please stop looking at me as a potential wife. It's clouding your judgment." She left the room.

16

Yvette's body was absolute perfection. Soft where it should be, smooth and lean where it shouldn't. Her legs went on forever, the miniskirt barely covering her ass. And what those fucking shoes did for her calves and thighs. Damn.

She moved with the grace of a dancer as she stepped into the foyer and gave Talen an up-and-down look. "This house is amazing."

"I'll give you the grand tour." Beginning with the hot tub. Talen took her hand and led her toward the back of the house. "You look amazing tonight."

"Thanks."

He stopped outside of the indoor pool room to open the door for her.

"Oh, I didn't realize we were going to be swimming. I didn't bring a suit." The expression on her pretty face suggested she wasn't at all concerned about having a bathing suit.

He opened the door, leading her inside with a hand on the small of her back, just above her round little ass. Weak by nature, he let his hand slide down, cupping the soft flesh as he followed her inside.

He'd never fucked Yvette. He'd scened with her at the club a few times, but he never fucked his subs there. He'd been hoping to take their relationship to the next level for a while, and was glad when their schedules had finally coincided.

Already sporting a painful hard-on, Talen eased her around to face him, then pulled her closer, until her small body was flattened to his, cupped the back of her head, and kissed her.

The kiss was everything he'd expected. It was nuclear hot. The way her body molded to his, the way she smelled, tasted, the sound of her little gasps.

He tilted his hips, pressing his erection against her, and she gave a little groan. Taking advantage of her open mouth, he slid his tongue into her sweet depth and savored her flavor. Her tongue found his, stroked along its length, making him hungry for more.

With great effort, he broke the kiss and stepped back. Up and down his gaze traveled, following the glorious curves of her body, emphasized by her snug black clothes. She'd dressed exactly as he'd asked. Ironically, he was already eager to get rid of the garments. They were in the way.

He hooked his fingers under the hem of her top and pulled it up, over her breasts—she wasn't wearing a bra—and over her head. Next, he rid her of her skirt. Then he knelt down and unbuckled her shoes, easing one foot out, then the other. Finally, she stood before him as he wanted, nude and proud and absolutely glorious.

"Now, this is hardly fair. Do I finally get to see you?" she asked, giving him a faux pout.

"I guess that would be okay." He let her undress him, enjoying the way she sprinkled little kisses on his exposed skin as she peeled his garments away. The minute she had his clothes off, he resisted the urge to sink his cock into her hot pussy and instead scooped her into his arms and jumped into the pool.

Cool water enveloped them, easing the simmering of his skin. Even though they were separated when they plunged underwater, she quickly found him the minute they both broke through the surface. She wrapped her legs around his waist, arms around his neck, and pressed her mouth to his.

Now this was the kind of swim he liked.

The water chilled his heated body as her slick breasts flattened against his chest. Thanks to her strong leg muscles and her buoyancy, he didn't have to hold her, allowing him to explore her back, shoulders, and, eventually, her ass while they kissed each other to oblivion.

They both moaned and groaned, petted, pawed, pulled, and clung to each other until he could hold off no longer. Grabbing her hips, he positioned her against his cock, warned her, "I can't wait another moment," then slammed his hips forward.

His teeth gritted with the agony of that first penetration. Her tissues gripped him like a tight fist.

Moving carefully, he walked to the edge of the pool and extended his arms to grasp the smooth surface for leverage. His hips slammed back and forth now, his possession of her feral. He couldn't help himself. It was her response, the gasps and pleas for more that drove him to the edge. His body was one big ball of knotted muscle. His nerves were on fire. His teeth were gritted.

So fucking good.

He was on the verge of coming. Already. She was trembling against him, her hot skin searing his.

"Ohmygod," she chanted. "More. More!"

With one hand, he reached down, found her anus, and pierced it with his index finger.

She shuddered against him, screamed his name. Her pussy

spasmed around his cock. He withdrew to the tip, then rammed deep inside. His cum was right there, ready to go. Almost there.

His fucking phone rang.

Ignoring it, he fucked her harder. She clawed at his shoulders, begged him for more.

All too happy to oblige, he added a second finger in her anus, sliding it in as far as he could.

She curled her legs up, hooked her knees over his arms, and contracted those hot tissues around his cock.

He shuddered, thrust once more, and his cum blazed down his rod and filled her.

Once again, her pussy spasmed, milking his rod and his fingers.

Now that was a fucking orgasm.

Feeling a little spent, he kissed her and pulled out. He was about to lift her up out of the pool when his blood turned to ice.

He was staring into the barrel of a gun.

There was a *pop* and Yvette's head slumped forward.

The water around them turned to blood.

Malek cussed at his phone and shoved aside the feeling of icy dread coiling deep inside. Talen hadn't answered, and he'd called six times. That wasn't anything unusual. Talen tended to leave his phone lying around. He shouldn't feel the way he did, so fucking anxious.

At least there was another way to get ahold of his pain-in-the-ass brother.

Malek wobbled to his computer and fired it up. After the Chimera's last attack, Drako had beefed up their security system and added a remote access feature to it, so any of them could see what was going on in the house at any time. Malek hit a few buttons, impatient with his sluggish computer.

Once the operating system loaded, Malek signed on to the

remote system and waited for the connection to link up. Finally, his screen clicked on, a view of the closed front door reassuring him that Talen was either intentionally ignoring his calls or had left his phone where he couldn't hear it.

Still, a niggling feeling made him change cameras.

The living room was clear, too. Empty. He used the mouse to adjust the camera's angle, checking the whole room.

The hallway upstairs was empty.

The outside looked good, too.

A check of the garage's camera confirmed Talen's car was there.

Where the fuck was Talen? Shower?

He hit the final camera, the one in the hall leading out to the back door. As the camera panned the wall of windows, opening to the swimming pool, his breath caught in his throat.

There was a man holding something at arm's length. That something looked a lot like a gun. And it appeared to be pointed at the swimming pool.

Malek hit a button, magnifying the image.

Yep, it was a fucking gun.

"No!" he said.

He grabbed his phone and dialed Drako's number.

Drako sounded sleepy when he picked up.

"Armed gunman in the house," Malek said.

"Which house?" was Drako's response. He didn't sound sleepy anymore.

"Ann Arbor. I'm watching now. Camera eight."

"Fuck. I'm signing in. Give me a minute."

Malek made some adjustments to the camera. The man had the gun pointed at Talen, who was in the pool. But it looked like Talen wasn't alone in the water. And what the hell was wrong with the water? Malek squinted at the slightly grainy black and white image. "We've got to do something about these fucking cameras."

"I didn't think it was worth it."

"I get what you're saying." The camera caught something dark in the water. "Shit, I think someone's already been shot."

"What the fuck is Talen doing?" Drako asked.

Malek shifted his focus back on Talen, catching him as he dove under the surface. "Trying to dodge a bullet?"

"No, he dove down once, then resurfaced. Now he's doing it again."

"What are we going to do?"

"There's nothing we can do. We can't call the cops." Drako's sigh was heavy. "We'll have to wait, see if they're Chimera. If they are, we'll be hearing from them soon."

"Bullshit." White-hot rage flared through Malek. He curled his hands into fists and fought to resist the urge to pound something. "I can't sit here and wait."

"Bro, you've just had surgery. You're in no condition to do a goddamn thing but stay where you are. And we don't need the Chimera taking down two of us. One's bad enough."

"I don't like this."

"Neither do I." After a beat, Drako added, "Talen knows what to do. We've all known this could happen to any of us at any time."

Malek cut off the connection. He couldn't watch it anymore. It was too horrific. He turned, teeth gritted, and tried not to vomit. "Goddamn it, Drako."

Talen couldn't believe it.

The guy with the gun had been telling the truth, and he held the proof in his hand: a syringe. Yvette had been about to inject him when she'd been shot.

So, there could be no doubt that Yvette had been there to do more than fuck.

But what about this guy?

The man in question clicked the safety and slid his gun back in the shoulder holster. He took a step back, giving Talen room to lever himself out of the pool. "Name's Canfield. Will Canfield."

Talen set the needle on the edge of the pool, then making sure to stay clear of it, pushed himself out. He snatched a towel off the rack and wrapped it around his waist. "Will Canfield, what are you doing in my house?"

"Besides saving your ass?"

Saving his ass. "Yeah."

"Tim Dickerson sent me over, in a way."

"What does that mean, sent you over? For what? I told him he was done with the job. I didn't need any more help."

"Yeah, so he said."

"So . . . ?" Getting the impression this guy was as dangerous as Yvette had been, he kept his gaze locked on that gun.

"So I came to tell you otherwise."

Talen made a beeline for the security panel, expecting the silent alarm to have been tripped. It hadn't been. "How did you get in?"

"Dickerson made a copy of his key. I stole it and used his code."

"He was told not to make a copy." Keeping one eye on his armed visitor, Talen punched keys on the panel, inactivating the security guard's code.

Canfield motioned to the security panel. "Now you see what I'm getting at."

"What are you saying?"

"I'm saying Dickerson was up to something, and I felt I should tell you."

"Why?" What did this guy want? Nobody came to a coworker's ex-client's house to warn him about something that might not be . . . all out of the kindness of his heart. Talen's gaze traveled up and down his visitor's form, noting the expensive shoes he was wearing, the watch, the sunglasses.

Had to be money.

A guy that willing to do something so potentially dangerous for money wasn't worth a fucking penny to him. After all, if he was willing to take money from him, how easy would it be for the Chimera to buy him for a higher price?

"Okay. Well, thanks." Leaving the system off, Talen escorted Canfield to the door. "I appreciate the heads-up."

"You're welcome." After stepping outside, Canfield handed him a card. "In case you need to reach me again."

"I'll hang on to it." Talen shut the door, then tossed the card in the trash on his way to the swimming pool. He was about to handle the ugly task of fishing his would-be assassin out when he heard his cell phone ring. He grabbed it, checked the number, and answered.

"What the fuck is going on there?" Malek snapped.

"Long story short, there's a dead woman in the pool, I think one of the guards was Chimera, and our new security system has been compromised."

"I'm coming home."

"No."

"But you're alone—"

"I'm fine. And you're not. No offense, but I don't need the added stress of having to watch out for your disabled ass right now."

"Dammit."

"Do us all a favor and stay where you are."

He heard Malek grumble something under his breath. "What do you know about the woman floating in the pool?"

"I've known her for almost a year. But I'll admit, I don't know as much about her as I should have. Obviously. I'll be spending today seeing what I can get on her. I'm guessing she's Chimera too."

"If she is, then we need to be extremely cautious. They aren't as disabled by Uncle Bob's death as we thought. What about the bastard with the gun?"

"Name's Will Canfield. Supposedly works for the security company Drako hired. He came over here to tell me Dickerson was dirty, made a copy of the house key."

"Hmmm. That sounds suspicious, too. Maybe Canfield and the dead woman were working together?"

"Maybe," Talen agreed. "If they were, then the arrangement didn't work out so good for Yvette. I definitely won't let my guard down again. Nobody steps foot in this house until I've personally run a full background check on them."

"I have a feeling you'll need to do more than that."

Talen knew what was coming next. He didn't want to think about it, but like every other aspect of their job, he'd been prepared for the eventuality of a move. Prepared, but always hopeful it wouldn't come to that.

For one thing, a move would leave them completely vulnerable until they'd reached their new home.

"You know, maybe Drako was on the right track," Talen said, thinking out loud. "Maybe we should go on the offensive, hunt down those pieces of shit and put a stop to them for once and for all. I mean, what do we have to lose?"

"Talen, don't do anything we'll all regret."

"Worst case, I die—"

"And there's nobody there to . . . water the plants."

"Fuck." Talen shoved his fingers through his hair. Malek was right, dammit. Naturally, watering the plants wasn't exactly what he'd meant. But they couldn't take any chances. For all he knew, Dickerson had planted some bugs when he'd been in the house, pretending to protect Malek.

"I'll do what I can from here," Malek said. "It's time to make the move."

"Shit. Okay. I'll call when I'm ready." He cut off the call.

He had a hell of a lot of work to do in the next few days. First thing—find some stiffs.

Malek had no idea what he was going to say. But he wasn't a pussy. Lei deserved to know what was about to happen. She deserved to know more than that, but he couldn't risk telling her everything.

He'd spent all night rehearsing what he'd say. Hadn't slept at all. It was morning now, just after nine. He figured she was up by now, rumpled and still sleepy, thoroughly sexy. But awake. He knocked again. This time he heard a soft rustle, the muffled rhythmic thump of footsteps approaching.

The door swung open.

Malek's heart slammed against his breastbone.

She looked exactly as he'd pictured, and still he could barely breathe. Her eyes were hooded, her hair sexy, mussed. And she smelled so damn good he couldn't help licking his lips. "What?" she snapped.

"I need to talk to you."

"What now?"

"It's important."

Her gaze narrowed. She stared him down for a handful of stuttering heartbeats, then stepped aside. "Fine."

As he meandered into her room, she put as much space between them as possible, standing clear across the room, next to the closet. He ventured deeper inside. "I'd prefer not shouting across the room."

She smacked her arms over her chest but didn't retreat when he moved closer. "Malek, I'm so done with all the drama."

"This has nothing to do with April or with my marriage."

"Oh." She plopped down on the chair behind her and looked up at him.

"You remember what happened this summer?"

"How could I forget? Rin was kidnapped by some psycho.

You and Talen and Drako were almost killed when you tried to rescue her. Why are you bringing that up now?" Her face paled. "Did something happen to Rin again?"

"No, she's safe. That's the primary reason why Drako took her out of the country, to keep her safe."

"From what? You told me that guy was killed."

"He was."

"So, does this have to do with me? With those bastards—"

"No, none of this is your fault." He reached for her, but when she flinched, he pulled his hands back. "Please, I don't want you feeling guilty for something that has nothing to do with you."

She threw her hands into the air. "Then what . . . ?"

"You won't be going back to school. It isn't safe."

Her expression darkened. "What do you mean? Is it because of all those dead girls?"

"No, the house was broken into last night. Talen was almost killed."

"I don't understand."

"I wish I could explain everything, but the less you know, the better."

"Okay. That's enough." Jaw clenched tightly, she stomped toward him, stopping a couple of feet away. "We've been attacked. Rin was kidnapped. You three seem fairly unfazed by it all, and you don't like to involve the police . . . are you spies?"

"No."

"Federal agents? FBI? CIA?"

"No."

"Criminals? Gangsters?" she asked.

"Not that, either."

"Were you witnesses to some crime? In a witness protection—"

"It doesn't matter why we have to make some changes," he interrupted. "What you need to understand is that we will be taking new identities. Me, my brothers, and your sister. I'm also suggesting you do, too. If you don't want to—at this point, you have a choice—we can take you anywhere you'd like to go and drop you off. And that would be it. The last time you will see us or your sister again."

"What?" Her pretty features twisted. Her eyes widened. Her face paled. "What the hell is going on? This is crazy. Who does that? Takes new identities and dumps family members by the side of the road?"

"I realize it sounds strange, but it's absolutely necessary. We have to get a new start. Nobody can know where we've gone or what our new identities are. It's as much for Rin's safety as ours."

"I don't know what to say."

"I should tell you, if you do decide to come with us, your death will be faked. And everyone you knew will believe you are dead. Including your family."

Lei stared down at the floor. She didn't move. Didn't speak.

"You can have some time to think about it."

"How much?"

Malek shrugged. "A week, maybe? It's going to take some time to make all the arrangements."

"None of this makes sense." She wouldn't look at him. And that nearly killed him. All he wanted was to pull her into his arms and promise her that everything would be okay if she'd just trust him. But he couldn't.

Frustrated and sad, he started toward the door.

"What about April? What will you tell her? And Brent? What about him?"

"Brent . . . I'm going to have to let go. I haven't decided yet about April."

"That's going to kill Brent. You know that, don't you?"

Malek's insides twisted. He did know that, but he had no choice. The fact was, he'd tried calling Brent last night, after he'd talked to Talen. Brent had told him to fuck off and never call him again.

"And weren't you planning on marrying April?" Lei asked. "As your wife, she'd have to come with you."

He didn't know how to answer that question. Had he been planning to marry April? Maybe. Did he want to? No. What did Lei want to hear? "That hasn't been decided yet."

She jerked her head up, meeting his gaze. "But I thought..."

"I know it's what you want me to do. I get that. Loud and clear." Leaving the door, he moved back toward her. "But there's a problem with that plan. It's not what I want." He grabbed her upper arms and yanked her toward him, then stared down into her wide, panic-filled eyes. "I hate that I want you as much as I do. Maybe it would be better if you didn't come with us. It would be easier for me to have another woman in my bed, instead of you, if I didn't have the reminder of what I was missing right in front of me all the time. But I'm trying not to be selfish, goddamn it. I know how much you and your sister mean to each other." He let her go and charged for the door, yanked it open, and slammed it shut behind him.

Of course, April was standing in the hall. Her expression was unreadable as her gaze jerked back and forth from Lei's door to his face. "Good morning," she said, a sweet smile spreading over her face. "Are you hungry for some breakfast?"

What the fuck was going on here?

Staring at the closed door, Lei paced her room. Back and forth, back and forth. None of this was making sense. Drako was a jeweler, for Christ's sake. And Malek was a writer. Talen...? She didn't know what he did for a living. Why the hell did it seem that danger was always lurking in their shadows? If it wasn't because of Holloway, why did it seem as though someone was out to kill them all the time?

Was Malek lying? To try to protect her from feeling guilty for bringing all this trouble to their doorstep?

Whatever the case, if it was true, this sort of sucked. She'd have to give up her classes, the only thing that gave her any kind of joy. But she had no choice. There was no way she could let Rin just disappear from her life forever.

Then again, maybe it would be a good thing. At least the whole faking-her-death part would make it hard for anyone, CIA agent or not, to hunt her down.

But Heather and Kate. What about them?

And then there was the other issue—regarding Malek and his marriage. When he looked at her the way he had a moment ago, she wasn't sure how she felt anymore. There'd been frustration in his eyes. There was no mistaking that. Or the anger. That didn't soften her resolve. It was the vulnerability, the pain that did. He'd told her he didn't want to marry April. There was no doubt he was telling the truth.

April wasn't the right wife for him.

That still didn't mean Lei was the right woman for him, either. But until he found the right woman to marry, neither of them would be comfortable living under the same roof.

The right woman. Yes, that was the solution. Lei needed to find him a better wife. He deserved someone who could be loving, affectionate, submissive, obedient, and sweet.

One major problem: She had less than one week to find that special woman, and she couldn't leave the house.

It was time to adopt plan B. She'd have to work with what she had. If the current April wasn't the right woman for Malek, maybe the new and improved April would be.

17

A few hours later, Lei saw her chance and went for it. Malek was taking a shower and she had April cornered in the kitchen, waiting for some coffee to brew.

"We need to talk," Lei said as she dug a couple of coffee cups out of the cupboard.

"About what?"

"Malek."

Silence.

Lei could appreciate why April was acting a little reticent. She would, too. Especially if she had any notion of the fact that Malek was probably in love with the other woman.

Come to think of it, this plan B was probably doomed from the start. But that didn't mean she couldn't at least try.

"Did you change your mind?" April asked, eyes narrowed to slits.

"No, not at all. As a matter of fact, I want to help you win him over. . . ."

April laughed. "You bitch."

"I didn't mean it that way."

"Righttt. You're just trying to be nice." She rolled her eyes.

"I am."

April got in her face. "Don't try to play the sweet, innocent, wounded-girl card with me. I don't buy your act. Not at all."

Wow. Lei'd dealt with women like April before. Plenty of times. Tough. Defensive. Proud. If she'd realized April was that way, she wouldn't have even considered plan B. Clearly, it wasn't going to work. Lei lifted her hands and took a step back. "Okay, forget I said anything. I didn't mean to insult you."

April filled her cup and stomped away.

What a great way to start the day.

It was no wonder Malek was second-guessing his decision to marry that woman. She was a snappy bitch. Jealous. Defensive.

Then again, who wouldn't be?

Now what?

Lei was brainstorming her other options when a wet-headed Malek came into the kitchen. He slid a half smile at Lei. "Afternoon." He made a beeline for the coffeepot.

"Hi." Trying to look busy, she went to the refrigerator and dug out some fresh vegetables to make a salad.

"April's a little fired up. Do you know anything about that?"

"Maybe." She dug through a cupboard, looking for a bowl.

He lifted a brow.

She sighed. "I know. I shouldn't have gotten involved. It's none of my business."

His other brow lifted.

She sighed again. "You've made it perfectly clear that you're not confident in your decision to marry her."

"I'm not."

"So, I thought I'd give her a few pointers, help her convince you that it wasn't such a bad idea. Naturally, she took it the wrong way."

Malek laughed. It was so good to hear that sound, to see the sparkle in his eyes again. "It's no wonder she's so wound up."

"I'm glad you can see the humor in the situation."

"Who wouldn't? It's funny as hell." He sobered slightly. "Thanks for trying, Lei. I'm sure you did it out of the goodness of your heart."

"At least you realize that." Lei grabbed a knife out of the knife block and started sawing at a carrot.

"Don't worry about April." Malek gently took the knife from her. "Here, let me help you. If you go at it like that, you're going to lose a finger." In seconds, he had the carrot sliced. "Seriously, don't worry about April. She'll get over it. I'm not concerned. Not a bit." He dumped the carrot slices into the bowl.

"But shouldn't you be?"

Malek's gaze snapped to Lei's. Her heart lurched in her chest. "Probably."

She grabbed a cucumber and smacked it down on the chopping board. "You really don't love her, do you?"

"Yes and no. I care about her. She's a close friend. But I'm not in love with her."

Lei concentrated on slicing the cucumber. Slow, even slices. One after another. "It doesn't seem fair that you have to get married now. I mean, we're in hiding. It isn't like you can go out and meet someone new. Shouldn't your brother take the circumstances into consideration?"

"No," he said flatly.

"But it isn't fair." A twinge of something shot through her body. Anger. Frustration. She slammed the knife down, grabbed a handful of cucumber slices, and tossed them into the bowl.

"What is fair?"

"So he'll make you marry a woman you don't love, no matter what?" she asked, that twinge amplifying.

Malek shrugged. "It isn't up to him. It's the way our trust is set up. If I don't marry, I'll be cut out."

"So what?" Why was this making her so angry? She was literally gritting her teeth. Her blood was pounding through her veins. This wasn't her business. It was Malek's. She shouldn't be so emotionally invested in what happened.

But she was. God help her, she was completely, thoroughly invested. To the point that she couldn't stand the thought of Malek marrying any woman but the one who would make him over-the-moon happy.

"What if you just walk away?" she asked. "You have book royalties, right? You would still get those if you don't take another identity. Better to be poor than to be locked into an unhappy marriage."

Malek's lips twitched. Something flickered in his eyes. "Lei, if this was just about money, I'd have no problem walking away. But it isn't. And I won't."

"But..."

"What?" Once again, he lifted one brow. He was adorable when he was looking at her like that. Amused. She entertained him. She could see it all over his face. "Do you have any other suggestions?"

"No."

"Okay, then that's that. Because of the situation, I'm pushing things up. I'm proposing to my bride-to-be today. And we'll be married tomorrow night."

"Tomorrow?" Her heart lurched. Her insides instantly knotted. "Tomorrow?" she repeated.

"Yes."

"But you have a week before you have to move, right?"

"There's no point in delaying the inevitable. I'm not going to find anyone else in a few days. Despite what you saw this morning, April is a decent choice in a wife for me. She'll allow me to enjoy certain liberties, which most women wouldn't."

Lei knew exactly what he meant by that. Instantly, the memory of the party she'd seen him at flashed through her mind. The image of Malek's gorgeous chest and shoulders. Of bodies entwined. A wave of heat pulsed in her pussy.

"I guess you've made your decision, then," she said. "I thought... I don't know what I thought. That you weren't okay with this. But you are. So I wish you both happiness." Her appetite completely gone, Lei left the half-made salad sitting on the counter and headed to her room.

She was doing the right thing by not marrying Malek. She couldn't be the wife he needed, he deserved. Right?

Yes, right.

Maybe.

April would make him happier than she would, right?

Yes. Absolutely.

Maybe.

She imagined him dropping to his knee, his hands gently cradling hers, his eyes filled with love as he whispered the words, "Lei, I can't live without you. Be my wife."

It would be selfish to get in the way of his happiness. To take what she wanted, even though he'd be happier with another woman, someone who was whole, who could at least provide for all his needs.

"Quit thinking about yourself, dammit," she mumbled. "Yes, he thinks he'd be happier with you. But he won't be. You know the truth. Don't fool yourself. Think of his happiness."

This was no doubt the hardest thing she'd ever done. She longed for the stability he could provide her. She ached for the gentleness, the peacefulness he emanated. But it wasn't fair for her to take him for herself. Not when she'd fail him on every level.

Blinking back tears, she dialed Rin's phone number. Maybe it was time to book a flight to Spain. She hoped she'd catch one before the wedding. She didn't think she had the strength to watch him say his vows.

He had the ring. It was as unique, as perfect as the woman he intended to give it to.

If only she'd accept it today. Right now. But he knew she wouldn't.

At the knock on his door, he put the box back where he'd hidden it, then went to let April in.

She wasn't happy, and it was his fault. He should've sent her home right away, instead of leading her on, allowing her to think there was a chance he'd marry her.

"You wanted to talk to me?" April said, arms wrapped around herself. She was standing stiffly, glaring at him.

"Yes, please sit." He motioned to the chair next to the bed.

"No thanks. Let's just get this over with, so I can go pack."

"Okay." Damn, this wasn't going well at all. But he deserved to be kicked in the teeth. "First, I'd like to apologize. I do care about you. I want what's best for you. And I realize this situation has been extremely painful and awkward."

She hiked up her chin. "I'm fine."

She was lying, but Malek had no doubt that was because she was trying to salvage what little of her pride she had left. "I'm relieved to hear that."

"Good. Now, if you're done—"

"I'm not."

She shook her head. "Malek, what do you want from me?"

"A favor. A big favor." He shoved his fingers through his hair and swallowed the lump that had congealed in his throat. "If I wasn't so desperate, I'd never ask for this. But it's the only way. And I feel like shit for even thinking about getting you involved after everything..."

April tilted her head and studied him for several excruciating moments. "Wow, I've never seen you like this. What is it?"

Malek tried to say the words. He moved his lips. He pushed air up his throat. But it wouldn't come out. And he knew why. This was wrong. He was being a selfish, conniving, deceitful bastard.

But he saw no other way.

"I need Lei to believe we're getting married."

"She already does. At least, I think she does."

"No, I mean, I want her to see me propose to you. . . ."

Her eyes widened, then turned hard and flinty. "You're insane."

"And maybe even begin the wedding ceremony . . . ?"

"Ohmygod." April burst into a fit of sardonic laughter. The spell lasted for roughly a lifetime. Then she stopped and shot him a dose of mean eyes. "I don't know a woman alive who'd do something like that. Not to mention, how would your dear, sweet Lei feel if she knew you were basically tricking her into marrying you? I bet she'd—"

"Name your price."

"This is going from bad to worse." She swung her arm in a wide arc. When her hand met his cheek, the sound echoed through the room. The pain followed.

He didn't flinch. Didn't blink. "I deserved that."

"You deserve more than that, but I won't stoop to such low levels." She spun around and stomped toward the door.

With nothing to lose, he offered, "Fifty thousand."

She halted but didn't turn to face him. "A hundred. Cash."

It was a small price to pay. Truth be told, he'd be willing to pay a million. Ten million. Every penny in his trust. "Done. I can have the money for you by tomorrow."

April slowly rotated around. "What do you need me to do?"

"I'll propose to you in the living room. In front of the fire. Can you pretend to be happy about it?"

"I'm sure I can manage."

Malek started pacing as he tried to play out the scene in his head. "Then again, maybe you shouldn't try so hard to look happy. Lei's convinced herself that I'm better off married to you, that I'll be happier. So if she sees I won't be—not that there's anything wrong with you—"

"Yeah, yeah, I get what you're saying." April gave an exaggerated sigh. "I'm not good enough."

"You are. It's not that. It's just I'm in love with Lei, and I can't think about any other woman but her."

"Damn." April shook her head. "I never thought I'd hear you say something like that. About any woman."

"I know, neither did I."

They exchanged a weighted stare.

He broke the silence. "The wedding is arranged for tomorrow. I have everything in place except your gown. I wasn't counting on you agreeing to do this."

"I'll go shopping this afternoon, after you propose."

"Good."

"Okay." She opened her mouth, closed it. "I guess I'll get going. I want to get cleaned up before the big event."

"April, I owe you."

The little muscle along her jaw clenched as she stared at him for about a million heartbeats. Finally, she said, "Just be happy. If you're not, I'll be fucking furious." She left.

That was one hell of a woman. She'd make some lucky man very happy some day.

And at least this way Brent wouldn't be alone when he learned...when Brent was told he was dead. Maybe, just maybe, Brent and April would end up together. They made a good couple.

Satisfied he'd made the right decision for everyone involved, it was time to convince Lei she needed him as much as he needed her.

* * *

Lei stopped in her tracks. Her heart literally stopped beating. She could swear it had.

Just her luck, she'd walked in on Malek and April, mid-proposal. He was on bended knee, in the living room, smack dab in front of the fireplace. He was holding a ring box in his hands and was looking up into April's eyes.

She gritted her teeth and tried to move. Dammit, her feet were glued to the fricking floor.

"You and I have shared a long history together, and now I'm asking you if you'd share my future, too," Malek said, his voice somewhat flat.

Weird. It sounded like he was reading a script.

Then again, she supposed he might not be one hundred percent enthusiastic about the proposal. He'd all but spelled out the fact that he wasn't happy about the situation. But wouldn't he at least try to make a small effort at appearing happy for April's sake?

April's response was even chillier, much to Lei's surprise. All she said was, "Sure. Thanks." She took the ring out of the box and put it on her finger.

Lei's feet began moving. She crept around the corner, counted to five, then headed back into the great room, hoping they didn't know she'd just witnessed the world's most pathetic marriage proposal ever.

When she entered the room, she found Malek sitting on the couch, next to April. April was staring at her ring, shifting it on her finger so the facets caught the flickering firelight. Lei inadvertently bumped a chair as she was crossing behind the raised breakfast bar, and both Malek's and April's gazes snapped to her.

"Hi," Lei said, motioning to the kitchen. "I... thought I'd better put away the salad."

April and Malek exchanged glances.

"It's official." April scampered over to her and flashed her ring finger. "We're engaged." Lei couldn't help picking up the heaviness in her tone.

Lei forced a smile. "Oh, wow! That's great! Congratulations!"

"Thanks."

Lei's gaze flicked to Malek. He was staring into the fire.

"The wedding's tomorrow," April added.

"Wow, so soon?" Lei's stomach twisted. "Tomorrow."

"Yes, Malek took care of most everything but the dress. I'm heading into town. Want to come with me?"

"I don't know . . ." Lei checked Malek again. Still staring into that fire.

"Okay, well, I'm going up to change into something more respectable and then I'm heading out. You can come along if you want. If you'd rather stay behind, that's your choice. If it were me, I wouldn't hesitate. We've been locked up in this freaking house for long enough." April hurried off to change.

Lei took this opportunity to check on Malek. She sat beside him and set a hand on his shoulder. "Are you okay?"

"Yeah."

She studied his profile. If he was trying to convince her he was okay with his decision, he wasn't a good liar. "April didn't seem all that emotional about the proposal. Is it because of your ambivalence to this marriage thing?"

"Probably. But I'm not going to lie to her. That would be unfair, to pretend. No, she knows exactly how I feel."

"What about her? Up until now I thought she genuinely cared for you, more than she dared admit."

"She does care for me. I don't doubt that. She's committed to marrying me and making it work for both of us. But she's not exactly thrilled about the situation either. You remember the 'booby prize' comment?"

This was so freaking wrong, forcing two people to get married.

Malek's gaze finally met hers. "Before you go off to chew out my brother for being unfair, remember, it's my decision to get married. He's not holding a gun to my head."

She wanted to smack him upside the head for that remark. "What kind of person would set such unreasonable conditions in his will?"

"The trust was set up many years ago, long before my brothers and I were born. It's completely legal and binding."

"But that's only if the trustee cared to enforce—"

"He will."

Could she be any more frustrated or confused? "Why?"

"Because it's what he must do."

That was the most noninformative response she'd ever heard. "Since when is everyone so goddamn honest and faithful?"

"In my family, as far back as I can trace."

"Then your family isn't normal."

"I never said we were."

Well, so much for that. Lei yanked her gaze away from the face she could stare at for the rest of her life and instead watched the flickering red and yellow flames writhe and dance in the fireplace. "You're going through with it."

"Of course."

"Even though you don't love her."

"That's right. But isn't that what you want? Up until now I thought it was."

"Yes, it was. But only if you couldn't avoid it. And only because I thought it was what April wanted."

"You heard what she said about thinking about it."

"Sure, but I thought that was just her pride talking. Her actions said something different. They said she was committed to you."

"The fact is, she is committed. But she's not in love with me. And that's why I'm semi-okay with this. If it were one-sided and she loved me, hoping I would reciprocate, I'd probably feel too guilty to go through with it."

"Ugh. How honorable."

He shrugged. "I'm who and what I am. Nothing more. Nothing less." He took her hand in his, his fingers loosely enclosing it. "I think we just need to put this subject to rest. I've decided to marry April. She's decided to marry me. Will you go shopping with her? I don't want her out alone."

"Is it safe?"

"If it wasn't, I wouldn't let you go."

"But that'll leave you here alone. You're hardly in any condition to fight off an attacker."

"Nobody knows we're here. We haven't had any problems. I'll be fine."

"Okay."

"Thank you." He gave her one last longing-filled look and then went back to staring at the fire. His fingers relaxed, and he released her hand.

A few seconds later, April came clomping down the steps in five-inch stilettos. "Lei, I'm ready to go. Are you coming?"

"Sure." As she headed toward the door, she looked over her shoulder, snatching one final glance of Malek before she left.

18

The next day was gorgeous. The sun was shining brightly, making the snow sparkle like a coat of pristine white diamonds. Birds were twittering cheerfully. And the air was fresh and clean, but not bitter cold.

Lei had been yearning for a day like this for several weeks. This year fall had been too short, too wet. The weather had gone from hot and muggy and soggy to frigid and snowy and wintry. This was better. This was nice.

Except . . . Malek was about to marry another woman in just a few minutes. And the kicker was, he didn't love her and she didn't love him.

Why exactly was she sitting there, watching him make this huge, colossal mistake?

He loves me. It's me he wants.

Lei's hands shook as she stepped into the living room, where the private ceremony was about to take place. Malek was standing in front of the windows, head tipped, talking with the minister, his voice too low for her to hear what they were saying.

She wanted to go up to him, ask him once more if there was

any way he could get more time. But she couldn't move. It was as if her feet were glued to the floor. And before she could get them unstuck, Malek had hit the remote and the room had filled with the hauntingly beautiful sound of Pachelbel's "Canon," and both men turned toward the back of the room.

Lei followed the direction of their gaze, finding April standing behind her. She had to admit, April made a beautiful bride. The dress she'd selected was simple, a floor-length sheath of white silk, but it fit her curves perfectly and made her picture-perfect body look even more stunning than usual. She smiled at Lei—the only witness, as well as bridesmaid—then motioned for Lei to start down the makeshift aisle. Lei shuffled into place in front of the minister, turning to watch the bride as she started slowly walking toward her waiting groom.

With every step April took, Lei's heart hammered against her breastbone at least a hundred times. The roar of blood in her ears was almost loud enough to drown out the music. But Lei didn't speak, didn't move to interrupt April's progress toward the minister and Malek. Over and over, she kept repeating to herself, *This is for the best, this is for the best.*

The music cut off several seconds after April had reached the end of the aisle. Lei stared at April and Malek. Were they happy about this at all? Either of them? Did they stand any chance of being happy down the road?

Malek flicked a gaze at her and her heart jerked. Even though he was smiling, his eyes were dark.

The minister started, "We are gathered here today—"

"Excuse me," Lei cut him off. Her voice was weak, shaky.

Three sets of eyes cut to her. Only one held any hint of surprise, and they belonged to the minister.

"Is there a problem?" the minister asked.

"Yes, there is," she said, still hardly believing she'd just said what she had.

Something flickered in Malek's eyes. Was it hope? Was it relief? Or were those the things she wanted to see? "Lei? What's wrong?"

"Malek, this is just... wrong." Her eyes started tearing up. She thumbed her lower lashes, catching the first tears before they dribbled down her cheeks.

April said nothing, didn't even look at her.

"April, do you love Malek?" Lei asked.

April didn't answer.

"Malek?" Lei asked. "What about you?"

"You know the answer to that question, Lei."

Her gaze hopped from Malek to April to the minister at least three times. She was so freaking confused. So torn. She had no idea what to do, what to say. She knew she probably should have just kept her mouth shut and let Malek marry April, like he'd planned. But she was weak. She couldn't do it.

"I'm sorry, Malek, for ruining your special moment." Thinking a hasty retreat might be the best idea for all involved, she back-stepped away from them. Her ass smacked against the chair and she lurched around, fighting to stay upright while scrambling to get out of the room.

Behind her, she heard Malek shout, "Lei, wait!"

But she didn't wait. She kept going, dashing as fast as she could in the stupid silver-gray dress and insanely high stilettos April had insisted she wear.

Malek caught her as she was stumbling down the hall. He grabbed her arm. "Lei, we need to talk about this now. Don't run away. If you do, you'll regret it. So will I."

Her vision blurred again as another fresh batch of tears gathered in her eyes. "What do you want from me?"

"I want you to be strong, courageous. For me."

"But I'm not strong. I'm weak. I'm broken. And I have no idea if I can ever be fixed. Why would you want me, when I can't give you everything you need? Everything you deserve?"

"You can. You will. If all you do is say yes. If all you do is promise to love me for the rest of your life. That's all I need. Nothing more."

"But—"

He pressed an index finger to her lips. "Shhhh. Don't talk yourself out of this. Listen to your heart. Don't think."

"That's easier said than done," she said, all too aware of his finger still resting lightly on her lip.

"You stopped the wedding. Now, what are we going to do next?" He let his hand fall to his side.

She glanced over his shoulder at the waiting minister. April had gone somewhere, out of sight. Guilt wound through her insides. "Where did April go?"

"Probably out to her car. She's leaving."

"But..."

"I'm not marrying her, and she knows it. I told her she was free to leave if you interrupted the wedding. Let me make one thing clear—she's extremely grateful." He extended a hand and smiled. "And so am I."

"But..." Reluctantly, she placed her hand in his. Okay, maybe she hadn't wanted to see Malek marry April. But she'd intended to just leave so she wouldn't have to witness it.

Oh hell, who was she fooling?

"We're making the minister wait." Ever so gently, he tugged on her hand, leading her down the hall. She let him walk her up to the minister, but she still wasn't sure if she was doing the right thing for either of them.

The minister's expression was serene and kind. "Now that we've taken care of that minor situation, are we ready to begin?"

Malek slid a sideways glance at her. "Lei? Is there something you'd like to ask me?"

"Are you kidding me?" She knew her eyes were bugging out of her head. He'd put her on the spot.

Granted, it was her fault, since she'd interrupted his wedding.

"Well?" he asked.

Could she do it?

She said, "You know what you're in for. If you ever throw this back in my face—"

"I won't. I promise."

"Okay." She turned toward Malek and he shuffled around to face her. "If you expect me to get on bended knee."

"No, that's for me to do." Grimacing ever so slightly, he started to lower himself down on one knee.

"Malek, stop. You're hurt."

"Hell no." He looked up at her with wide eyes. "I'm feeling just fine, Lei." He nodded. "Okay, I'm ready."

"Malek Alexandre." Her throat constricted. She inhaled. Exhaled. Inhaled again. "Will you . . . marry me?"

"Yes." Malek pushed back up to his feet, beaming one of the most breathtaking smiles at her that she'd ever seen. His eyes were full of joy, so different from how they'd looked just a short time ago. He turned to face the minister. "Please continue."

The minister launched into a speech about the meaning of love, reciting that familiar passage that begins, "Love is patient . . ."

As he spoke each word, her doubts began to fade. Yes, she wasn't perfect. She had her problems. But Malek's love was everything it should be. It was patient and kind and hopeful and beautiful, and she should never have doubted his ability to wait for her to heal.

With happy tears, instead of sad ones, she recited her promise to Malek, to love him, honor him, and keep him for the rest of her life. After he promised her the same, he pulled a beautiful ring from his pocket and slipped it on her finger.

It was done. They were now bound together for the rest of their lives.

The minister said, "You may now kiss the bride."

Malek used his index finger to tip her chin up and brushed his lips across hers in a sweetly seductive kiss. "Now, you're mine," he said, staring deeply into her eyes.

"Yes," she said, breathless, trembling all over, from head to toe.

The minister clapped Malek on the back and offered his congratulations. They signed all the required paperwork, making the marriage legal; then the minister left.

They were alone now. Married.

Lei knew Malek wasn't going to haul her to bed like a caveman and have his way with her. Not knowing how she'd react. But she did appreciate the fact that he might have some expectations when it came to his wedding night.

If he did, he kept those thoughts to himself. They shared a romantic dinner in front of the fire, fat white flakes drifting to the ground outside, blanketing everything in glittering snow. It was one of the most peaceful, serene moments in her life. And she realized then, as they later relaxed on the ginormous couch, cozy and comfortable in sweatpants and T-shirts, bellies full, exactly how stressed out she'd been over the last few days.

"Well," she said, glancing down at the stunning ring on her finger, "today wasn't what I'd expected."

"Is that so?" His voice was light, bubbling with laughter.

"So glad you think that's funny."

"I don't think it's funny." He swiveled to face her, took her hands in his, and kissed the back of each one. "I'm just so happy, Lei. I wanted you to stop the wedding, but I wasn't sure if you'd do it. Thank you for being brave for me."

"You're welcome." Her gaze wandered over his face for a moment, taking in all the glorious details that weren't as noticeable from a distance. The thick lashes framing his eyes. The sexy little mole sitting high on his cheekbone. The arch of his eyebrows. The curve of his lip. And the fine lines bracketing his eyes.

That was a face she would wake to every morning for the rest of her life.

She reached for him, tracing his square jaw with the tip of her index finger, and she let herself wonder what their children would look like. Would they have his wavy, soft hair or her straight, slick hair? Would they have his deep blue-black eyes or her brown? Would they have his angled face or her softer, rounder one?

"Lei, if you don't stop that, I'm going to lose control," he murmured, his voice rumbly and thick and masculine.

She pulled her hand back. "Sorry."

"No, I'm sorry." He shoved his hands through his hair. "I should have more self-control. I shouldn't get hard when you just look at me like that. But I've tried to stop it. I can't."

"I should be flattered."

"I won't tell you everything. You're not ready. Suffice it to say I'm suffering, but in a good way." As if he wished to lighten the mood, he winked. "Don't worry. I won't do anything to hurt you. Not mentally. Not emotionally. Not physically. I can't. I love you too much."

"I believe you. I... trust you."

They shared a look.

"Can I kiss you?" she asked, finding herself already leaning in.

"Hell yes."

She moved slowly, tipping her head, inching closer, closer, until she felt his breath tickling her lips. Finally, she closed that miniscule distance between them.

The second their mouths met, her heart started pounding. Her blood warmed. Her body tightened. The kiss was sweet, lingering, a tease. She pulled back and looked at his face. So handsome. Utter perfection.

"Is that it?" he asked, eyes still closed.

"Are you disappointed?" A giggle slipped up her throat. She skimmed along his cheekbone with her index finger, tracing the angles that haunted her dreams. He had such a strong face, masculine features that appeared so hard they could have been carved in stone. But underneath, he was so different from his appearance—kind, gentle, patient.

"Disappointed? No." His eyelids lifted partway, revealing half of his eyes. He looked sleepy, sexy. He cupped her cheek, brushed his thumb over her lower lip. He tipped his head, moving in for another kiss.

Holding her breath, she closed her eyes and waited. That fraction of a second, between knowing he would kiss her and when their mouths met, seemed to last a lifetime. Finally, their lips touched.

This kiss was nothing like the last. It was a possession. It was hot and sexy, and it stirred the heat simmering in her blood to new heights. His lips worked over hers smoothly, seductively. His tongue traced the seam of her mouth, and she trembled from head to toe.

God help her, she wanted this man. She wanted him to be her husband—in all ways, in every way. Including the ways she wasn't ready to accept yet.

A moan bubbled up from her chest, echoing in their joined mouths. He groaned, flattened his other hand against the left side of her face, caging it between both hands, and deepened the kiss. His tongue caressed and tasted and took. It plundered and possessed and seduced. And she surrendered, drinking in his intoxicating flavor, and lifting her arms, draping them over his shoulders.

The ache between her legs was getting stronger, and she was getting more breathless, more dizzy with each stroke of his tongue. She needed to be touched. Her breasts. Her pussy. Everywhere. But she was afraid.

Hoping it would help, she took his hand in hers and moved it down, down, until it was hovering over her tingling nipple.

Malek broke the kiss. "Lei?" he asked, sounding as breathless and desperate as she was. "What are you doing?"

"Let me control it."

"Okay." His gaze lowered to their hands.

Shivering, she pressed his palm against her breast and waited.

A little zing of anxiety buzzed through her system, but when Malek crushed his mouth over hers, it evaporated. Once again, his tongue and lips were the center of her universe; nothing else mattered. Her body burned with each thrust, each caress, each nip. And the warm hand covering her breast only added to her pleasure. When his fingers started moving, she struggled to inhale. But she didn't pull his hand away. Instead, she pressed harder, pushing it into the softness, and arched her back.

"Dammit, Lei." Kissing a fiery path along her jawline, he kneaded her breast, and her fingers dug into the back of his hand. Her pussy clamped around the throbbing emptiness inside, and a gush of warm fluid trickled out, coating her labia.

Dammit was right.

She tipped her head to the side and moved his hand down lower, letting it skim down the concave hollow of her stomach until it reached the bottom of her shirt.

Could she? Would it be the end of this incredible moment?

She swallowed a huge lump that had congealed in her throat, reached down with her free hand, and pulled the bottom of her shirt up a little, exposing her stomach.

Malek resisted when she tried to push his hand up under the knit material. "No."

That, she hadn't expected.

"I'm not going to push this." He leaned back, grabbed the remote, and an instant later, the room was filled with the sound of a sultry jazz tune. He stood, pulled her up off the couch, and led her to an open area of the room. "We haven't had our first dance yet."

"Ah, you're right." Slightly unsteady, she stepped into his arms and rested her cheek against his chest. Their bodies fit together so perfectly, her soft curves against his hard angles. And they moved together perfectly, too.

Swaying in time to the music, she relished the sensation of his heat, the scent of his skin, the sound of his heartbeat pounding beneath his shirt. His arms were cradling her ever so gently, supporting without restricting. She felt safe—wonderfully, amazingly safe. And special, cherished.

To think this moment might never have happened if she hadn't found the courage to stop him from marrying April.

He kissed the top of her head. "This may be a stupid question, but how are you doing?"

"I'm good. Very good."

"Excellent." He tightened his hold, which made her heart jerk a few times. But before she had a chance to react, he swirled her around the room again and again and again, until the music stopped.

Dizzy and giddy, she laughed and clung to him, afraid she'd fall. Probably the result he was looking for. Once she was sure she wouldn't topple over, she let go and stepped back. "Now, that was a dance I won't ever forget."

"Good. I want every day to be a day you won't ever forget. I still can't believe you did it, Lei. You married me."

"A part of me can't believe it either. I hope you don't regret—"

He cut off her sentence by kissing her yet again. And with the first sweep of his tongue, whatever she'd been about to say vanished from her mind. Lots of other stuff did, too, as the kiss went on and on. When it ended, she was more than a little dumbstruck and shaky.

"So..." she said. "We're here all alone...and it's our wedding day. Night. Whatever."

"I don't expect sex tonight."

That was both a relief and a disappointment. They were married now. She knew from talking to Rin that the Alexandre brothers married with the primary purpose of fathering children. Surely Malek had that goal in mind. Not to mention, he was very clearly displaying the need to fuck. The bulge in the front of his pants was unmistakable.

Already, she was letting him down.

"We can try," she suggested.

"No." He took her hand in his and walked back to the couch. He sat, pulling her down with him. "It's not going to be like that. Like it's something you have to get done and over with." He shook his head. "Damn, I never thought I'd say something like that, but with your past and..." He visibly grasped for words.

She supplied them for him, "You mean, you don't want to be my next John."

"I didn't mean it like that, no." His gaze swept over her face, and she couldn't help seeing the worry in his eyes. "I know I'm not a John to you. I know you care about me, or you never would have married me." He smoothed a strand of hair back from her face. It was a sweet, caring gesture. So Malek. "But I don't want you to feel anything but pleasure when we finally do make love. At this point, I can't be sure of that." He stretched. And before she could come up with a response to his very selfless gesture, he stood again. "I'm tired of sitting around in this house. Let's get out for a while, go for a walk."

"Are you sure you're well enough?"

"Absolutely, as long as we don't go far."

They donned heavy winter coats and boots, hats, and gloves, then stepped out into the quiet, snowy early evening. It was glorious. The air was dry and crisp and fresh. Fat flakes were falling. Bare tree limbs were heavy with snow. And the light of the full moon reflected all around them, illuminating the world in that magical winter glow. Walking with Malek, Lei felt as if they were the only two people within miles. Probably because they were. The house was set on dozens of wooded acres.

"This way." Malek offered a gloved hand and she took it, following his lead. "The property in Ann Arbor is pretty. But it's nothing compared to this."

"Will you miss that house?"

"I will."

"What about all your friends?"

"You mean the people at the dungeon?"

She shrugged.

"Like Brent?"

"I get the impression you were very close to him."

"I was."

"Do you miss him?"

Malek didn't respond right away, and that made Lei regret asking the question. "I do."

"You're really not going to tell him where we are? When we change our names?"

"No. If I did, that could put us all in danger."

Reading between the lines, she caught a hesitation in his voice. "But . . . ?"

"I worry about him. He doesn't have a lot of people he can trust in his life." Malek stopped, lifted a fallen tree limb high enough for Lei to duck under, and motioned for her to go first.

"I know the feeling," she said, ducking under the tree. She turned to watch him, and within seconds, she was practically nose-to-chest with her husband.

He cupped her chin in his gloved hand and stared into her eyes. "I am going to wipe away every shadow I see in those eyes, Lei. If it takes me the rest of my life."

"You're a good man, Malek Alexandre."

His smile was slightly rueful. It made her feel a little wobbly. "I'm not always good."

She had no doubt that was true. A little charge of sensual electricity sparked between them and her breath caught in her throat. Malek's gaze focused on her mouth, and instinctively, she licked her lips.

He said, "I've wanted you to be mine for months. I've dreamed about you. Fantasized about you."

Lei felt her cheeks heating up, a blush creeping up her face. "I noticed you right away, too, but I knew I wasn't what you wanted. What you needed."

He bent down, inching closer, closer still. "You are all I can think about, the only woman I want in my bed."

"But what about all the things you'll be giving up?"

He jerked back a little, his brows furrowed. "What will I be giving up?"

Now she was confused. Of course he was giving certain things up. Or did he mean to find a new dungeon once they were settled? Would he expect her to become his submissive eventually? Or would he find a new gay lover since he'd had to give up Brent? "I know you enjoy having an extra man in bed with you sometimes. And what about the bondage? The domination and submission?" A breeze sent her hair whipping across her face. As she pulled it aside to clear her vision, she said, "This is stuff we should have talked about before we were married, I know. But there wasn't really time..."

Malek nodded. "You know exactly what my lifestyle was like before we left Ann Arbor. And to be honest, I did think once that I might be able to have an open marriage where certain activities might be accepted, given specific conditions. But that was before. I couldn't expect that from you."

"Would you have expected it from April?"

"Maybe. I can't say for sure."

Her gaze dropped to the ground. "You're making me feel a little guilty. I'm keeping you from something that was such a big part of your life."

He cupped her chin, tipping it up until her gaze met his again. "A big part, Lei, yes. But not an essential one."

"You understand, I can't submit to you. I can't do it."

"I understand." He released her chin, but his gaze remained locked to hers. "But you realize you are by nature a sexual submissive?"

Her heart jumped. She'd never admitted that to anyone, not even herself. Not so bluntly. Yes, she'd found Malek's brand of dominance mesmerizing. She'd fantasized a few times about relinquishing all control over to him. But that didn't necessarily mean she was a natural submissive. She'd never had that urge with anyone else, male or female. "I don't know that, Malek."

"Okay." He took her hand in his again and began walking, following a narrow winding pathway through shrubs and trees.

As they walked, a dark thought kept crossing her mind. Before she could stop herself, she blurted, "Please tell me that's not why you married me. Because you thought I'd someday be able to fulfill that need for you."

"Of course, I didn't."

The conviction in his voice was convincing. "Okay. And you're sure about Brent?"

"I'm concerned about him, but that doesn't mean I want to make him a part of our marriage. That's two very different things. That stage of my life is over, Lei. And I'm ready to move on, to make you happy, to help you heal, and, God willing, to start a family. Brent will have April. I think she'll be enough for him."

They broke through some dense growth and stopped.

Lei's breath caught in her throat. They were standing on a ridge overlooking a snow-covered lake. Skirting the water was forest as far as the eye could see. "Wow."

Standing behind her, he slid his arms around her waist, holding her flush to him. "You like this spot?"

"I do."

"What do you think about having a view like this from our bedroom?"

"I think I might never want to leave."

"That's exactly what I hoped you'd say." Using her shoulders, he turned her to face him. "Look, I know things are going to be rough for us for a while. I'm prepared to help you through all your issues. But I have absolutely no regrets. I love you, Lei. Being your husband is all that matters to me. Nothing else. And nobody else."

And then he kissed her. In that magical place, where everything was quiet and perfect and beautiful. And she pressed her body against his, looped her arms around his neck, and held on while his tongue did decadent, naughty things in her mouth. When the kiss finally ended, she was dizzy and warm.

She looked into his eyes and saw something, a tiny shadow. "Are you tired? We've walked a pretty long way."

"A little."

"Let's go back. You should rest for a while. Or turn in early."

"Only if you join me." He beamed a wicked grin at her. "We have some nights to make up for. You remember, don't you?"

How could she forget? A part of her warmed at the thought of lying in bed with Malek again. "I guess I could do that."

Another part chilled.

She had heard what he'd said, that he'd be patient, wouldn't force her to do anything she wasn't ready for. But he was a man. With needs. And every man had his limits. How long would it be before she pushed him to the end of his?

19

Malek gritted his teeth as he toweled off. He'd thought a long, cold shower would help. It hadn't. His balls were still aching like a son of a bitch, and all he wanted to do was throw his wife onto the bed and show her how much he loved her.

Not happening.

Thinking about the succulent woman lying in his bed, waiting for him, he tied the towel around his hips and brushed his teeth. It would probably kill him, but he was determined to keep things under control. Lei was obviously suffering from post-traumatic stress disorder. She hadn't spelled it out for him, but the signs were there. Fortunately, he knew all too well what PTSD did to some people, and he had some notion of how to help someone suffering from it. He'd done a lot of reading on the subject in the last couple of months.

Systematic desensitization, that was the clinical term for what he was doing. The non-clinical: a slow, painful seduction. Either way, it would work, if anything would.

He checked his reflection in the mirror, combed his fingers through his damp curls, and opened the door.

She was lying on her back, staring straight up at the ceiling. The covers were pulled up to her chin.

He cleared his throat and she glanced his way. Her eyes widened. She visibly swallowed. And then she jerked her gaze back to the ceiling. She was acting like a virgin on her wedding night. He felt his lips pulling into a smile as he let the towel drop on the floor, walked to the bed, pulled back the covers, and climbed in.

"Now that we're married, some things are going to change," he said.

"What things?" She scrambled out of bed, pulled the drapes, and switched off the bedside lamp. The room went dark.

"You won't be sleeping with me like this."

"What do you mean, 'like this'? Do I smell bad?" Giggling nervously as she settled back under the covers, she flicked a curious look at him.

He tugged at her T-shirt sleeve. "With clothes on."

"Ohhhh." Her cheeks turned the sweetest shade of pink. He had to admit, he loved to see her blush. For a woman who'd once been a prostitute, Lei was extremely easy to embarrass.

"Yeah," he said, trying not to laugh.

"Okay." Once again, she sprang from the bed. She shuffled into a dark corner at the far end of the room.

"Where are you going?"

"Nowhere. I'm just undressing."

He turned on the lamp, washing the room in a soft gold glow. "That's better. I couldn't see you."

Her cheeks turned an even brighter shade of red. Her top lifted to expose her stomach, and she visibly swallowed.

"Go ahead." He reclined back against the headboard.

She yanked her shirt off and dropped it on the floor. And then, hopping and jerking stiffly, she disposed of her pajama pants and dove under the covers in her bra and panties.

They were nice. Better than nice. They were lacy and sweet. But they had to go, too. "You still have clothing on," he pointed out.

She sighed. "Malek, I don't sleep nude. It isn't comfortable."

"You'll get used to it."

Her sigh was highly exaggerated. "You're doing this on purpose."

No use denying it. "I am. I'm torturing you. I know you're uncomfortable, but in the long run, it's for the best."

She mumbled something under her breath as she wriggled and shimmied. A moment later, she waved the scraps of lace and satin at him, then tossed them on the floor. "Happy?"

"Yes, thank you."

She motioned to the lamp. "I don't think I can sleep with the light on."

"I guess I can go without." He shut off the lamp, then slid down deeper into the bed.

Now, this was heaven, lying in bed with Lei, her scent on his sheets, the soft sound of her breathing filling the silence. He smiled to himself and closed his eyes, trying to ignore the raging erection that was making his balls ache.

"Lei, I love you," he said.

He heard her sniffle. Was she . . . crying?

"Lei?" he said when she didn't respond.

"I'm so afraid, Malek."

"Of what?"

"Of letting you down, of disappointing you."

"You aren't letting me down. What made you think you are?"

"It's our wedding night and I can barely stand getting naked in front of you."

"It's okay. I understand."

"What if I never get over what happened? What if I never learn to enjoy sex again?"

"We'll deal with the what-ifs when the time comes, if the time comes. Right now, you need to concentrate on what we have, our reason to celebrate. I love you, Lei. I will love you for the rest of my life, whether we make love or not. That's only one way of expressing love, my precious wife. Only one. There's a great many other ways." He reached out for her, found her hand, and their fingers wove together. "Please, don't get down on yourself already. We've just begun our journey. I'm happy, baby. Very happy."

"I can't believe you're real."

"I am. Real. But far from perfect."

For that comment, he received a sweet chuckle.

"Now, that's better. Today is a happy day. It's a time to look toward a wonderful future, not a time to worry about the what-ifs."

"You're right." She sniffled again. "Thank you."

"For what?"

"For loving me like nobody has ever loved me before. I love you, too."

His heart took flight. And though he'd never admit it, a few tears gathered in his eyes, too. This woman, with all her imperfections, had brought out a very different side of him, one he hadn't realized he had before now. He'd always known he was protective. As a dominant, that was one of the traits he'd seen in himself most. As he pushed his submissives to the edge of their limits, he always felt a sense of protectiveness, of responsibility.

But this was different. With Lei, he not only wanted to protect her, to take care of her, but to also help her become whole again. He was more patient, more caring.

She made him a better man.

He squeezed her hand and she returned the gesture.

"It's hard for me to be touched," she said, her voice low and husky. "But I want to do something special for you tonight. Something to show you how much I care about you, how much I respect you." After a beat, she added, "How much I want you. You decide. What will it be?"

A few possibilities flashed through his mind. She liked to watch him. He knew that. So asking her to watch him masturbate was his first thought, but he shoved it aside. That would be too easy. No, he wanted to bring her a little out of her comfort zone, but not too far. He could also ask her to give him a hand job or suck his cock. But he thought that might take her back to her old life.

No, he wanted her to enjoy the experience, to get all the pleasure. How could he do that without touching her?

"I want to watch you come," he said.

He counted eight heavy heartbeats before she answered, "O-okay."

"I won't touch you. I'll only watch."

"I think I can handle that. Lights?"

"Off."

He heard her sigh of relief and almost laughed. He rolled onto his side, facing her, and pulled the cover aside, exposing his wife's gorgeous body. The room was cloaked in shadow, but he could still make out the silhouette of her curves and the contours of her face. His heart rate kicked up a notch as he watched her hand glide down her stomach, toward the juncture of her thighs.

Thinking she might need some lube, he said, "Hang on." He log rolled toward the edge of the bed and fished out a tube from the nightstand drawer. After returning to her side, he set the tube on her chest, in the valley between her breasts. "I thought you could use this."

"Thanks."

The sound of lube squirting echoed in the heavy silence. A

softer sloughing of skin against the sheets followed as she bent her knees and dragged her feet apart.

How he wished he could bury his face between those thighs. Lap away every drop of her sweet juices. And come to the sound of her screaming his name in ecstasy. Someday, he hoped those wishes would come true. Until then, he would be satisfied to watch her.

Even if his balls ached for years.

"Do you want music?" he asked, hoping she'd say no.

"No, that's okay."

He tracked the motion of her hand as it moved down her body, finally becoming engulfed in the deep shadows between her legs. His blood warmed at the sound of her breathing. His mouth dried. He licked his lips, wishing he could taste her.

In his mind's eye, he saw her part her labia, exposing her plump little clit. Watched her slender index finger glide back and forth, back and forth. Watched the rise and fall of her breasts as her breathing deepened, sped up.

He inhaled deeply, catching a tiny whiff of the sweet scent of her desire. He pulled in another breath, eager to gulp it in.

Moving cautiously, so she wouldn't hear him, he inched his hand down, to grasp his erection. He had no lube, so he had to stroke slowly, but that was okay. The luscious sight of his wife taking her pleasure was enough to make up for it. With the poor light, he couldn't see every detail of her body, but his mind easily swept aside the dark shadows hiding her from him. And he saw her in all her glory, her pussy lips wet and swollen, the finger of one hand sliding up and down, tormenting her clit while the finger of her other hand inched into her cunt.

He hadn't touched her. Hadn't laid a single finger on her. Hadn't licked or nibbled or kissed or sucked an inch of her flesh. And yet his cock was painfully hard, the fire in his blood was raging, and his balls were so tight he had to grit his teeth against the agony.

His senses picked up each and every sign of her passion: the scent of her juices perfuming the air; the sound of her quickened breathing; her skin rubbing against the sheets as she rocked her hips up and down; the almost imperceptible feel of her trembling as it reverberated through the mattress.

He quickened the pace of his strokes, silently vowing someday all his touches would be for her. He would focus every ounce of energy on her pleasure. When she was ready to accept him.

He inched one arm closer to her, feeling the heat radiating off her skin, the slight bounce of the mattress. She was shaking all over, her skin probably coated in a sheen of sweat. Her pussy lips were probably puffy, her channel slick and ready for him.

"I'm going to come," she whispered.

He said nothing, afraid even a single word might break her concentration and ruin the moment. Instead, he let all the minute sensations feed his desire, and stroked his cock until he was straddling the brink of orgasm. Tight. Hot. Burning. He could come. One more stroke. Only one.

But he would wait.

"Ahhhh..." she whispered as she started thrusting her hips up high in the air.

Malek slid his fist down his shaft. His insides exploded. Cum burned up the length of his cock and sprayed into his cupped hand. Again. And again. His body jerked. His insides spasmed. Liquid heat blazed from his center out to the tips of his fingers and the soles of his feet.

Relief.

He drew in a deep breath and let it out.

"Are you okay?" she asked.

"Yep, fine."

"You're breathing a little heavy."

"Yes, I am." He sat up and reached for a tissue to clean his hand.

"Did you masturbate, too?"

"I did." He tossed the used tissue into the trash and settled back down.

"I like to watch you."

He liked the way her voice sounded when she said that. "You can watch me anytime you want."

She rolled onto her side and propped up her head. "Now?"

He chuckled. "You'd have to give me a little bit of time to recover."

"I was just joking." She leaned over him and pressed her soft lips to his. Her kiss was sweet. Pure temptation. "Sleepy?"

"A little."

"Me too." She laid her head down and flopped an arm over his stomach.

Hoping she'd leave it there, he didn't move, barely breathed. He closed his eyes, knowing very soon she'd be thrashing and screaming in terror.

Lei was smiling. Oh yes, she was. Smiling. And satisfied. But more than that, relieved.

Maybe she hadn't made the worst mistake of her life. Maybe everything would be okay.

Oddly, it was this little masturbation scene that had given her some hope things would turn out okay. Malek had proved he could be patient, creative, resourceful...and yet quietly dominant. The end result was her first orgasm in ages. A blast-off-to-the-stars climax that made her toes curl. She was still warm and tingly all over as she lay next to her husband, listening to his slow, even breaths.

A few niggling doubts and questions still remained, but for the most part, the worst of her worries had been laid to rest.

She was ready to relax, face the future as it came. For once, she felt the chains tying her to her dark past could be broken. Holloway was still out there somewhere. And she hadn't heard a word from Vasquez in days. But she was safe. Malek was safe. And soon they would be starting a new life together.

Relaxed, she let her dreams carry her off.

20

The next morning, Lei left their bedroom feeling a little anxious but also a little excited. Her husband—would she ever get used to saying that?—had already proved himself to be a very clever man. Without laying a hand on her, without speaking, he'd given her the most sensual experience of her life last night. What would his wicked mind come up with next?

Because she wanted to feel pretty today and as relaxed as possible, she ran some water for a bath in the master bathroom. As the tub was filling, she went back to the bathroom she'd once called hers, in search of her personal items. But when she returned, arms loaded with all her stuff, she discovered Malek had made himself comfortable. In her full tub.

"Well, I guess I'll wait to take my bath later," she said, laughing.

His grin was pure evil. "Oh no, you won't." He scooted toward one end and flipped his head. "Come on in. There's plenty of room."

There was plenty of room, under normal circumstances. The sunken bathtub was one of those nifty oversized jet tubs, made to accommodate two people, as long as those two people didn't mind touching and weren't the size of a polar bear, like Malek.

"Lei," Malek lifted an arm, draping it over the tub's edge. "The water's getting cold. This place has an old water heater. If you don't bathe now, you'll be taking a very chilly bath later."

"Are you even supposed to be taking a bath? What about your stitches?" She set all her bottles and jars and tubes on the counter and, avoiding meeting his gaze, stripped off her bathrobe.

He pointed at the bandages. "They're dry. That's why I didn't fill the tub all the way." He reached for her hand, holding it and easing her into position in front of him. She sat with her back to him, her legs bent, knees in front of her chest, her butt between his spread thighs.

Malek poured some bath gel into a net pouf and started lathering her back. "Last night, when you were touching yourself, what did you picture in your mind?"

"Nothing."

"Nothing?" he echoed. The pouf swirled in circles over her back, round and round. It felt so good. "Your mind was blank?"

"I try not to think. If I do, it gets in the way."

"I see."

"What about you?" she asked as she let her chin rest on her bent knees.

"My mind wasn't blank, if that's what you mean."

"What were you visualizing?"

"You."

Lei's heart jerked.

"I watched your sweet little nipples harden. Your stomach clench. I saw your fingers slide between your slick, swollen tissues to find your clit."

"You saw all that?" she asked, growing breathless. Her pussy was getting warm. Her blood, too. It was the way he talked, his voice so low and rumbly and masculine. He might talk her into an orgasm.

Before today, she'd gone months, make that years, without coming. She'd thought she might never have an orgasm again. And here she was, panting at just the sound of his words.

"I did," he said. "And it made me hard."

An image flashed through her mind, of Malek standing before her, completely nude, rivulets of soapy water glistening on his golden skin. "I . . . you have quite an imagination."

"Yes, I do." The pouf skimmed along one side of her body, coming close to the side of her breast.

She sucked in a little gasp.

"Did that hurt?"

"No."

"Good. Now it's my turn." Before she could ask what he meant, he reached over her shoulder and dropped the pouf into the water.

His legs disappeared from either side of her, and the water started splashing as he repositioned himself. She turned around to find he was now facing the wall. She took one look at his broad back and fished in the water for the lost pouf.

His skin was smooth, a golden tan that suggested he spent a lot of time shirtless in the sun. And under that satin velvet skin rippled bulging, defined muscles that would make most men green with envy.

This was a man who was powerful, strong, maybe even a little dangerous.

He said nothing as she scrubbed his back, working from his broad shoulders down, down, down. He stopped her when she reached the level of his narrow waist. "Your turn again." Moving quickly, he grabbed the pouf out of her hand. "Don't move."

Sitting exactly where she was, Lei watched Malek stand up. Water shimmered in the light, emphasizing every curve and bulge of his muscles. Naturally, her gaze went right to his groin when he turned around. His cock, the base covered by coarse black curls, was fully erect. Thick. Long. Lei yanked her gaze away, dropping it to the white frothy water.

He sat, loaded up the pouf with more fragrant gel, and said, "I'm going to wash your front now."

She closed her eyes and nodded.

"Open your eyes, Lei."

She didn't want to, but she did it.

His I'm-going-to-eat-you-alive smile was gone, replaced with an expression that was much less threatening. He reached out, centering the pouf on her chest, just below her chin. "Touching isn't always sexual, Lei. Everyone needs to be touched."

"I know. In my head. But when someone touches me, something clicks inside, and I start to panic." Her gaze dropped to the water again. It was hard to look at him, to see the wanting in his eyes. He was a man. He had the same needs as any man. As the men who had once paid to own her. "I mean, I've heard about infants dying from lack of human touch. It's frustrating that I can't just get over it and go on with my life."

"I'm going to help you." His hand moved in slow, small circles. The scratchy plastic netting abrading her chest, then her shoulder, then the other one. It moved toward the center again. Down between her breasts to her stomach. "This is okay, right?"

"I'm okay."

It swirled round and round for a while on her stomach, moving up and down. It never reached her breasts and never descended as far as her mound. It stayed in safe territory. Nonsexual territory.

He motioned for her to scoot back a bit, away from him, and extended a hand. "Your leg."

She did exactly as he asked and lifted a leg. He began at her foot, scrubbing the sole, working his way up toward her thigh. It felt wonderful, and not once did she feel that awful gut-twisting sensation in her belly. Relaxing, she leaned back and closed her eyes.

"Yes, that's it," he said. "I'm glad to see you're enjoying this."

"I am. I really am."

He moved to the other leg without ever reaching too-close-for-comfort territory. "That's exactly what I want to hear."

"But I worry—"

"Don't. You know what your problem is? You overthink things. You need to turn off the brain and focus on sensation."

He was right. Though she'd never realized it before. "Easier said than done. Thinking comes naturally to me."

"Your eyes are closed. What are you feeling?"

She thought about his question.

"Don't think. Just describe the sensations."

"Okay. I'm feeling the scratchy netting abrading my skin, making it warm."

"What else?" he asked.

"I feel your fingers on my calf, your hand supporting my leg."

"And . . . ?"

"The warm water rippling when you move, caressing my skin." She inhaled deeply. "And I smell the lavender. In the bath gel."

"Good. Now you're getting it."

"And I hear water dripping. The echo of my voice against the tile." She licked her lips. "And I taste soap."

"Now, how do you feel?"

Again, she started thinking.

"No, don't think about your answer. Describe how you feel."

"I feel warm and wet. My body feels heavy. My heart is beating slowly, the pulse thumping through my head. Content. Happy."

A soft splash told her he'd dunked the pouf into the water again. But it didn't return to her leg. His hand did. It skimmed up, from her ankle, over her shin, to her knee.

"How do you feel?" he asked again.

"A little less relaxed," she admitted, aware of the muscles in her leg tensing.

"What do you feel?" he asked as his hand inched a little higher.

"A hand moving slowly up my leg. Over my knee."

"What else?"

"My muscles tightening. Calf. Foot. Thigh."

His voice was smooth and deep, calming, soothing. "Relax your feet. Your legs. Your arms. Your face." As he said each body part, she focused on it, loosening the muscles. "Yes, that's the way." His hand inched higher. It skimmed her lower thigh. "Relax your stomach. Your back. Your chest. Breathe in, out. Slowly."

She did exactly as he said, and the little bit of tension that had started to wind through her body melted away. To her utter amazement, a very different kind of tension began coiling deep inside her body, the good kind. "Wow," she whispered.

"What is it?" His hand stopped, his fingers a few precious inches from the flesh that was warming between her legs.

"Don't stop." Again, she focused on what she felt, the pulse beating in her neck, the almost imperceptible caress of the water, the sweet scent of lavender. The smell of his skin. Her husband. Hers.

She reached out, covered his hand with hers, and eased it between her thighs. A rush of erotic heat blazed through her body the instant his fingers grazed her labia. She gulped in a shallow breath.

Disjointed images flashed through her mind. Ugly. Horrid. She shoved them out and focused on the pleasure of his intimate touch. Using her fingers, she moved his, making his index finger slip between her labia to find her clit. A hard tremble shook her.

"There," she whispered. "They never touched me there." She moved her hand away and parted her legs for him.

His touches were soft at first, little flicks back and forth, up and down. They sent mini storms of white-hot pleasure zinging through her body like electricity. Her nerves jumped. Her muscles clenched. It was delicious.

He added a second finger, slowly sliding in and out of her pussy, knuckle scraping that special spot that made her toes curl. In and out, in and out it went. The other one danced over her clit. Together, they sent pulses of wanting through her body. She was getting hot. Too hot. Too tight. She wanted more. She wanted to be filled.

"Malek, I need you." She heard the desperation in her own voice.

He scooped her out of the water as if she were weightless, and both dripping wet, rushed out of the room, back to the bed. As he laid her on the mattress, she lifted her eyes to his.

He was staring down at her with such raw emotion the sight nearly took her breath away.

She lifted her arms to him. "Hold me. Like a man who loves his wife."

He crawled onto the mattress and hauled her into his arms. For the first time in many months, an embrace didn't feel like an entrapment. It felt wonderful. It felt safe. A warm cocoon. A sanctuary.

She'd come to associate all touches with the horror she'd endured those many months she'd spent in slavery. But now, she could feel the difference. Not all touches were the same. Malek's touches weren't the same. His were healing. His soothed her soul.

She slid her arms around his waist and hugged him with all her might. She turned her face, nuzzling the crook of his neck while one of his hands skimmed up and down her back in a slow, steady rhythm.

Could it be this simple? That she'd be healed so easily? Just from the power of an embrace?

God, she hoped so.

He cupped her chin, lifting it. Her gaze followed. From his neck to his adorable chin. To his kissable lips. To the straight blade of his nose. Over to the hollow line of his cheekbone. And finally up to his eyes.

"Say the words, my wife. Tell me you're ready, and we'll complete the vows we spoke yesterday."

"I want to belong to you. Only you," she whispered. "You are my sanctuary."

He kissed her.

21

Malek's balls were so tight and high, he was choking on them. And his blood was burning through his body like molten lead. But he wouldn't let himself lose control. Oh, hell no. Not after waiting and working, patiently, all this time.

At last, he had what he'd been hoping for. He had her in his arms. And, oh yes, it was heaven.

Despite his determination to maintain control, his kiss was anything but controlled. His lips crushed hers, the kiss hard, feral. His tongue pushed into her sweet depth, stroking, tasting, drawing her flavor into his mouth. She was so sweet, intoxicating, he couldn't get enough.

Her fingers curled, her nails digging into his shoulders. The pain only amplified his need. The sound of their gasps and sighs filled their joined mouths. And that did nothing to help him keep his tenuous grip on his self-control.

Keep it real. Show her how you feel.

He broke the kiss and dragged in a few much-needed deep breaths. "I love you, Lei. More than words. More than life."

"I love you, too, Malek. You make me want to be a better

person. You make me want to be whole again." She took his hand and placed it on her breast. His balls tightened even more. "I'm ready, Malek."

"Are you sure?" If she wasn't, he would have to find the strength, from somewhere, to put on the brakes. He prayed he wouldn't have to do that. Already, he was in agony.

Her lips curled into a soft smile. She nodded. Then, using her hand, she began moving his back and forth across her breast. Mesmerized and completely lost in his need, he let her take complete control. She manipulated his hands, allowing him to caress her breasts, tease the nipples until they were pointy little succulent peaks.

"Can I taste you?" he asked, his voice husky.

"Yes." She arched her back, pushing her breasts higher into the air, bringing them closer to his mouth.

He bent over her, inhaled. She smelled so good, like woman and desire. His mouth watered as he angled lower, lower.

At the first flick of his tongue, she clamped her fists in his hair. His heart jumped in his chest. His cock jerked. He froze in place.

"Don't stop," she whispered. "Please."

A zing of sensual heat pulsed through him at the need in her voice. He pulled her nipple into his mouth and suckled hard, and she whimpered, arched her back even more, and tightened her hold on his hair.

Damn did he love how responsive she was. The sound of her little gasps and whimpers was like the sweetest music to his ears. And her taste. Damn. She was sweet and salty, utter perfection. Using his teeth, he grazed the turgid flesh.

"Oh God!" she murmured. "Ohmygod! Yes. Again."

He nipped then laved, nipped then laved, and each time she cried out for more, more, more.

He moved to the other breast, repeating the process, while

she writhed and quaked beneath him. She was like no woman he'd ever fucked—responding to his every touch as if it were her first. It was enough to make him almost lose control.

Her pleasure first, Malek. Always her pleasure first.

Just when he thought he might lose his mind, she yanked his head away, dragged him up so they were nose-to-nose, and kissed him roughly. Her tongue shoved its way into his mouth, tangling with his. He couldn't help but meet her thrusts, giving exactly what he was receiving. He tasted, teased, tormented her, and she did the same. Within minutes, they were both gasping, covered in a light sheen of sweat, and desperate for more.

Still, Malek resisted the instinct to take control. He ached to feel her hand cupped under his balls, those decadent lips circling his throbbing cock. But he could do nothing but tremble and ache and allow her to shove him back until he was lying on his back and she was straddled over him.

His gaze raked up and down her body. She was absolutely perfect. Everything about her. Her tits were high and full. Her little hard nipples puckered and tempting. Her waist was slender, her hips flared out just enough to make her feminine. Her thighs were slender, the lines of her muscles visible under her smooth skin.

"I admit, watching you fuck makes me wet," she said, her voice husky. "Almost as wet as watching you dominate a submissive. That drives me crazy." As she spoke, her hand was gliding down her stomach, toward her smooth-shaven mound.

Talk about driving someone crazy.

His gaze inched lower, to her moist nether lips. They gleamed, slick with her juices. Out of instinct, he licked his lips.

"Are you hungry?" she asked.

"Oh yes."

Her hand cupped her cunt. "For this?"

"Yes."

"Hmmm." She parted her fingers, pulling the puffy outer lips apart. She stroked her clit with the index finger of her other hand, back and forth.

His throat practically closed up, and a surge of erotic hunger blasted through his system. "Come here," he said, voice hoarse.

She lifted one brow, gave him a seductive smile, then walked on her knees up his body.

Finally, her pussy was right there, above his mouth, her thighs straddling his head. He inhaled, drawing in her luscious scent.

"It's yours," she said as she pulled her labia apart for him.

His mouth flooded with saliva. Finally, he would taste her.

"Thank you, baby." Placing his hands on her hips, he pulled her down until she was practically sitting on his face. With his tongue, he explored her folds, and his mouth filled with her delicious flavor. When he finally found her little clit, she reached back and fisted his cock.

He growled as an almost overwhelming flare of heat blazed through his body. "Fuck. You're going to pay for that."

"For what?" she asked, donning a devil-made-me-do-it smirk. She flicked her fingertip along the flared ridge circling the head, and he bit back a curse.

"You know what." Tipping his head slightly, he nipped the juncture of her thigh, and she shivered, a coat of goose bumps covering her leg.

"Malek," she whispered. Her little fist tightened around his cock, amplifying his need.

Her pussy was wet for him. The air was thick with the intoxicating scent of her need. And damn if he didn't want to shove his cock inside her slick heat and find out how tight and hot she was.

But he couldn't.

It seemed all those years of honing his control, of mastering his own body, would pay off today. Clearly, his wife wasn't going to make it easy on him.

"Taste me, please," she murmured.

He tasted her, but not where she wanted. His tongue flicked up and down along the inside of one thigh, then the other. As he worked, his nose filled with the smell of her arousal. His mouth with the flavor of her need. His eyes with the sight of her surrendering to her body's demands.

"If you're going to be so stubborn, I'll do it myself." She reached between her legs, but he grabbed her wrist and pulled it away.

"No, you won't." He released her wrist immediately, fearing any restraint might ruin what was quickly becoming the most erotically charged experience of his life. He couldn't remember the last time he'd felt like this.

"Fine, I'll do one better." Walking on her knees again, she moved backward, taking that decadent pussy out of his reach. She stopped when she reached his hips. Smiled. Took his cock in her hand and dragged it up and down her folds until the head was coated in her slick heat.

Malek groaned, reaching up to grab her hips.

Inch by inch, she lowered herself down, taking him deep. Her slick pussy walls opened to accommodate his girth, then clamped tight.

A deep moan shot from his chest as she lifted her hips and slammed down again.

"How's that?" she asked, her voice a taunting siren's call.

He couldn't stand it. He had to take control.

"What's wrong?" she asked. She lifted her hands to cup her breasts.

His throat constricted and he swallowed hard. "Not a damn thing."

She shot him a wicked grin, then, moving carefully, rotated

around, his cock still deep inside. Now he had a full view of her back and ass as she rode him hard. That ass slapped the base of his stomach with each bouncing descent. The sound of skin striking skin seemed to reverberate through his whole body. With each sharp slap, a blast of erotic heat shot from his center.

Surrendering to his own overpowering need for release, he rocked his hips, meeting his wife's strokes, driving himself deeper into her tight little cunt. His muscles were tightening, his breathing growing ragged. So hot. Trembling. On the verge of orgasm.

Now.

No.

His cum was there, at the base of his cock. One more thrust. Just one more. And it would be over.

Not yet!

Moving swiftly, he sat up, tackling her onto her back and pinning her arms over her head. He panted as he stared into the wide eyes of his wife and struggled to recover. Beneath him, Lei wriggled, fighting to regain control of him.

That wasn't going to happen.

"Now it's my turn."

Lei couldn't breathe. The air had been sucked from the room. A brief memory flashed through her mind, but as quickly as it came, it vanished, and she was left lying on her back, staring into Malek's dark eyes, her body a big tangled mass of wanting and needing.

She'd pushed him to his limit; then she'd pushed him more. And this was what she got.

Not that she was surprised. Or disappointed.

This felt good, lying beneath him, vulnerable and powerless. It felt right.

Malek gathered her wrists into one hand, placed his free hand on her left breast, and smiled. "Your heart's pounding. Your face is flushed a pretty shade of pink. And your pussy is wet. This is what you want, isn't it, Lei? You were pushing me, taunting me, because you wanted me to lose control, didn't you?"

"Yes, Malek."

With an index finger, he drew little swirling lines down her center, from her breastbone down her belly, over her belly button, to her mound. "This beautiful body is mine now. Mine to touch. Mine to worship." His finger skimmed back up, circled a nipple.

She smiled as her gaze meandered over his face. It was hard to believe that this gorgeous, patient, loving man was her husband. That she would spend the rest of her life in his arms. Her sanctuary. Her salvation. Someday, she would hold their child, would look into their son's eyes and see his father. This was just the beginning of their journey, and already she couldn't wait to see where they would go from here.

"Malek, I need you."

"I need you, too, Lei. More than I have ever needed another person." He eased her legs apart. "Your pussy is so tight. I can't stand waiting another minute." After positioning his hips between her thighs, he scooped her ass into his hands, lifting it up. "Look me in the eyes as I enter you. Don't hide."

She locked her gaze on his eyes.

"Yes, just like that." He kissed her gently as his cock filled her.

"Ohhhh," she said into their joined mouths. It felt like a hot wave of water had washed over her. Her chest felt warm. Her face too. She rocked her hips up and down, meeting Malek's strokes, taking him as deeply as she could. He fit her perfectly. He held her perfectly. He kissed her perfectly. He possessed her perfectly.

It was as if he'd been created to be hers and hers only.

She wrapped her legs around his hips, locking her ankles. So right. So . . . beautiful.

With his body, his hands, his mouth, he made love to her. He cherished her. He worshipped her. He claimed her. And he brought her to that incredible pinnacle where the whole world narrowed to a pinpoint, and all that existed were the sensations he stirred inside her.

Harder, he thrust, his cock shoving inside her, caressing every sensitive inch of her canal. And at that glorious moment, when his cock thickened before he climaxed, she tumbled over the crest. She cried out his name as her body shook with pleasure. Her pussy convulsed around his cock, and his cries joined hers. His cum filled her, and his hard, rough thrusts shoved her over the edge again. A second climax tore through her body, and she clamped her arms around his neck and clung to him.

He slid his hands underneath her, wrapping her in a tight embrace. Gently, he kissed her forehead. "Are you okay?"

"Better than okay."

He sandwiched her face between his hands. "I love you."

"I love you, too." A loud bang cut her off, and she flinched. Her heart started thumping against her breastbone. "That sounded like it was inside."

Malek's eyes widened. He stilled, listened. A second thunk echoed through the house. He rolled off her, grabbed a pair of sweatpants, and stuffed his feet into them, pulling them up as he ran toward the door. "Go hide. And whatever you hear, don't come out until I tell you it's safe."

"Should I call the police?"

"No, not yet. Could be a raccoon or something in the garage."

A cold sweat prickled her skin as she scampered around, grabbing clothes and looking for a place to hide.

A raccoon? God, she hoped so.

22

What was this?

A strange man was standing in his fucking garage, like he owned the place. Correction, not a strange man. It was one of the assholes who'd nearly killed him. "Who are you and what the hell are you doing in our garage?" Malek asked.

The man's lips curled in a hint of a smile. "Why don't you ask your lovely wife."

"What do you mean by that? Who are you?"

"Do I need to spell it out for you? First letter, C. H. I. M. E. R. A."

"Lei would never. No." Malek couldn't believe what this stranger was saying. It was a lie. It had to be. Lei loved him. She would never lead his enemy to his front door. Not knowingly. "You tricked her. Lied to her."

The man laughed. The sound was hollow, mocking. "Did you ever fall for her shit? That bitch is good. Damn good."

Rage surged through Malek like a thrashing river. His arm swung back, then forward, his fist aimed for the intruder's nose. But before it hit its mark, the man ducked and planted his fist in Malek's stomach. The pain forced Malek over. White hot. Searing. He gasped for air and his knees buckled.

Standing over him, the attacker crossed his arms over his chest and clicked his tongue. "Oh, damn, you had surgery not long ago, didn't you? I forgot. That must've hurt."

Stars twinkled in Malek's vision, and he shook his head to try to clear it. He needed to get up, off the fucking floor, before the bastard beat him to death. He needed to protect Lei.

"I owe Lei for this. She's a damn good actress, isn't she?"

"You're lying."

"You still think so?" The man squatted. "How else do you suppose I found you?"

"I don't know." Malek fought to breathe. The pain was getting worse, not better. He wondered if something had broken open inside. He wondered if he might die there, lying curled up like a damn baby. His brain was getting foggy from the pain and he couldn't think. "Maybe it was April."

"She's dead. Dead women don't talk."

"Dead? When? How?"

"She had a little accident. You should ask your lovely wife about that one, too."

"I don't believe you."

"Well, then I guess we need to go in and talk to her. Get to the bottom of this." He hauled Malek to his feet and shoved him forward.

Walking blindly, his legs heavy, Malek stumbled into the house.

Lei was standing just inside the door. Her eyes were round. Her lips pulled tight. "Malek." Her gaze jerked from his face to the attacker's.

"Your husband has a few questions to ask you, Lei."

"You didn't tell him—" She cut herself off and visibly swallowed.

A tiny thread of doubt began winding through Malek's mind.

Had this bastard told him the truth? Had Lei known who he was? "Lei?"

Her gaze jerked to the stranger again. "I'll talk to him alone. Leave us."

"Whatever." The attacker stepped back, lifting his hands as if to say he wouldn't interfere.

Lei wrapped one slender arm around Malek's waist and supported him as he hobbled to the couch and sat. She sat next to him. "I'm so sorry, Malek. So, so sorry."

"What the hell is going on?"

Lei blinked a few times and lifted a trembling hand to her mouth. "I don't know where to start." When he didn't give her any direction, because his throat had become completely cut off, she continued, "That man is Nate Holloway, an agent in the CIA. Or so he claims. I met him when I was . . . working."

"Okay."

"He did a favor for me. Actually, he did several. And he told me not to worry about paying him back. He said we'd figure it out later. I had no idea I was making a deal with the devil. I swear." She was sniffling now. Shaking all over. But it was clear she wasn't exactly denying what that bastard had told him.

"So, it's true? What he said?"

She dragged her hand across her face. "I don't know what he told you."

"You led him here."

"I might have. Somehow. Not intentionally. I don't know." Her gaze dropped to her hands, clasped in her lap. "I refused to help him. But then the girls started dying. And Eve's grandmother. She was such a nice woman. She'd never hurt anyone."

"Okay." He still didn't understand. What did the dying girls and an old lady have to do with the Chimera? With him?

"He was sending me a message," she said between sobs and hiccups and sniffles. "And it was killing me, seeing them pay the price for my refusing him. Oh, God." She covered her face, shoulders quaking, gut-wrenching sobs tearing his heart into pieces.

His insides felt like they were being slashed apart. Whatever was happening, it was more than Lei could handle. "Lei, I'm having a hard time understanding. Start again. From the beginning. You said he did you a favor. What did he do?"

Once again, she was overcome by tears. She tried to talk, but just mumbled and blurted things. He caught bits and pieces. "I had no idea. I wouldn't have asked him for help." Her hands, still cupped over her face, muffled her sobs and her words. He struggled to hear, to make sense of what was quickly becoming incoherent babbling. "I didn't know what to do. I was trapped. I do love you, Malek. I honestly do."

"Time's up!" the attacker said, charging toward them.

"No! Please!" Lei flung herself over Malek, begging, crying. "Please! Just a few minutes more."

"No, I've wasted enough time here." When Lei didn't move, the man tore her off, shoving her back. She landed on the floor with a heavy thud, her head slamming backward, striking the coffee table.

Malek's heart stopped. Completely. He dove toward her, but the bastard caught him in the gut, this time with a booted foot.

He saw black.

The pain.

Confusion.

Lei's mind suddenly cleared and she remembered falling, recalled watching that bastard Holloway grabbing her husband.

This was all her fault. Everything.

Her vision was blurry. But she could make out the ceiling up above. She was in the living room. Alone? She tried to sit up, but her stomach lurched and acid swept up her throat. She rolled onto her side and dry heaved again and again and again.

By the time she stopped, her thoughts were clear, but she was sick and shaky.

Was Malek dead already? Where was he?

Oh God, what have I done?

Moving as fast as she could with her skull threatening to split apart, she went in search of her cell phone. It was in her room. And there were messages. Several.

The first was from Rin: *When you get this message call me! Something's happening.*

The second, Rin again: *Lei? If something's happened to you, I don't know what I'll do.*

The third, Rin again: *Dammit, call me.* She was crying, and it was almost impossible to understand her.

The fourth was just a *click.* No message.

Lei started to dial her sister's number, but stopped.

Already, she'd fucked up Malek's life. Wasn't that enough damage? Wouldn't it be better if she just disappeared off the face of the earth right now, before she could hurt anyone else?

Everything was all fucked up.

Lei sank to the floor, wrapped her arms around her bent knees, and cried. It had all started out as such a good thing. She'd found a way to help some girls who desperately needed it. They were too weak to handle the stress, willing to do anything to escape from the clutches of those people. With Holloway's help, she'd been able to rescue four girls, to help them escape, get out of that hell. She'd never imagined such a good deed would end up costing her such a dear price.

Malek was a good man. An honorable one. Kind.

Whatever this thing with the stupid ancient relic or whatever, it couldn't be worth killing people for. Who did that? It was crazy.

At first she'd simply refused to do what Holloway said. But then the first girl was reported dead. And the second. He wanted to make sure she knew the rest would die, too, if she didn't fall into line and keep up her end of the bargain.

They were innocent. Mothers. Sisters. Daughters. They didn't deserve to be caught in the middle of anything. And she'd promised each and every one of them that if they trusted her, they would be safe.

That was the hardest part about the situation, knowing she'd failed them.

And then there'd been the attack. She'd turned to another stranger for help. So far, he'd done nothing. Not a fucking thing. Except maybe tell Holloway how to find her.

What a fool she'd been to think it was over, that hiding would work. Yeah, that was the ticket. That sure worked. There she was, sitting in the middle of the floor, married to a man she loved.

And soon to be a widow.

The heaving started again.

Struggling to stand, she ignored her cell phone as it started ringing once again. She just wanted it all to end. The pain. The hollow darkness inside. There was only one way.

Pills. Malek had a boatload of them in his bathroom.

The hell would be over soon. And it would be over forever.

So. Fucking. Cold.

Malek's jaw hurt, his teeth were chattering so hard. With each breath, a white cloud of mist obscured his vision. The floor beneath him was like ice, the chill seeping into his bones. And the pain in his gut was almost unbearable.

He was in hell. And not just because of his physical discomforts. The heartache, the emptiness inside was far worse.

Lei had led the enemy right to his front door. Why? How could she tell him she loved him one second and then betray him the next? She'd tried to explain, but her words had only made him more confused.

The lock on the door to his cell clicked and opened. Holloway strolled in, dressed in a parka like he was going camping in the arctic.

If Malek hadn't been chained to the fucking floor, he'd rip that fucking coat off the bastard and let him freeze his balls off, too. Then he'd shove them down his throat.

"Glad to see you're awake. Take a nice nap?" he asked.

Malek said nothing.

Holloway grabbed the shitty chair sitting against the wall, set it down closer to Malek, and sat. He crossed his legs. "Not in the mood to talk?"

Malek said nothing.

"We're just having a friendly conversation here. No reason to give me the silent treatment. How's the pain? Would you like something for it?"

Again, Malek said nothing. He knew what the bastard was after, and the hell if he was going to give it to him.

"Okay. Well, let's see if this inspires a little attitude adjustment." He pulled a small remote out of his pocket, clicked a button, and a television screen descended from a slit in the ceiling. Another click and there was an image displayed on the screen. One that made his blood turn to ice.

Talen. Beaten. Bloody. Sitting on a chair. Arms pressed against his side, as if his hands were tied behind his back.

Malek swallowed hard. For many years, he'd lived with the knowledge that something like this could happen, that he might watch his two brothers die. Or they might watch him die. All those years of knowing, of preparing, hadn't made this moment any easier. Not at all.

His stomach lurched.

"Now, I ask again, how is your pain? Would you like anything for it?" Holloway said, enunciating each word clearly.

Malek stared at the image, but said nothing. It was the right thing, the only thing he could do.

Protect The Secret. At all costs.

He prayed for strength.

Holloway shook his head and produced a cell phone from another pocket. He poked a button, said, "Phase one," and clicked off. He clicked the remote again.

Now the image was in real time, a video, not a still image.

Malek fought the urge to panic and focused instead on the room his brother was in. The floor, he noted, was exactly like the floor in the room he was being held. The walls, the same sterile white. Was he close by? In the same building?

Two men entered Talen's room, and Talen didn't move, didn't speak. One of the two men slid a white hood over Talen's head. Still, Talen said nothing, did nothing. They pushed Talen off the chair, positioning him on the floor, on his back. Again, Talen put up no fight.

Malek knew what was coming. He had to assume Talen did, too. Boarding, as it was called, was a legal, though questionable, interrogation technique. Some called it torture, inhumane, cruel. And it had been outlawed by President Obama shortly after he took office. Outlawed for most agencies.

Not the CIA.

And evidently not the Chimera either.

A moment later, two more men entered, carrying buckets of water.

With Talen bound, his head held in place so he couldn't turn away from the torrent, one of the men began pouring water onto his face.

Holloway turned to Malek. "One word. Say one word and we'll stop."

Malek bit his tongue and jerked his gaze away from the screen.

"Really? You're that much of a sissy that you can't watch what *you're* doing to your brother?" the asshole said.

Him? He wasn't the one dumping gallons of water in Talen's face. It was them. Those fucking bastards doing it. Torturing his brother. But he did feel guilty for being such a chickenshit. He dragged his gaze back to the screen.

Damn, that was a lot of fucking water.

They were still pouring a steady stream in Talen's face. And Talen wasn't lying still anymore. He was jerking, arching his back. His fingers were curled into tight fists. His survival instinct was kicking in.

Holloway hit the button on the phone. "Phase two."

The man stopped pouring water. The others, who had been holding Talen down, released him and moved back cautiously. Still wearing the hood, Talen hacked and sputtered and gasped, the sound hitting Malek in the gut.

"It's unfortunate we have to bring your wife into this, but we're talking about national security, Mr. Alexandre. We must get some answers. But the good news is, once you've told us what we need to know, you'll be free to leave. With your wife. No one will bother you again."

And Armageddon would begin.

Hoping the bastard was bluffing about Lei, Malek remained silent.

Holloway hit his little remote and all hope vanished.

Lei was lying in a room that looked a lot like the one Talen was in. She appeared to be sleeping. Just the sight of her, so still, so vulnerable, made his heart jerk in his chest. No matter what she'd done, he couldn't hate her. Even if she'd delivered both him and his brother right into this bastard's hands. Even if she had done the worst, pretended to love him to gain his trust.

He loved her. He would die for her. End of story.

His hands ached with the need to touch her, his arms to embrace her tiny frame and cradle her to him. The instinct to protect her was almost overwhelming.

"She's a little sleepy," Holloway said. "She has about ten minutes before it's too late."

He wasn't one hundred percent sure what that meant.

A knock sounded on the door.

Holloway shouted, "Clear."

The door opened. One of the men who'd been restraining Talen set an amber plastic pill bottle on the table in front of Malek. The agent slowly turned it until the label was facing him.

It was his prescription. There'd been at least twenty pills in that bottle last time he'd checked. It was empty now.

But would they force her to overdose? Wouldn't it have been easier for them to inject her with something?

"We found the bottle in her hand. She left something else." The agent handed him a piece of paper.

Right away, he recognized her handwriting. It was not a forgery. It read:

> *There have been a lot of things I've regretted in my life. But this one horrible mistake has left me with nothing. No hope. No love. No future.*

Malek's insides twisted.

"She told us she took at least twenty pills and has refused treatment. Give us the information we need and we'll make sure she lives."

Shit. This was an impossible choice: between duty and love. He bit back a curse and let his head fall forward.

He might save her life if he told them where The Secret was hidden. Might.

But once The Secret was unleashed upon humanity... nobody could be saved.

"I get the feeling you've made a decision?" the agent asked.

He nodded.

"Will you save her life?"

"I will," Malek said.

Relief flickered across the agent's face. He pulled up a chair and sat, leaning forward. "Okay, so where is it?"

Malek shook his head. "I wish I could help you, but I can't."

Into his phone, the agent said, "Phase three."

The lights went out.

23

Her head was going to explode. She was sure of it. And her stomach.

Oh shit, she was going to be sick.

A wave of overwhelming heat crashed through her system. Instantly, her entire body covered with sweat. Her throat constricted and she heaved. Nothing came up. Nothing. Her mouth was dry. Her eyes were blurred with tears.

Why the fuck was she still alive? Why?

The creak of a door opening made an explosion of white light flash behind her closed eyelids. Next, she heard the slow, steady tap, tap, tap of footsteps.

"How are you feeling, Mrs. Alexandre?" It was a woman's voice. A kind one. A nurse?

Lei pried her heavy eyelids up, squinting against the horridly bright light that was melting her retinas. Her gaze hopped from the woman's face to her arm—restricted and an IV tube taped to the inside of her elbow—to the bed's safety rail. She tried to talk, but no sound came out.

"You had a very close call," the nurse said as she fussed with the IV bag hanging at the head of the bed. "Your husband is going to be happy to hear you're conscious."

"Husband?" Lei repeated.

"He's been waiting to see you." The nurse gave her a pretty smile as she hung a fresh bag next to the empty one. "You're a lucky woman. He didn't leave your side, not until I finally insisted he get something to eat. He was this close to passing out." She indicated a fraction of an inch with her finger and thumb. "He'll be back in a moment."

A knock sounded at the door, and a pair of men dressed in suits came into the room. She didn't recognize either one, but immediately she assumed they worked for Holloway. Like Holloway, their eyes had an eerie, almost inhuman darkness.

Her body was instantly coated in sweat again.

"Hello, Mrs. Alexandre," the taller of the pair said, stepping up to the bed. "How are you feeling?"

Like he cared. "I'm tired," she croaked.

"Yes, I'm sure you are." His smile was broad, but it was far from genuine. Like a crocodile's grin—all teeth, no feeling. "We will make this as quick as possible."

"Okay, Mrs. Alexandre, I'll be back in a little while," the nurse said as she headed toward the door.

Now she was alone.

Barely alive.

And staring into the eyes of monsters.

She watched the man warily as he pulled a chair up to her bed. Next, he poured some ice chips into a paper cup and scooped some into a plastic spoon, offering them to her.

"No thanks," she said.

"All right." He set the cup of ice chips on her tray and wheeled it into position so she could reach it herself. "Now you can help yourself."

"Where am I? What's going on?" she asked, her throat burning with each word. Why she was so hoarse, she didn't know for sure, but she could think of a possibility or two. The last she remembered, she'd been lying in the bed she'd shared with Malek. Her body had felt so heavy, as if it was made out of concrete. She felt herself suffocating. Everything going black.

"We have some concerns about your husband," he said, ignoring her questions.

"I don't know anything," she said.

"We need your help."

Shoot me now. "Agent . . . ?"

"Ewoldt."

"Agent Ewoldt, first, I don't know anything about anything. And second, I am almost certain my husband hates me after what happened. Really, I'm useless. You should have left me where I was."

"You're wrong. It's quite clear from his response to your suicide attempt that he still cares for you. Very much."

"Either way, I can't help you. There's nothing I can do."

"There is," he said, enunciating every word very carefully, "and we expect you to do it."

"Or else another girl will die?"

He didn't speak, but that didn't mean he didn't say anything. Oh no, his message came through loud and clear.

"Bastards." Tears gathered in her eyes. This was so unfair! They'd used her, made her lose everything that mattered, and then when she'd tried to end it all forever, they'd dragged her away from a peaceful end back into hell. What had she done to deserve this? What? "I've lost everything because of you and some stupid artifact. Everything. Maybe I don't care anymore."

He pulled out his phone. It was one of those big smartphones. Touch screen. He poked at it a few times, then set the phone on the tray in front of her.

She refused to look. She knew whatever he was about to

show her wasn't going to be pleasant. "I would strongly suggest you watch," Ewoldt said, his voice cool, his tone clipped. "It's not one of your whores."

She couldn't stop her gaze, it snapped to the phone.

She sucked in a breath. On the screen was Rin, strolling up to a pretty house in a country-like setting. Lei had seen that house before. It was the one they were staying in right now. The bastards had found her.

"She's looking very well," Agent Ewoldt said. "She has a certain *glow* about her. Wouldn't you agree?"

He knew Rin was pregnant.

"Is there any low you assholes won't crawl to, to manipulate people into doing your dirty work?"

He tsked. "I believe you've jumped to some hasty conclusions."

"You know that's a lie. Hasty conclusions. What a joke." She forced a few mirthless guffaws out to illustrate her point. "Before I agree to anything, where are Kate and Heather?"

Ewoldt shrugged. "I assume at home."

"They're not dead?"

"Not that I'm aware of." He picked at a fingernail. "We decided to take our investigation in a new direction."

"Then who was the dead girl most recently found?"

"I don't believe she's been identified yet. We have no interest in that case, if you get my drift."

She got it, all right. The dead girl, if he was telling the truth, wasn't anyone she knew. "And speaking of murder, what about the murder charges?"

One brow rose slightly. "What murder charges?"

"Holloway told me I was being framed for Eve's murder."

"I believe the Ann Arbor PD has taken their investigation in a new direction as well."

That was a small relief. Kind of. She hoped that didn't mean someone else, someone innocent, wasn't being framed for the crime. "So, what do you want from me now?"

He leaned forward, his elbows on his knees. "We don't want anything from you, Mrs. Alexandre."

"Riiiight."

"We have your husband in custody. But we would be willing to bring him here to talk with you."

"And you're doing that out of the kindness of your hearts?"

"You could take it that way."

She rolled her eyes. "What do you want me to say?"

"I'm not going to tell you what to say. But if you would like to see him free, and your sister safe, all he needs to do is tell us where he has a certain item hidden."

"Ah, so you haven't been able to get him to talk?"

Ewoldt said nothing.

"Maybe that's because he doesn't know? Or maybe there's no such thing as whatever that stupid thing is called."

Whatever it was, they were pretty damn desperate to get their hands on it. Desperate enough to have innocent women killed. And if they would kill innocent women, what else might they do?

She glanced down at his phone again. The video of Rin was still playing. She was working in a garden now, on her knees. Sunlight flashed blue in her dark hair as she bent down to dig a hole in the earth.

If she didn't help them, Rin and the baby could die.

"What if he doesn't know anything about it?" she asked. "What if there's no such thing?"

"We have proof of its existence. And we have further proof that your husband and his brothers are in possession of it. But we've already searched their property in Ann Arbor, as well as the house out here. It isn't in either of them. None of the brothers has bank deposit boxes registered in their names. No commercial properties. No other real properties either."

That wasn't true, but she wasn't about to tell him that.

"I'm telling you, my husband has never said anything about a secret relic, about hiding something. I'm not convinced he knows anything about any such thing. He's a writer. His brother is a jewelry maker. And his other brother...? Well, I have no clue what Talen does. Maybe you need to ask him."

"We believe all three brothers know about it. We believe they are the entity that's known as the Black Gryffons."

"Black Gryffons? This whole thing seems too ridiculous. Like some silly game or movie."

Ewoldt hit the button on his phone, pausing the video. "Where do you think those people get their inspiration? Reality can be stranger than fiction."

"So I've heard," she mumbled, staring at the image of Rin. She seemed to be staring right at the camera, as if she knew she was being filmed.

"Can we count on you?" he asked, palming his phone.

"To do what?"

"Talk to him."

"I'll talk to him. But that's as far as it goes. I'm not lying anymore. And I'm not keeping secrets."

"Of course, you'll tell him we're watching?"

"Of course."

Ewoldt stood and put his phone to his ear. "Bring him in." He strolled toward the door, stopping before exiting. "I know you don't believe what I've told you, but our country's safety is in your hands, Mrs. Alexandre. Every man, woman, and child will benefit once we have the relic in our possession. But if we don't...and it falls into the wrong hands..." He shook his head. "Those films you saw of the nuclear fallout in the former USSR will look like Disney films." He left.

Lei's hands shook as she grabbed the cup of ice.

* * *

Malek's heart thumped hard against his breastbone as he fought to take in a deep breath. He knew what the bastards were up to, that they were making him see her, be near her, so he'd be more vulnerable. Dammit, the sons of bitches knew exactly how to manipulate him. And of course, they were making it out like they were doing him a huge favor by letting him visit her. Like it was some extraordinary kindness. A goodwill gesture.

Standing outside her room, waiting for Holloway to remove his handcuffs, Malek struggled to think of what he'd say to her, how he would warn her what would be coming next without them knowing. She'd tried to kill herself once. Clearly, she didn't care if she lived or died. But that didn't mean she was ready to face what those heartless bastards would do to her when he refused to cooperate. He couldn't imagine watching her be tortured.

Holloway jerked his head toward the door. "Have a nice visit." He sneered and gave Malek a little shove.

Malek sucked in a breath—which hurt like a sonofabitch—let it out, and opened the door.

She was lying in a hospital bed, looking small and defenseless and vulnerable. Her head rolled to the side. A soft smile pulled at her lips. "Malek." Her face was pale. Her hand shook as it lifted, fingers curling around the metal and plastic safety rail.

His gut did several somersaults. "Lei. Oh, dammit."

She blinked several times, and with each blink, her eyes became redder. "Malek, I . . . I don't know what to say."

"No, don't." He hurried to her bedside, took her little hand in his, and brought it to his mouth. He brushed his lips over the back, then, unable to stop himself, flattened it against his mouth and shut his eyes. He focused on the scent of her skin, the softness. How could he hold those sensations inside forever? So he would never forget how she smelled, how she tasted, how she felt? His eyes burned. His nose was running. He sniffled.

Damn those fucking bastards. Damn them to hell. They were destroying so many lives by their greed. Why couldn't they see that? Why wouldn't they believe the truth?

"I'm the one who should apologize," he whispered.

"Are you crazy?" she asked. "I lied to you."

"About what?" He met her gaze. "About loving me? Did you lie about that?"

"No, not that."

"You love me." He released her hand, but only long enough to pull a chair up to the side of her bed; then he took her hand again.

"I do." She blinked twice and a tear seeped from the corner of her eye. "That's why I... that's why I didn't want to live anymore. I thought I'd lost you forever."

"No, you haven't lost me."

"But you looked so angry, so hurt."

"I was confused. You tried to tell me what happened, but I didn't understand."

She pulled a tissue from the box on her bedside tray and dabbed at her bloodshot, watery eyes. "It wasn't so much that I told you untruths, more I deceived by omission. There are so many things I didn't tell you."

"Why?"

"Because I was afraid. Because I believed Holloway's threats. Because I was worried you would get hurt. Or worse. But everything I feared has already happened. There's no reason to keep secrets anymore." She sucked in a deep breath. Exhaled. "Those women, the ones who died recently, were murdered. By people I thought I could trust. And they were killed because I wouldn't do certain things."

"What things?" he asked, feeling his grip on her hand

tighten. His heart began thumping heavily in his chest as anxiety crept through his body, spreading like a disease.

"They wanted me to do whatever it took to gain your trust, including sleep with you. But I refused."

"Why did they want you to do that?"

"I guess they thought you'd tell me about... about some secret relic they think you're keeping."

"A secret relic?" he echoed. The pieces were all falling into place, and the picture was crystal clear. Somehow Lei had become tangled up with the Chimera. How? How had they found her? "So all those excuses, about not wanting to marry me and about not being able to be touched, they were lies? You were saying those things because you didn't want to help them?"

"To a small degree, I guess. I didn't want to help them. For one thing, they never convinced me that you and your brothers were hiding something. And secondly, I hated what they were doing to blackmail me. They killed innocent women and have threatened to do the same to two more. But as far as my personal issues go, they aren't an act. I do have problems. Maybe the guilt made my problems worse."

"I see now."

"I didn't want to become your wife just because it would allow me to search your home undetected. Or access your bank safe deposit boxes and other personal possessions." She dragged her hand under her eyes, smudging the tears streaking from the corners. "I didn't want our marriage to be a lie. And then, when they took you, I knew they'd use me to get to you. Even though I fought it, they still got what they wanted. Now I'm a tool for them, and a vulnerability for you. Before they had the chance to do anything, I did what I thought was best. I... I..." She sobbed. "I'm sorry I failed. Now they're using me to blackmail you. Aren't they?"

He nodded.

Her gaze dropped to their hands, hers cradled in his. "Is there really a secret relic?"

"I couldn't tell you if there was."

Her gaze jerked toward the right-hand corner of the ceiling. Then she leaned in closer and whispered, "What is this thing? Why can't you just give it to them?"

"I can't."

Her face paled. Her eyes widened ever so slightly. "Even if it means you'll die?"

"I've always known I would die eventually. Everyone dies."

"There really is a secret thing, then? A relic or something? You are hiding something?"

He looked into her wide eyes and tried to force the lie past his lips, but he couldn't. She'd just confessed to dozens of lies and deceptions. She'd just laid the truth out, the whole ugly mess. She had finally proved her trust. He couldn't keep this secret from her. Not while telling her he loved her, trusted her.

No, he had to tell her.

The Chimera were listening in, watching, hoping he'd give them some kernel of information that would lead them to it. He scooted over so his back was facing the camera. Before he spoke, he scanned the room for others. "It's real."

"The CIA is looking for it. Central Intelligence. They've gone to a lot of trouble trying to get it. Why? Is it dangerous?"

"In the wrong hands, maybe."

Lei didn't speak for a long while. Finally, a little louder, she said, "They're going to kill Rin next—and the baby—if they don't get what they want."

Her words hit Malek like a kick in the groin. He'd hoped, prayed that Rin and Drako were still safe, being so far away. How had the fuckers found them? "Are you sure they know where she is?"

Her eyes reddened even more. "I saw a live video feed. They're watching her every move."

"Fuck." He shoved his fingers through his hair. This was a no-win situation. Either Rin, his brothers, and Lei would all die now, or they'd die soon after. Along with millions of other people as all the ancient prophesies came true.

The end took on different names and faces. The horsemen of the apocalypse. The Mayan end of the World Age. But all the stories stemmed from one truth. And that truth was what he and his family had been protecting humanity from for millennia, since the Great Flood.

There was no way he could let The Secret fall into Chimera's hands. He had to protect it. At all costs.

She whispered, "What would happen if you gave it to them, Malek? Wouldn't it be better if you just handed it over? At least you'd all be safe. And my sister, too. The baby."

"Lei, I love you. With every cell in my body. And it will be your face that I will focus on when I take my last breath."

She gasped. She choked. "You're . . . there must be something? My sister. The baby."

"No, Lei. There's nothing I can do."

She blinked once, twice, clapped her hands over her face and sobbed. The sound cut straight through him, each ragged breath sawing at his insides. It was excruciating to hear. He gathered her into his arms and stroked her hair, wishing he could protect her, comfort her.

If only there was something he could do.

If only some magical powers would come to him, like they had Drako. Since that day, not so long ago, he and his brothers had wondered how Drako had suddenly gained magical power after he'd married Rin. Where had the fire come from? And would he and Talen possess it, too, once they were married?

Lei shoved him. Beat on his chest. Screamed every curse word known to man. And he took every blow, knowing he deserved all that pain and so much more. He'd dragged her into this. He should have refused to marry and accepted the consequences. If he'd done that, she wouldn't be here now, about to die, and knowing her sister would soon die, too. She was hurt and confused and angry, and he could have spared her all of it. He'd gained her trust. And look what had come of it.

"I hate you!" she screamed, her words broken by sobs and hiccups. "I hate you, Ihateyou." As if all her strength had been drained from her body, she slumped forward.

The door swung open. Holloway strolled in and hauled Malek to his feet. "Time to go." As they moved toward the door, two more men entered. They brushed past, making long strides toward Lei's bed.

Holloway jerked him around to face her. "They won't make this pleasant."

Lei's gaze snapped to his. "Malek, what's happening?" The look of utter panic made his insides go instantly ice cold.

"I love you, Lei. Dammit." His nose burned. He blinked, but his vision was blurred. He couldn't tear his gaze away. Not when the men dragged her off the bed. Not when they struck her with their fists. Not when she screamed in pain and fought for her life.

"You can end this right now," Holloway said in his ear. "Save your wife. I know it's what you want to do. It's in your blood. Save her."

"I am."

One man threw her on the bed and ripped her hospital gown down the middle. Malek knew what was coming next. His fingers curled into tight fists. Every muscle in his body tensed. Moving swiftly, he threw a punch at Holloway, but he was anticipating it. Holloway dodged the blow and slammed Malek back against the closed door. Fists flew. A few brain-rattling blows were exchanged. Malek gave as well as he got, but within seconds, he was on the floor, pinned down by three men. Breathless. In pain. And wishing it could just be over.

"Fucking do it," he said, intentionally taunting them. "Kill me now. I'm not giving you what you want."

One of them blasted him in the groin and his vision went black. While he was blinking and fighting to drag in a breath, he heard Holloway say, "Dammit, Ewoldt. Hold off. I want him to see."

Malek heaved a few times before his lungs finally filled with air. Seconds later, he was pulled upright. His legs were soft, couldn't hold his weight. Holloway supported him on one side, another guy on the other.

"Okay, now," Holloway said.

The asshole who was about to rape Lei sneered and shoved her beautiful legs apart. She wasn't fighting anymore. From his position, he could see her eyes were open. She seemed to be staring straight up, at the ceiling. He guessed she was in shock.

She rolled her head to the side, and mouthed, "I love you." Then she closed her eyes. A single tear leaked from the outer corner of her eye and dribbled down over silken skin.

"I'm gonna fuck every hole in this whore," the bastard said as he jerked his zipper down. His cock sprang out, hard, ready. "Aren't I lucky? I get to be the last to fuck this little cunt. It's mine."

"You might fuck me," Lei said, her voice low, barely above a whisper, "but I will never be yours. I belong to Malek. I trust only Malek."

Something inside Malek snapped. Wild rage ripped through him, exploding through his body like a nuclear blast. A surge of electricity charged through his system. He lifted his arms, throwing them backward, and both men who'd been holding him slammed through the wall. Hopped up on adrenaline, he ran full speed at the bastard who was about to rape his wife, grabbed him by the shoulder, and shoved him; the guy sailed through the air, his body hurtling across the room like a ragdoll. Malek scooped his wife and a blanket into his arms and ran toward the door. One kick and it was open and he was in the white-walled hallway. The sound of alarms blared, and security guards stormed at him from every direction, but he charged forward like a raging rhino, barreling through them, through doors, through a wall.

And next thing he knew, they were outside. A blistering cold wind knifed through his clothes, and Lei shivered.

He ran.

His wife was safe.

Nothing else mattered.

24

Lei wasn't sure what had just happened. She could have sworn Malek had just tossed three grown men around like toys, kicked his way past at least six more, slammed through several locked *metal* doors and one wall, and was now running faster than a man should be able to, all while holding her so gently she felt as if she were wrapped in a cocoon.

What the hell?

It was dark outside. Bitterly cold. Nighttime. That was actually a good thing. At least it was dark outside.

They just ran past a Suburban. The truck was moving at a good clip. Maybe thirty-five miles per hour. No human being could run that fast.

She glanced down at the ground. It was whizzing past so fast it made her dizzy.

"Malek, what's happening?" she asked.

"I'm getting you to safety." He didn't even sound breathless. How could that be? "You need to be safe. Safe," he repeated, over and over. "Safe."

Adjusting her position, she looked over his shoulder. "I don't see anyone following. I think you can slow down."

"No, not yet." He picked up speed, zooming down a quiet residential street, zigging and zagging between parked cars. "Need to get you somewhere warm."

"Where will we go?"

"Don't know."

In the distance, a police siren shrieked. Malek stopped. Frozen in place. "Fuck."

"Do you think they're looking for us?"

"I don't know. Could be. I'm not taking any chances." His gaze swept up and down her body. "You're hurt."

"I'm okay. Bruised. Sore. But okay. What about you?"

"I'm fine." Turning down another residential street, he started running again, but at a slower pace. "Rest, Lei. You're safe now."

"Are you serious?" She chuckled. "You're carrying me down the street. We just broke out of some... I don't know what kind of place that was. We're being hunted. We have nowhere to go. And my sister is their next target."

"Yeah, I see your point." He halted next to a parked car and glanced at it.

"What are you doing?" she whispered, her eyes darting from one shadow to another. She half expected a CIA agent, or whatever they were, to jump out at them at any second.

"Can you stand?" He was staring at the car.

"I think so. But—"

"You need to rest," he said as he set her on her feet. He supported her until she was steady, then pulled open the car's door. "It's unlocked. No alarm."

"Yeah, but—"

"Get in." He motioned to the passenger's side.

She ran-walked around the car on legs that felt like wet noodles. By the time she'd dived inside, Malek had the engine started. She was still buckling her seat belt as he was pulling the car away from the curb.

"Better?" he asked.

"You stole a car. Isn't that a good way to attract attention to ourselves?"

"We'll ditch it as soon as possible. I need to get more miles between us and them. If that's possible."

"What does that mean, 'if that's possible'?"

"It means..." He shook his head. "Nothing. Rest, Lei. Close your eyes and get some sleep."

"No." She shot him some mean-eyes. "You need to stop keeping secrets and come clean if we're going to have any hope of saving our asses... and the rest of our family."

Malek angled a look her way. "I like this feisty side of you."

"I'm sorry, Malek, but I'm pissed. If you'd been upfront with me, explained all this secret shit, and warned me, I might've done things differently. For one thing, I would have warned those girls right away."

His expression softened. "You're right. But I wasn't sure what you felt about me, whether I could trust you."

"I can see your point. What a mess. What a fucking mess. Ironically, if I hadn't done what I did for those girls, Holloway wouldn't have had anything to hold over my head—"

"Don't blame yourself. I love you for what you tried to do for those girls. And I know those fuckers will burn in hell for what they've done. You're right. If I was going to put you in danger the way I have, I should have told you what you could be facing once I knew you really did love me. But I was trying to protect you, to shelter you."

"And that was sweet."

"Stupid."

"So, are we turning a new leaf? Making a fresh start?"

At a light, Malek glanced at her, smiling. "This is one hell of a time for this, but what the hell?"

Lei offered a hand. "I'm Lei. Former sex slave with enough baggage to fill a jumbo jet, a sister I love more than life, and a checkered past that makes Mata Hari look like an angel. While I was working as a high-priced whore, I worked out a deal with a man who said he was a CIA agent to get some girls rescued from the business. And now he's forcing me to help him. He wants me to fuck you and find out where you and your brothers are hiding some supposedly secret weapon of mass destruction."

Malek took her hand in his. "And I'm Malek, second of three members of a secret order called the Black Gryffons. My brothers and I protect something called The Secret, which, in reality, is an ancient non-exhaustible energy source. We have been hunted by members of another group, called the Chimera. They have been trying to steal The Secret from us and our family for millennia. We have vowed to die if necessary to protect The Secret. But in the meantime, our duty is to marry and produce the next generation of Black Gryffons. Sons who will carry on our work."

"That's one hell of a story you have there, Malek." She couldn't help smiling as she shook his hand. It was great having the truth out there. No more secrets. "But I wonder, how did Holloway know about my connection to you? He was working with me weeks before Rin married Drako."

"I'm guessing he didn't. The Chimera dug into your past, linked him to you, and is paying him to help them."

"I guess that makes sense. But what are we going to do about your brothers, my sister, and the first member of the next generation of Black Gryffons?"

"I have no clue."

"Well... okay." As the car rolled by a Starbucks, she said, "Then it's time to get some chocolate and caffeine. Those always help me get the neurons firing. And we need to find a phone, to call Rin and Drako. Please tell me you have some cash on you . . . ”

“Yes, cash and a phone. That’s a good place to start. I can handle that.”

Twenty minutes later, their stolen car was idling outside of a coffee shop. Lei was staring into the bottom of an empty paper cup. Her stomach was full. Her head had cleared somewhat. And they had the start of a plan. It seemed, to her relief, the Alexandre brothers did plan ahead for certain situations. In this case, that planning meant they could access a pretty sizable sum of cash and a secured cell phone by paying a trip to a fitness center not far from the coffee shop. Hoping there hadn’t been a “breaking story” on the news, with their photographs plastered all over the TV, they took the risk of being recognized and went to the gym, one of the smaller ones that catered to serious weight-lifter types.

After parking outside the fitness center, Malek kissed her, told her not to leave the car—not a problem, since she was still dressed in a hospital gown—and hurried inside. Lei didn’t breathe, not one single inhalation, until he had returned. He was carrying a gym bag and was smiling.

As he tossed the bag into the backseat, she glanced over at him. “Got it?”

“We’re good. There’s not a huge sum here, fifty-thousand. But that’ll get us where we need to go. I called Drako. No answer, so I left a message. Don’t worry. I’m sure they’re okay.”

“Don’t worry? I can’t believe you just said that. I won’t stop worrying until I talk to Rin.”

“Then I’ll have to make sure you do. Soon. Oh, I also have new driver’s licenses and passports for *both* of us. We’ll be joining them soon.”

“Oh, really? Passports for both of us?” This surprised her.

Not that his new identity had; he'd mentioned a move and name change. But at the time he'd told her about that, she hadn't been part of the plan.

"Before you ask, no, I wasn't expecting you to marry me. But I was hoping. And I'd planned accordingly." He pulled the car out of the parking spot, turning it toward the road. "As it turned out, that was a good thing."

"I guess so. Um, what's my name?"

"Bai." He stopped the car, looking left and right for a break in traffic.

"Bai," she echoed. "Bai."

He pulled the vehicle out into traffic, hitting the gas to accelerate. "Do you like it? I chose it for you. It means—"

"Pure," she finished, a tear trickling from her eye. She wiped it away with the pad of her thumb.

"Yes, pure." His gaze flicked to the rearview mirror. His expression changed.

"Is something wrong?" she asked.

"No, but we need to dump this car and get something else."

"A rental?"

"That's risky."

"Oh, yes. Credit card."

"No, that's not a problem. I have one in my alias. But we should change our appearance before doing something like renting a vehicle. Too much paperwork involved. It would be too easy to track us down if our aliases are blown."

"Got it. So, what's next?"

"We're going to dump this car as soon as we can and find somewhere quiet to hole up for a little while. Just until I can make some changes."

"And then?"

"Then I go back. To get Talen."

"Talen? They have him, too?" Lei's stomach surged up her throat. "They'll catch you."

"They might." Pulling off the freeway, he glanced in his rearview mirror again. "Drako wouldn't agree with me, but I think it's better all three of us die, rather than only one or two. If one survives, he becomes an easier target. He'll have no one to back him up. To help protect The Secret. If we're all gone, The Secret should remain safe. At least for a while. It's well hidden."

With every word she heard, Lei's insides knotted more. She was very likely going to lose Malek. Soon. Much too soon. "Are you sure, Malek? Wouldn't it be better if one of you remained?"

"No, it should be three or none."

Her nose began burning, and another deluge of tears threatened to bust free. Here she'd just started to feel like they might be safe, that they might have a future together. Though she suspected it would be nothing like she'd ever guessed. But now... as Malek pulled down a rural road, she told herself she might be counting their time together in minutes. Not hours. Not days. Not years.

"I saw a hotel a ways back," he said. "We'll dump the car out here somewhere and cut across the fields."

"Okay."

Malek turned the car down a rutted dirt road that cut through a thick forested area. They bounced and skidded along at less than five miles an hour for a while. Finally, he turned off the road, driving through a clearing that was just barely wide enough for the car to pass. It took some real skill to maneuver between trees, but Malek managed to drive a decent distance from the road before giving up and cutting off the engine.

He swiveled to look at her, cupped her cheek, and said, "I love you, Lei. And if you'll let me, I want to take the next couple of hours to show you."

She placed her hand over his, leaned in, and kissed him.

The kiss started out gentle—lips meeting, grazing against

each other—but with each second that passed, her heartbeat sped up a little more, and her temperature inched a smidgen higher. When his tongue traced the seam of her mouth, a wave of need rippled through her. Her lips parted and a moan slipped up her throat, echoing in their joined mouths.

Their tongues stabbed and stroked, their hands explored, grasping, clawing. Not once did even a flicker of anxiety creep through Lei's body. Only sweet, glorious wanting. Desire. Hunger.

Malek broke the kiss and stared into her eyes. "I don't want it to happen like this. Come on." He unlocked the door and ducked out of the car. While she exited, he grabbed the bag from the backseat, then checked the trunk. "You're freezing."

Lei's teeth chattered as a bitter cold wind cut through the flimsy hospital blanket and torn paper-thin gown. "It's a little chilly," she said.

Finding nothing, he slammed the trunk closed and hauled her into his arms.

She sank into his embrace, grateful for the ample heat coming off his body. And when he started running, this time at a more human pace, she looped one arm around his neck to hold on. She felt so safe, protected, cherished in Malek's arms, and her heart ached at the thought that after tonight, she might never feel that way again. She snuggled in, closing her eyes, and drew in his scent, committing it to memory.

Before she knew it, he was setting her on her feet outside of a hotel, behind a large garbage Dumpster. "You'll draw attention if you go inside like this. I'll check in and come and get you."

"Okay." Now missing his warmth, she wrapped her arms around herself in a failing attempt at shielding herself from the wind and dropped into a squat. Malek's footsteps crunched on the frozen ice that had collected on the parking lot. Eventually, the sound faded away, and she was alone in the dark, counting every second, anxious for Malek to return to her. And, once again, breathless with fear.

When she heard footsteps approaching, she peered out from her hiding place.

A man, wearing some kind of coverall, was walking toward her. She immediately jerked back, hiding behind the Dumpster.

"Miss?" the man said, footsteps approaching faster.

She stood in place, frozen by indecision. Run and risk Malek coming back and not finding her? Stay put and hope he would be back before the man called for help?

As the stranger turned the corner, she stepped into the deepest shadow, which put her at a complete disadvantage. She was wedged between the huge metal garbage container and a brick wall. There was nowhere to go.

"Are you all right?" the man asked, halting a few feet in front of her. His gaze jerked up and down her body, taking in her nearly nude form, bare legs, feet and arms. "Where did you come from?"

"I'm fine," she said, knowing he wouldn't believe her. Who would? "I know it looks weird, me standing out here in the cold," she said, her teeth chattering nonstop, "but there really is an explanation."

The man's eyes narrowed. "Such as?"

"I was"—she glanced around, then pointed at the closest vehicle, which happened to be a minivan—"cleaning out our van, throwing away some trash. Fast-food wrappers. And getting our luggage. My husband went inside to check in." Not in one million years did she think he'd buy that lie. But she had no other choice.

The man's eyes narrowed even more. He opened his mouth to say something; then his face went blank and he sank to the ground.

Lei sucked in a horrified gasp, clapped a hand over her mouth, and slammed her back against the wall. And then she saw Malek hefting the man over his shoulder.

"What does he know?" Malek asked her.

"N-nothing."

"You're sure?"

She swallowed a lump the size of a Hummer and nodded.

"Okay." He set the man down next to the Dumpster and grabbed Lei's hand. "I'd rather play it safe, not take any chances. If he sees a picture of you on the eleven o'clock news tonight, he might remember you."

She glanced over her shoulder. "Are you saying you want to . . . ?"

"I won't do it. Let's go. Before someone else sees us." He hurried her toward a set of stairs that angled up to the second floor. Like most motels, this one had open outdoor hallways with the room doors opening directly outside. That part was convenient. No need for her to traipse through a hotel lobby.

Their room was dark and warm. Malek shepherded her toward the bathroom for a hot shower, promising to be back within a half hour. After making her promise at least a dozen times that she wouldn't open the door for anyone but him, he kissed her until she saw stars, stuffed some of the money from the gym bag into his pocket, and left.

As Lei latched the security chain on the door, she prayed her sister was safe and her husband would return to her. And she would have at least an hour or two to show him exactly how much he meant to her.

25

The second Malek entered the room, arms loaded with Walmart bags, Lei hurled herself at him.

She kissed his face. His cheeks. His eyes. "Thank God you're back," she repeated over and over and over, legs wrapped around his waist.

He chuckled. "Now this is the kind of greeting I like." Wrapping one arm around Lei's waist, he turned, pinning her between the wall and his big, hulky body. "I guess I don't have to ask if you missed me."

"I did. I really did." She planted a kiss on his lips and he growled. She liked the sound of that growl—low and deep and sexy.

"Wife, if you don't stop that, our food is going to get cold."

"To hell with the food." She bit his neck. "We don't have a lot of time. I want to make every minute count."

"We'll have plenty of time." He cupped her chin and looked deeply into her eyes. "Don't you worry about that."

She wanted to believe him. Absolutely. But there was no guarantee. There never was. And with all the death and danger she'd seen lately, she was even more appreciative of that fact. "Have you heard from Drako? Is Rin safe?"

"I did, and she is. For now."

She was so relieved to hear that. Even the thought of losing Rin made her insides twist. Now she was free to concentrate on Malek, on making every precious minute with him count. She rocked her hips forward, grinding her bare pussy into him. "Make love to me, Malek."

His arms slid down and cupped her ass. "Hmmm. That's a mighty tempting offer."

"That's no offer." Knowing he was playing, she grabbed two fistfuls of hair and pulled until their mouths were a fraction of an inch apart. "It's a demand."

"There's only one dom in this family, baby. And it isn't you."

A zing of heat buzzed through her body at his words. "Is that so?"

"It is so." Another wave blasted through her when he crushed her mouth with his and showed her exactly who was boss.

His kiss was not soft. It was hard. A possession. A domination. And she shuddered and quaked in his arms as wave upon wave of desperate wanting washed over her.

God help her, he was right. Being dominated by this man thrilled her. More. She wanted more.

Seeming to read her mind, he caught her wrists in one big fist and pinned them behind her back. He carried her to the bed and gently laid her on her back, angling over her. "I'm going to spend the rest of my life showing you the pleasures of submitting."

She looped her arms around his neck. "That's one promise you'd better keep."

Again, he kissed her, but this time his lips weren't as hard. And while they sent her to oblivion, his hands did wonderful things to her breasts. He kneaded and stroked and pinched and caressed. And with every touch, every stab of his tongue, her body burned hotter, her pussy wetter.

Whimpering, she pulled on his neck, coaxing him to settle over her. She longed to be held in his arms, to feel his weight on her.

But he broke the kiss.

"Malek?" she asked.

His lips curled into a half smile. "I'm still wearing my clothes." He gave her a do-something-about-it look.

She was all too happy to help him. She knelt on the bed, grabbed his shirt, and yanked it over his head. Then, just because he was so gorgeous and right there, she licked and nibbled and kissed her way down the bumpy terrain of his shoulders, chest, and stomach. The man had the most beautifully sculpted body this side of heaven. Even with the scar slicing down the center of his abdomen.

The scar.

She trailed her finger down the healed wound. "Malek, it looks completely healed. How could that be?"

"I don't know."

"I'm glad." She kissed the freshly healed skin. "How strange. I didn't even think about it when we were running. Do you think they did something to make it heal?" Next, she unbuttoned his pants and pulled them down. His snug boxer-briefs were last; then he was standing before her nude. A picture of pure masculinity. Of latent power. "You're beautiful."

"I'm not beautiful. And I'm not cute." He bent over her, crowding her and forcing her to lean back. "I'm dangerous. I'm sexy. I'm your master."

By the time he'd said that last word, she was lying flat on her back, legs dangling over the edge of the bed, and he was on all fours, looking hungry and hard and ready. He wedged a knee between her thighs and pushed, easing them apart.

Her heart rate kicked into double time.

She reached for him, but he caught her wrists in one hand and once again lifted them up over her head.

He said, "I'm in control. Me. You touch me only when I say."

A raging inferno shot through her body, and she sucked in a huge lungful of air. What a wicked thrill, to have this gorgeous, dangerous man taking command of her body. The sound of that sharp edge in his voice made her blood burn. The feral look in his eyes made her nerves tingle. And the way his mouth possessed hers when he kissed her made every cell in her body vibrate.

When he broke the kiss and looked into her eyes, she whispered, "Malek, I want to have your baby. I need to have your baby. That way . . . if . . . if . . . I'll have a piece of you. One tiny, perfect, sweet piece."

"Lei . . ."

"It's the right time. I've prayed for a miracle."

He entered her slowly, and she shuddered at the excruciating pleasure. How perfectly he filled her. His cock stretching her pussy, grazing that secret spot inside as it gradually withdrew, then pushed back inside.

Lying on her back, she skimmed her hands up and down his smooth back and nibbled on the thick muscle of his shoulder. He murmured sweet words in her ear as he rocked his hips back and forth, back and forth. Her body fell into pace with his, her stomach clenching, tipping her pelvis up so she could take him as deeply as possible.

Their bodies moved as one. They inhaled at the same time, exhaled. They both were stroking, kissing, nipping, pushing each other toward that glorious crest. It was lovemaking. Sweet, pure lovemaking. A testament to their love. Their commitment. Communication on a level that could not be understood, could only be experienced.

Lei's blood pounded through her body, and with each heartbeat, the heat swirling deep inside increased. Her muscles tightened. Her fingers. Her feet. She clawed at Malek's smooth back and begged, "More. More!"

Sensations battered her, the scent of Malek's skin blending with the perfume of their pleasure. The sound of Malek's heavy breaths and her soft moans and whimpers. The taste of him on her lips as her tongue swept across them. The feel of his hard, strong body possessing hers. His heat soaking into her. His desire pulsing along her nerves.

Malek's thrusts turned hard, fast, as together they rocketed toward orgasm. He kissed her, his tongue sweeping inside, filling her mouth with his decadent flavor. A huge surge of erotic heat blasted through her and she tumbled over the edge. She moaned into their joined mouths, the sound echoing in her head, blending with Malek's as he growled. He withdrew his cock and plunged one last time, and her pussy filled with his cum. They kissed through all the quakes and tremors of their orgasms. And they didn't stop until they were both breathless and dizzy and spent.

Remaining inside her, Malek eased onto his side, taking her with him. He laid a thigh across her hip. "I love you," he said, over and over.

"I love you, too."

His stomach rumbled, and he laughed. How she adored that sound! "Now, I've got to eat." He rubbed his flat stomach. "You're going to wear me out."

"Well, at least you'll always be smiling." She wrapped her arms around him, refusing to let him go. A tiny pang of fear hit her at the thought that soon he'd be walking out that door, and she had no idea if he'd come back.

"You bet I will." He gently disentangled himself from her. "Just as soon as I take care of this one last thing, we'll be ready to start our new life. Husband and wife. In a new city. New home. A fresh start."

"That sounds wonderful." Smiling, she ran her hand over her belly as she watched her husband get dressed, wondering if maybe that fresh start might involve a new life, a child.

After stuffing a sandwich down his throat, Malek kissed her, promised he'd be back as soon as he could, told her he loved her, and handed her the cell phone. "So you can stop worrying." He left.

"Malek Alexandre is on the property."

Holloway glanced at monitor one, then smiled. "Good. Is Talen ready?"

"Yes."

"Excellent."

"Are you sure this is the right way to go?" Ewoldt asked, shifting his gaze to monitor two as they followed Malek's progress. "We could have them both in custody. That's two out of three. And we know where the third one is, too."

"No, it's obvious they aren't going to tell us where the weapon is. We're going to have to let them lead us to it."

"We could *question* them some more." Ewoldt weighted the word *question,* indicating the form of questioning he'd like to take.

Holloway shook his head. "We've already water boarded Talen and gotten nowhere. We've threatened the wife. And a pregnant woman. They aren't going to talk."

"Tight-lipped bastards," Ewoldt grumbled.

"If they were on our side, I'd respect them for it."

"Their story's pretty convincing—that using the weapon would be dangerous. Clearly, they believe it."

"That's because that's what they've been taught their whole lives. How could a non-exhaustible power source be dangerous? It would shift the world's economy, putting the U.S. in control of the world's power supply. But that would be a good thing, since right now it lies in the Middle East and so much of that territory is a political and military hotbed. From what I've read, it's a clean power source, too. No more carbon emissions. I see no downside to it. None whatsoever."

"Maybe they know something about it we don't. Why else would they hide it?" Ewoldt asked as they turned their attention to monitor three.

"I don't know."

"I mean, if they used it to generate power and then sold that power back to the power company, wouldn't they stand to gain a hell of a lot?"

Holloway shrugged. "Sure."

"So... why haven't they done it?"

"Again, they've been brainwashed into believing it'll destroy the world." Holloway rolled his eyes, then turned his focus on monitor four. He'd told his men before Alexandre was spotted to prepare for him, to put on a show of trying to capture him, but to allow him to rescue his brother and escape. So far, things were going exactly as he'd planned. Two men down. Not too horrible a loss. He figured he'd lose maybe ten more by the time the brothers were off the compound. "Come to think of it, I wonder if the Alexandre brothers haven't found a way to harness some of the weapon's power already. Did you see what that bastard did when he broke out?"

"Yeah, I thought maybe it was adrenaline."

"I've seen what a man can do when he's pumped up on adrenaline. What he did went way beyond that," Holloway said.

"Yeah, I saw the video of the oldest brother frying Oram to a crisp, too. I thought that was one hell of a trick. That maybe he was hiding some kind of flamethrower."

"Me too. But seeing what Malek did earlier... they're tapping into the weapon's power somehow. Another reason why we need to get our hands on it. Can you imagine what we could do with it militarily? Imagine if every soldier in our forces was as strong as that," Holloway said.

"Still, we're taking a risk by letting them go."

"A small one. Neither brother knows what we've done. Talen Alexandre will lead us right to it."

"I hope you're right."

Holloway cringed as two more men were thrown like fucking toys, their bones snapping as their bodies slammed into a wall. "I have to be right. Almost seven billion people are counting on it."

Not much farther.

Malek's senses were hyper-alert. It seemed the tiniest sound and the slightest scent were amplified a thousand times. His muscles were tight, ready. His heartbeat was racing. Already, he'd barreled through several doors, tossed a handful of men aside, and was following the scent of his brother as he stormed down the white-walled corridor.

He paused at the end of the hallway, turning his head left and right, trying to catch the scent. Just as he stepped to the left, something whizzed past his ear. A second one followed. In front of him, a hole instantly appeared in the wall. Then another.

Fuck! They're shooting at me.

Malek dove around the corner. But as he was flying through the air, something hard slammed into his shoulder. Pain exploded through his body, the world became a blur, and then his body hit something bigger, harder.

The floor.

Blinking, fighting to see, he scrambled to his feet, his arm held tight to his side.

Talen's scent was strong now.

"Talen!" he shouted.

"Malek?"

He kicked open the door on his right. Talen was lying on a bed, looking like hell. Malek hauled him up off the bed, and once Talen was standing, turned and faced three men, all of them with guns pointed at him.

Shitpissfuck.

Malek's heart jerked in his chest. He hadn't come this far to get caught now.

"Rin!" Lei couldn't help it. A sob of relief tore up her throat as her fingers constricted around the phone. "You're safe!"

"Yes, we're okay. Drako caught someone watching the house. That guy's history. And we've moved. It was horrifying, but we're both okay. He won't tell me. What's going on?"

"I don't know where to begin."

"Are you okay?"

"I'm safe. For now."

"What's that mean?"

"I..." She swallowed. Hard. "I tried to commit suicide."

"Why?" Rin shouted. "Lei, ohmygod."

"It's a long story. And you only know part of it. I don't want to hash it out now."

"Does it have anything to do with... you know?"

"In part."

Rin didn't speak for several seconds. "I wish you'd come to Spain."

"A small part of me wishes I had, too." Her hand skimmed over her flat stomach. "But another doesn't."

"Malek?"

"Malek." Lei could feel the smile pulling at her lips. "We were married."

"Oh, Lei! Are you okay?"

"I'm better than okay, though I don't know what's going to happen from this point on. He went back to where those men had been holding us all hostage.

Whoops.

"Hostage? What?"

"No need to panic. I'm okay. I swear. But Malek . . . he said he had to try to get Talen. I don't really want to think about what might be going on right now." Her voice trembled. She cleared her throat. "Some of the best moments of my life have been with that man since you left. If I'd gone with you . . ."

"I get it. You love him, don't you?"

"Yes, but . . ." Lei blinked and fought the wave of tears threatening to spill from her eyes. "Dammit, why couldn't he have just been a writer?"

"I know. It's hell having to live like this."

"Do you have any regrets?"

"No, Drako is my soul mate. He's the only man for me. I can't even imagine being married to anyone else."

"I feel the same way about Malek. I trust him. Only him. I doubt that'll ever change."

"Then we live with the rest and take each minute at a time."

"Yeah." Lei heard a low rumbling voice in the background.

Rin giggled. "I gotta go, Lei. But before I hang up, tell me you're okay, that you won't try hurting yourself again."

"I promise." Her hand stroked over her belly. As long as there was even the slightest chance she might be carrying Malek's child, she wouldn't even consider it.

"I don't believe you."

"I *promise,*" Lei repeated. "Malek risked his life to save me. I won't ever forget that. And I couldn't throw away what he's done for me. That's exactly what I'd be doing if I killed myself now."

"Then I thank God for Malek."

"So do I."

* * *

The minute the call ended, Lei was in hell. With nobody to talk to, time dragged. Minutes felt like hours. Hours like days. She fought through wave upon wave of panic. Despair followed. Then anger. And then she was back to panic again. She paced. She cried. She prayed. She promised. Still, she heard nothing from Malek.

Dawn came, and still Lei was alone. How long had he been gone? How many hours? Surely she'd have heard something from him by now, if he was okay.

A tiny voice in her head whispered something she wasn't ready to hear, and she grabbed the TV remote and powered up the TV. The room filled with the news anchor's voice, drowning out that irritating little voice that she hated.

She paced back and forth as the TV news reported on local traffic, weather. They reported a few school closings, then moved on to some local news. There was no mention of an arrest. No talk of a big CIA takedown. No word on Malek.

By ten, she was sitting on the bed, frozen by fear. He wasn't coming back. She could feel it in her gut. Something had gone wrong. He was gone.

She glanced at the bag of money. Fifty thousand wasn't much to start a new life with. Where would she go? How would she face even one day without her husband? One hour? One minute?

I can't.

You must.

What if he's gone?

She ran to the door and yanked it open. "Malek, where are you? I need you."

Her gaze scanned the parking lot. The field beyond. No Malek. "I need you!" She slammed the door. Her head was pounding. She felt sick. Exhausted. Petrified. She forced herself to cut off the TV and shut off all the lights. Then, all hope lost, she buried herself in the bedding, where she could at least catch the scent of him on the pillow, and closed her eyes.

She had just started to doze off when the door lock rattled. Instantly, she was awake. She scrambled from the bed and charged at the door. In her head, she screamed, *Let it be him! Let it be him!*

She reached the door at the exact same time as it swung open. Her gaze jerked up.

Malek.

He was alive.

A sob tore up her throat and she threw herself into his arms.

He scooped her up, cradling her in his arms. "Lei, it's okay..." He murmured soothing words to her as he carried her across the room. But she was so overwhelmed with relief, she didn't hear what he was saying. The voice in her head was too loud. *He's safe. Thank God, he's safe. Alive! Thankgodthankgod-thankgod.*

He sat on the edge of the bed, still holding her. He cupped her chin, lifting it. "Baby, do you hear me?"

"You're okay?" Feeling something wet, sticky on his arm, she looked at her hand. "You're bleeding?"

"I'm fine. It's just a small scratch."

Another sob cut off the next question sitting on the tip of her tongue.

"Everything's okay now," he said, smoothing her hair back from her face. "Do you hear me? We're going to be okay."

"Talen?"

"Safe."

"Are you hurt anywhere else?" She studied his face, what little of his body she could see.

"No, I'm okay."

She flung her arms around his neck again and squeezed as hard as she could. "I was so scared. It took you such a long time."

"I'm sorry, baby. I got back here as soon as I could. I wanted to make sure Talen was safe before I left him." He cupped her cheek. "It's all over now. I have a car, and we're all set to hit the road. After we get some rest." He stood up again, carried her around the end of the bed, and set her down once again. Then he stripped off his clothes and lay with her, pulling her into his arms.

She felt nothing but absolute joy and peace as she snuggled up to his warm, hard body. He had done exactly what he'd set out to do. He'd healed her broken soul and made her whole again. And now, as long as he was at her side, she knew her nightmares were over.

26

Beautiful.

Exquisite.

Thoroughly, utterly, intoxicatingly sexy.

As deadly as a cottonmouth.

And as fiercely protective and powerful as a lion.

That was her husband, summed up in twenty concise words.

Lei couldn't believe she was actually about to do this. Such a short time ago, it would have been impossible. She wouldn't have been able to even consider it. But slowly, gradually, Malek had helped her work through her fears. The walls around her heart had come tumbling down. And she was free at last.

Free to love.

Free to belong.

Free to submit.

Free to become Mrs. Malek Alexandre in all ways.

She smoothed her hand over her stomach and smiled at her reflection in the mirror. The start of a baby bump was just beginning to show. Their child was growing inside of her.

And that was just one of the changes that had happened lately.

To sum things up succinctly, everything was different.

The shadows in her eyes were gone. The scars had faded, and even though the memories of the dangers they had faced were still fresh, she wasn't afraid anymore. She had a new name. She had a new home.

But it went deeper than just a name and address. She was a new woman, a strong, intelligent, capable woman who knew what she wanted, what she needed, and was able to accept it. She could finally be the wife Malek deserved, and the mother their child would need.

Dressed in nothing but the flowing, translucent silk gown her husband had given her for Valentine's Day, she padded barefoot down the staircases to their private dungeon where he waited.

Outside the door, she took a final deep breath.

This was it. The time had come. She was ready to give him her most precious gift: her submission.

In she went.

The room was dimly lit, flickering candlelight creating just the right ambiance. The room smelled sweet, like vanilla and leather, and she couldn't help inhaling deeply, especially when a set of hungry male eyes settled on her.

Lei's gaze wandered up and down his body, taking in the full glory of his heavily muscled form. Just as he had been when she'd watched him at the public dungeon, he was wearing a black knit shirt and tailored trousers. And just like that day, he mesmerized her like no other man had ever done.

This man was not just any dom. He was *the dom*. Her master. Only hers. Always hers.

Primal heat sparked in Malek's gaze, igniting a fission of erotic need inside her. Heat blazed through her body in response. How she wanted to just throw herself into Malek's arms and beg him to take her! And yet, she couldn't. Not until she had submitted fully.

This was the first time. She'd waited so long for this moment. She couldn't let a little impatience ruin it.

Feeling the corners of her mouth lifting in a soft smile, she walked to the center of the room. Her gown fluttered about her as she moved, the gentle currents carrying the whisper-thin fabric fluttering around her legs.

She gave Malek one final look, took a few deep breaths, and bowed her head.

She was about to do the one thing she'd sworn she'd never be able to do. And she wasn't nervous or scared or hesitant at all.

She eased herself down onto her knees.

There.

At last.

She'd knelt before her master. Her husband.

Eyes closed, she felt at peace. Completely and utterly calm.

Malek stepped forward. "Lei, before we begin, I need to ask you one final time. Are you certain you're ready for this? Are you sure you can relinquish control to me? Can you trust me fully?"

"Yes, there's not a doubt in my mind. I trust you completely. I'm ready."

"Very good." He circled around her, making a full three-sixty. "You look more beautiful today than I've ever seen you."

"Thank you."

"No, thank you. For trusting me when it wasn't easy. For fighting so hard for us."

"I needed you as much as you did me." Breaking protocol, Lei lifted her gaze. She was glad she had. Their gazes tangled, and she was overwhelmed by the love she saw in Malek's eyes.

There could never have been any doubt that he loved her. He would protect her. He would cherish her. He would always think of her needs first, before his own.

A tear slipped from the corner of her eye. "Look at me, I'm getting emotional already."

Malek squatted down. His eyes were a little pink and watery, too. "You're not the only one," he whispered. He cupped her cheek. "My wife. Forever mine."

She laid her hand over his. "Forever yours." She pulled his hand from her face and kissed his palm. "I'm proud and eager to serve you. As master. As husband. I trust you with my body. My heart. My soul. My life."

He returned the favor, adding a line of soft kisses up her wrist. Instantly, little tingles of pleasure prickled her skin. "And I'm proud and eager to worship you, my wife, my soul mate." He set her hand in her lap and straightened up. "Now we begin a new journey together." Once again, he walked around her. But this time, he stopped directly behind her. Her back warmed, as if his gaze heated it.

She arched her spine and waited, breathless and excited and impatient.

What would he do next? What pleasures would her husband, her master, show her today? Tomorrow?

She couldn't wait to find out.

Turn the page
for a sizzling special excerpt
of Kate Pearce's

SIMPLY VORACIOUS

An Aphrodisia trade paperback
on sale now!

1

1826, London, England

"Are you all right, ma'am? May I help you?"

Lady Lucinda Haymore flinched as the tall soldier came toward her, his hand outstretched and his voice full of concern. She clutched the torn muslin of her bodice against her bosom, and wondered desperately how much he could see of her in the dark shadows of the garden.

"I'm fine, sir, please..." She struggled to force any more words out and stared blindly at the elaborate gold buttons of his dress uniform. "I'm afraid I slipped and fell on the steps and have ripped my gown."

He paused, and she realized that he had positioned his body to shield her from the bright lights of the house and the other guests at the ball.

"If you do not require my help, may I fetch someone for you, then?"

His question was softly spoken as if he feared she might flee.

"Could you find Miss Emily Ross for me?"

"Indeed I can. I have a slight acquaintance with her." He

hesitated. "But first, may I suggest you sit down? You look as if you might swoon."

Even as he spoke, the ground tilted alarmingly, and Lucinda started to sway. Before her knees gave way, the soldier caught her by the elbows and deftly maneuvered her backward to a stone bench framed by climbing roses. Even as she shrank from his direct gaze, she managed to get a fleeting impression of his face. His eyes were deep set and a very light gray, his cheekbones impossibly high, and his hair quite white, despite his apparent youth.

She could only pray he didn't recognize her. No unmarried lady should be loitering in the gardens without a chaperone. Somehow she doubted he was a gossip. He just didn't seem to be the type; all his concern was centered on her, rather than making a grand fuss and alerting others to her plight. He released her and moved back, as if he sensed his presence made her uneasy.

"I'll fetch Miss Ross for you."

"Thank you," Lucinda whispered, and he was gone, disappearing toward the lights of the ballroom and the sounds of the orchestra playing a waltz. She licked her lips and tasted her own blood, and the brutal sting of rejection. How could she have been so foolish as to believe Jeremy loved her? He'd hurt her and called her a tease. Had she encouraged him as he had claimed? Did she really deserve what he had done to her?

Panic engulfed her and she started to shiver. It became increasingly difficult to breathe and she struggled to pull in air. Suddenly the white-haired stranger was there again, crouched down in front of her. He took her clenched fist in his hand and slowly stroked her fingers. She noticed his accent was slightly foreign.

"It's all right. Miss Emily is coming. I took the liberty of hiring a hackney cab, which will be waiting for you at the bottom of the garden."

"Thank you."

"I'm glad I was able to be of service."

With that, he moved away, and Lucinda saw Emily behind him and reached blindly for her hand.

"I told my aunt I was coming home with you, and I told your mother the opposite, so I think we are safe to leave," Emily murmured.

"Good."

Emily's grip tightened. "Lucinda, what happened?"

She shook her head. "I can't accompany you home, Emily. Where else can we go?"

Emily frowned. "I'll take you to my stepmother's. You'll be safe there. Can you walk?"

"I'll have to." Lucinda struggled to her feet.

"Oh, my goodness, Lucinda," Emily whispered. "There is blood on your gown."

"I fell. Just help me leave this place." Lucinda grabbed hold of Emily's arm and started toward the bottom of the garden. She could only hope that Jeremy had returned to the ball and would not see how low he had brought her. She would never let him see that, *never*. With Emily's help, she managed to climb into the cab and leaned heavily against the side. Her whole body hurt; especially between her legs where he had...She pushed that thought away and forced her eyes open.

It seemed only a moment before Emily was opening the door of the cab and calling for someone named Ambrose to help her. Lucinda gasped as an unknown man carefully picked her up and carried her into the large mansion. Emily ran ahead, issuing instructions as she led the way up the stairs to a large, well-appointed bedchamber. The man gently deposited Lucinda on the bed and went to light some of the candles and the fire.

Lucinda curled up into a tight ball and closed her eyes, shutting out Emily and everything that had happened to her. It was impossible not to remember. She started to shake again.

A cool hand touched her forehead, and she reluctantly focused on her unknown visitor.

"I'm Helene, Emily's stepmother. Everyone else has left, including Emily. Will you let me help you?"

Lucinda stared into the beautiful face of Madame Helene Delornay, one of London's most notorious women, and saw only compassion and understanding in her clear blue eyes.

Helene smiled. "I know this is difficult for you, my dear, but I need to see how badly he hurt you."

"No one hurt me. I slipped on the steps and..."

Helene gently placed her finger over Lucinda's mouth. "You can tell everyone else whatever tale you want, but I know what has happened to you, and I want to help you."

"How do you know?" Lucinda whispered.

"Because it happened to me." Helene sat back. "Now, let's get you out of that gown and into bed."

She talked gently to Lucinda while she helped her remove her torn gown and undergarments, brought her warm water to wash with, and ignored the flow of tears Lucinda seemed unable to stop.

When she was finally tucked in under the covers, Helene sat next to her on the bed.

"Thank you," Lucinda whispered.

Helene took her hand. "It was the least I could do." She paused. "Now, do you want to tell me what happened?"

"All I know is that I am quite ruined."

"I'm not so sure about that."

Lucinda blinked. "I'm no longer a virgin. What man would have me now?"

"A man who loves you and understands that what happened was not your fault."

"But it was my fault. I went into the gardens with him *alone,* I let him *kiss* me, I *begged* him to kiss me."

"You also asked him to force himself on you?"

"*No,* I couldn't stop him, he was stronger than me and..."

"Exactly, so you can hardly take the blame for what happened, can you?" Helene patted her hand. "The fault is his. I assume he imagines you will be forced to marry him now."

Lucinda stared at Helene. "I didn't think of that." She swallowed hard. "He said we needed to keep our love secret because my family would never consider him good enough."

Helene snorted. "He sounds like a dyed-in-the-wool fortune hunter to me. What is his name?"

Lucinda pulled her hand away. "I can't tell you that. I don't want to have to see him ever again."

"Well, that is unfortunate, because I suspect he'll be trying to blackmail his way into marrying you fairly shortly."

Lucinda sat up. "But I wouldn't marry him if he was the last man on earth!"

"I'm glad to hear you say that." Helene hesitated. "But it might not be as easy to avoid his trap as you think. You might be carrying his child. Does that change your opinion as to the necessity of marrying him?"

Lucinda gulped as an even more nightmarish vision of her future unrolled before her. "Surely not?"

"I'm sorry, my dear, but sometimes it takes only a second for a man to impregnate a woman," Helene continued carefully.

"I will *not* marry him."

"Then let us pray that you have not conceived. The consequences for a woman who bears an illegitimate child are harsh." Helene's smile was forced. "I know from Emily that you are much loved by your parents. I'm sure they would do their best to conceal your condition and reintroduce you into society after the event."

Lucinda wrapped her arms around her knees and buried her

face in the covers. Her despair was now edged with anger. If she refused to marry her seducer, she alone would bear the disgust of society, while Jeremy wouldn't suffer at all. It simply wasn't fair.

Eventually she looked up at Madame Helene, who waited quietly beside her.

"Thank you for everything."

Helene shrugged. "I have done very little. I wish I could do more. If you would just tell me the name of this vile man, I could have him banned from good society in a trice."

"That is very kind of you, Madame, but I'd rather not add to the scandal. I doubt he would relinquish his position easily, and my name and my family's reputation would be damaged forever."

"And, as your father is now the Duke of Ashmolton, I understand you all too well, my dear." Helene stood up. "But, if you change your mind, please let me know. I have more influence than you might imagine."

"I'd prefer to deal with this myself." Lucinda took a deep, steadying breath. "I need to think about what I want to do."

Helene hesitated by the door. "Are you sure there isn't another nice young man who might marry you instead?"

Lucinda felt close to tears again. "How could I marry anyone without telling him the truth? And what kind of man would agree to take me on those terms?"

"A man who loves you," Helene said gently. "But you are right to take your time. Don't rush into anything unless you absolutely have no choice. In my experience, an unhappy marriage is a far more terrible prison than an illegitimate child."

Lucinda looked at Helene. "Emily told me you were a remarkable woman, and now I understand why. I'm so glad she brought me here tonight."

"Emily is a treasure," Helene replied. "I only tried to offer you what was not offered to me—a chance to realize that you were not at fault, and a place to rest before you have to make some difficult decisions. Now go to sleep. I will send Emily to you in the morning, and I promise I will not tell her anything."

Lucinda slid down between the sheets and closed her eyes. Sleep seemed impossible, but she found herself drifting off anyway. Would any of her partners have noticed that she hadn't turned up for her dances with them? Would Paul be worried about her? She swallowed down a sudden wash of panic. If anyone could understand her plight, surely it would be Paul....

Paul St. Clare prowled the edge of the ballroom, avoiding the bright smiles and come-hither looks of the latest crop of debutantes. Where on earth had Lucky gone? She was supposed to be dancing the waltz with him, and then he was taking her into supper. It was the only reason he was attending this benighted event after all.

Unfortunately, since the death of the sixth Duke of Ashmolton, speculation as to the new duke's potential successor had alighted on Paul, hence the sudden interest of the ladies of the *ton*. He'd grown up with the vague knowledge that he was in the line of succession, but hadn't paid his mother's fervent interest in the subject much heed until the other male heirs had started to die off in increasing numbers.

And now, here he was, the heir apparent to a dukedom he neither wanted nor felt fit to assume. It was always possible that the duke would produce another child, although unlikely, because of his wife's age. But Paul knew that even beloved wives died, and dukes had been known to make ridiculous second marriages in order to secure the succession. Paul's own father, the current duke's second cousin, had only produced one child before he died in penury, leaving his family dependent on the generosity of the Haymores for a home. In truth, Paul considered Lucky's parents his own, and was very grateful for the care they had given him.

Paul nodded at an army acquaintance, but didn't stop to chat. All his friends seemed to have acquired younger sisters who were just dying to meet him. In truth, he felt hunted. If he had his way, he'd escape this gossip-ridden, perfumed hell and ride up north to the clear skies and bracing company of his best friend, Gabriel Swanfield. But he couldn't even do that, could he? Gabriel belonged, heart and soul, to another.

Paul stopped at the end of the ballroom that led out on to the terrace, and wondered if Lucky had gone out into the gardens. He could do with a breath of fresh air himself. He was about to pass through the open windows when he noticed a familiar figure standing on the balcony staring out into the night.

Paul's stomach gave a peculiar flip. The sight of his commanding officer, Lieutenant Colonel Constantine Delinsky, always stirred his most visceral appetites. Of Russian descent, Delinsky was tall and silver-eyed with prematurely white hair that in no way diminished his beauty. Paul always felt like a stuttering idiot around the man.

Delinsky was looking out into the gardens of the Mallorys' house with a preoccupied frown. Paul briefly debated whether to disturb him, but the opportunity to speak to someone who wouldn't care about his newly elevated status was too appealing to resist.

"Good evening, sir."

Constantine turned and half smiled. "Good evening, Lieutenant St. Clare. I didn't realize you were here tonight. Are you enjoying yourself?"

"Not particularly," Paul said. "I find all these people crammed into one space vaguely repellant."

Again, that slight smile that made Paul want to do whatever he was told. "I can understand why. As a soldier, I always fear an ambush myself."

"Are you waiting for someone, sir?" Paul asked.

"No, I was just contemplating the coolness of the air outside, and deciding whether I wished to stay for supper or leave before the crush." Delinsky's contemplative gaze swept over Paul. "Did you come with Swanfield?"

"Alas, no, sir. Gabriel and his wife are currently up north taking possession of his ancestral home."

Constantine raised his eyebrows. "Ah, that's right, I'd forgotten Swanfield had married."

"I'd like to forget it, but unfortunately the man is so damned content that I find I cannot begrudge him his happiness."

"Even despite your loss?"

"*My* loss?" Paul straightened and stared straight into Delinsky's all-too-knowing eyes.

Delinsky winced. "I beg your pardon, that was damned insensitive of me."

"Not insensitive at all. What do you mean?"

Delinsky lowered his voice. "I always believed you and Swanfield were connected on an intimate level."

Paul forced a smile. "There's no need for delicacy, sir. Gabriel was happy to fuck me when there was no other alternative. He soon realized the error of his ways, or more to the point, I realized the error of mine."

Delinsky continued to study him and Paul found he couldn't look away. "Perhaps you had a lucky escape, St. Clare."

"You think so?"

"Or perhaps the luck is all mine."

A slow burn of excitement grew in Paul's gut. "What exactly are you suggesting, sir?"

Constantine straightened. "Would you care to share a brandy with me at my lodgings? I find the party has grown quite tedious."

Paul wanted to groan. "Unfortunately I accompanied my family to the ball. I feel honor bound to escort them home as well."

"As you should." Constantine shrugged, his smile dying. "It is of no matter."

Paul glanced back at the ballroom and then at the man in front of him. Despite Delinsky's easy acceptance of Paul's reason for not leaving with him, Paul desperately wanted to consign his family to hell and follow this man anywhere. Gabriel was lost to him. He needed to move past that hurt and explore pastures new. And when it came down to it, he had always lusted after Constantine Delinsky.

"Perhaps you might furnish me with your address, sir, and I can join you after I've dispensed with my duties."

"It really isn't that important, St. Clare."

"Perhaps it isn't to you, but it is to me," Paul said softly. "Give me your direction."